A marauding monkey, a ~~murder~~, middle-aged (hula) maidens, and mugs full of Mai Tai's.

Just another day in Tiki Goddess Paradise . . .

Crime-solving sleuth Em Johnson and her Uncle Louie, owner of the famous Tiki Goddess Bar on Kauai, head for the Cocktail Shake Off Competition in Honolulu. What is supposed to be a fun trip to a mixologist contest turns weird when Louie's legendary "Booze Bible" is stolen, and Em's ex-husband winds up dead—with Em the number-one suspect. Sexy Kauai detective and part-time fire dancer Roland Sharpe rushes to Em's side along with the unpredictable Hula Maidens, whose detective skills are even more haphazard than their dance routine at the island tiki bars. Toss in an escaped monkey and a killer who wants to make this the Last Call for someone's honky-tonk tiki-tossing night out, and it's going to be another wild escapade for Em and her Hula Maidens.

The Tiki Goddess Series

Too Hot Four Hula

Book 4: The Tiki Goddess Mysteries

by

Jill Marie Landis

Aloha!
Jill Marie Landis

B

Bell Bridge Books

Bell Bridge Books
PO BOX 300921
Memphis, TN 38130
Print ISBN: 978-1-61194-460-0

Bell Bridge Books is an Imprint of BelleBooks, Inc.

We at BelleBooks enjoy hearing from readers.
Visit our websites
BelleBooks.com
BellBridgeBooks.com
ImaJinnBooks.com

10 9 8 7 6 5 4 3 2 1

Cover design: Debra Dixon
Interior design: Hank Smith
Photo/Art credits:
Tiki god (manipulated) © Annsunnyday | Dreamstime.com
Drink (manipulated) © Svetlana Gucalo | Dreamstime.com
Monkey (manipulated) © Dannyphoto80 | Dreamstime.com

:Lhtf:01:

"Crime never takes a vacation."
— Kiki Godwin, Leader of The Hula Maidens

1

Hilton Hawaiian Village
Waikiki, Island of Oahu, Hawaii

I'D RATHER DRINK soy sauce.

Em Johnson, manager of the Tiki Goddess Bar on Kauai's North Shore considered herself a people person, but she'd rather be talking to anybody other than her ex, Phillip.

"Thursday at eleven thirty is fine," she said into her cell. "I'll see you then."

She slipped her cell in the pocket of her capris and turned to admire the view of Diamond Head and the skyscrapers of Waikiki spread out along the crescent of white sand. Breakers rolled in slow and easy, the perfect size for a multitude of fledgling surfers and their beach boy instructors.

From the twentieth story of the Ali'i Tower at Hilton Hawaiian Village, the surfers on their boards looked like matchsticks bobbing on the water. The ocean was crystal clear and aquamarine blue, the coral reefs shadowy stains beneath shimmering blue-green glassy water. If you knew what to look for, it was easy to spot the occasional sea turtle, even from this height.

She turned away from the luscious view to continue unpacking. She'd accompanied her uncle Louie Marshall, owner of the Tiki Goddess Bar on Kauai to the Western Regional Division of the National Cocktail Shake Off competition.

The mixologist who concocted the winning cocktail would go on to compete in the nationals in St. Louis. Anyone who'd ever visited Louie's famous Tiki Goddess watering hole figured he had the contest in the bag. Not only had he been concocting outstanding cocktails for at least half a century, but he'd written a legend about his inspiration for each and every one.

She'd just tucked her cosmetic bag into the top dresser drawer when the connecting door to the sitting room in the suite she shared with her uncle banged open. Louie Marshall came rushing in.

"It's gone!" he shouted.

Louie's thick, silver-white hair was always perfectly combed, but not now. It stood out as if he'd been pulling on it. His face was florid. Her uncle wasn't given to high drama, so Em was immediately alarmed.

"What's gone?" Em turned, took one look at his florid face and said, "Maybe you'd better sit down."

Until now, her uncle had been riding the crest of a wave of fame ever since the reality show *Trouble in Paradise* spotlighted his bar and the Hula Maidens, a group of enthusiastic, if not talented, mostly senior aged dancers. Now he looked like he was going to stroke out.

"My Booze Bible! I just finished unpacking my stuff, my lucky cocktail shaker and my promotional swizzle sticks. I picked up my satchel and thought it felt kinda empty. Because it is empty! My notebook is gone."

Em reached for her cell. "Stay calm, okay? I'll call Sophie and tell her to FedEx your copy over. It'll be here tomorrow." As she started to hit the number for the Goddess, he whispered something.

"What did you say?"

"There is no copy."

"What?" Em realized he'd never definitively answered her when she'd asked about making a copy of his recipe notebook before they left Kauai.

Her uncle sank into a chair, rested his elbows on the nearby desk, and cradled his head in his hands.

"I never had a copy made." He gazed up at her, looking sheepish. "I was afraid to take it to the business center. I thought someone might steal my recipes now that we're all so famous."

"And now they have. The whole notebook." It was all handwritten. There was no file on a computer, no back up.

"Who would do such a thing?" he moaned.

"Your competition for one."

"You think so? I haven't even gone down to the registration area yet. How would they even know I'm here?"

"Well, there *was* that minor ruckus in the lobby when we checked in. Who doesn't know we're here?"

2

Sixteen Hours Earlier
Tiki Goddess Bar, Island of Kauai, Hawaii

"TOO HOT FOR hula? Are you kidding me? It's never too hot for hula, Em. Never."

"Sorry, Kiki." Em added a shrug to her apology. She should have known she'd hit a nerve when she casually asked Kiki Godwin, the overenthusiastic, self-appointed leader of a troupe of senior hula dancers, if it was too hot for the old gals to dance tonight.

"I don't want any of you passing out on stage," Em added.

"As if."

Em knew Kiki would never call off a Hula Maiden performance even if Kauai was in the middle of a Category Five hurricane and especially not tonight when they were giving Uncle Louie a big send off to the Western Regional Shake Off Competition.

Em lingered with Kiki in the open doorway to the ladies' room the Maidens used as a dressing room. Kiki was encased in red faux-velvet from the neck of her ruffled muumuu to her bare toes. She pulled a wet paper towel out of her low-cut bodice and blotted a bead of perspiration headed down her temple. Her neck was wreathed in three thick strands of colorful plumeria lei, and clusters of plumeria and various varieties of ferns covered the entire left side of her head.

"That heavy dress must be murder." Em regretted uttering the word murder aloud. The bar had become as famous for its connection to homicides as it was for the outstanding food and beverages they served.

"Okay, I'll admit, it is hotter than Hades under this dress." Kiki fanned herself with the crumpled towel. "But the show must go on. Besides, this isn't tonight's performance costume. I wouldn't dare parade around in that before we take the stage."

"Of course not."

Em followed Kiki's gaze and checked out the bar. Every table was full to overflowing. One man seated near the stage had been forced to balance his dinner plate on his knees, but he was still chatting and smiling away. Every carved tiki barstool was occupied. A standing room only crowd filled tables and milled around on the outdoor lanai.

"Looks like the entire North Shore is in the house," Kiki noted with smile.

"Along with any tourists who talked their way into a reservation," Em added.

"Nothing like a party to bring all kinds of folks together. What a tribute to Louie. Everyone expects him to win, you know."

"I hope so," Em said. Especially since she was going to go with him and would be there to see it.

Kiki reached up and gingerly patted her floral hair adornments.

"I think I'd better go put a couple more bobby pins in my flowers. See you after the show." She hurried back into the ladies' room where the other dancers were busy with their own last minute primping.

Em would have said break a leg, but where the Hula Maidens were concerned, anything could happen and usually did.

Thankfully things had been pretty calm over the last few weeks. The bar was in the black financially for the first time in years, and business showed no signs of slowing down.

Em left the small alcove near the ladies' room, and deciding she'd never make it through the throng to the table where Louie was presently holding court, she slipped behind the long koa wood bar where bartender Sophie Chin was a symphony in motion.

The young woman automatically grabbed glasses, lined them up on a waiting tray and filled them with ice. Not once since she started working at the Goddess had the twenty-three-year-old lost her cool. Even the overflow crowd lined up three deep around the bar didn't fluster Sophie. She had come in early that morning to help set up, and she was still going strong.

"How are you doing?" Em asked her.

She looked up at Em. Her right brow was studded with silver rings.

"I'm hanging in. I don't think one more person can squeeze into this place. I hope the fire marshal doesn't stop by."

Em laughed. "He's already here with his entire *ohana*. They got here two hours ago to score a table together. He doesn't look concerned."

"He and Louie must go way back, I hear."

"Who doesn't go way back with my uncle? He never met a stranger."

Seated up front near the stage, the still handsome seventy-two-year-old Louie laughed along with a couple seated at his table. The middle-aged snowbirds from New York called Kauai home when their home state was buried in snow.

"How is the drink special going over?" she asked Sophie.

The two-for-one they were featuring was Louie's famous "Great Balls of Fire," the cocktail created in honor of a neighbor whose body ended up in the pit where they roasted luau pigs behind the building.

Sophie shrugged. "What's not to like about two kinds of rum and Triple Sec mixed together with ginger syrup infused with Tabasco?"

Em watched her assemble an order for ten more Great Balls. "You're not using paper umbrellas?"

"We ran out twenty minutes ago," Sophie said.

"Flora may have some in stock, but if we get them from her shop we'll have to pay retail. She doesn't give *kama'aina* discounts." Flora Carillo, one of the Hula Maidens, owned a trinket shop in the little town of Hanalei a few miles down the road.

"True dat." Sophie picked up an open bottle of Tabasco and shook it over the glasses lined up on the tray. After she set the bottle down she took a second to glance over at Em.

"Mahalo again for trusting me to run this place while you and Louie are off island."

"You've thanked me enough." Em smiled.

Sophie shrugged. "I never thought I'd be assistant manager of anything, let alone a place as popular as the Goddess. I can sure use the raise."

"There's no one else we trust more, believe me. The downside is that you'll have to stay at the house while we're gone and bird-sit David Letterman."

"Funny"—Sophie shook her head—"I don't see a downside to housesitting on the beach, listening to the sound of the waves hitting the reef out front, lying in the sand looking up at the stars after work, feeling the trades drifting in off the water. All I have to put up with is one very spoiled macaw."

"Spoiled? Dave's worse than spoiled. Just remember not to put your fingers anywhere near the cage."

"Louie left me some tongs for putting food into the feeder."

"Did he leave a list of Dave's favorite drinks?"

"Yep."

Once the reality show centered around the Goddess, *Trouble in Paradise*, hit the air, "David Letterman," Louie's taste-testing macaw, became as famous as the rest of the Goddess *ohana*. Louie depended on

David Letterman to help him tweak his recipes until perfected. The sight of the parrot passed out on the floor of his cage assured Louie that another legendary cocktail had been born. The parrot was so popular Flora couldn't keep plush Letterman toys in stock in her gift shop.

Sophie signaled to a tall, thin man with a gray ponytail. Buzzy, the waiter with no last name, had to squeeze his way thought the crowd to get to the bar and pick up the tray of drinks. When he finally made it to the bar, Buzzy fumbled his notepad and finally tore off three more pages of orders for Sophie to fill. He smiled at Em then concentrated on lifting the heavy tray to his shoulder.

She'd hired the aging hippie to officially wait tables until their return when she promoted Sophie last week. Buzzy was always around, though not always sober, but he was trustworthy and always voluntarily pitched in bussing tables whenever they were slammed. Em was confident Buzzy would stay on the wagon until the end of his shifts. If not, Sophie would fire him.

"If you can juggle this place while we're gone, I'm sure you can handle Letterman." Em watched Buzzy scan the room with a befuddled expression. "I hope he can get those to the right table," Em said. "I'm not so sure he's cut out for official employment."

"Not to worry. Tiko will be full time until you get back."

The diminutive local gal from Wailua was scooting through the crowd with a megawatt smile that never dimmed. Tiko usually filled in part-time but with Em leaving, there was no way Sophie and Buzzy could handle busy nights without another waitress on the floor.

"How are you doing?" Sophie glanced at the next order and grabbed some rocks glasses.

"I'm baking in here." Em picked up a napkin and dabbed perspiration from her brow and her throat.

Sophie reached over and pulled a scrap of paper napkin off Em's neck. "You know you're having fun when you've got a napkin stuck to your neck. Louie said this is your first trip off island since you moved over from the mainland. You excited?"

"I was until I got a phone call from my ex. Phillip read about the Regional Shake Off in the *LA Times*. Louie was featured prominently, of course. It turns out Phillip's going to be in Waikiki when we're there and wants to see me. He has something to tell me."

Ever since the reality show aired they'd all had more time in the spotlight than Em wanted or needed, but unlike her, the Maidens thrived on celebrity and so did Louie in a more casual way.

"So are you going to meet up with him?"

"My gut reaction was to say no, but things ended so badly between us that it would probably be a good idea to have some closure. Hopefully things are looking up for him. He was broke when we divorced. We both were. So I agreed to meet him for lunch, put the past to rest."

"Good luck."

"I'll take it, but I hope I won't need it."

"Maybe if you settle the past, you'll be able to heat things up with your detective." Sophie winked.

"He's not *my* detective," Em said.

"So you say. Seems like it to me."

Em couldn't deny sparks flew whenever she was around Roland Sharpe, the tall, dark, and handsome *hapa*-Hawaiian detective who moonlighted as a fire knife dancer at luau shows. But it was too soon after a messy divorce to ride that wave again.

"Where is he? I thought he'd be here tonight," Sophie said.

"He ended up on a case."

"Wonder if it had anything to do with all the cop cars that raced by headed north a few minutes ago?"

"Probably. He called about forty minutes before. That would have given him time to drive out here."

"Too bad he won't be here." Sophie nodded toward the ladies' room door. "Looks like the old girls are good to go. Kiki said she has a special number planned."

"When doesn't she plan something special?"

"Hopefully they won't set the place on fire tonight."

"I told her all dances that involve flaming coconuts or anything to do with fire are *kapu*. Don't let them try anything dangerous while we're gone."

The last time Kiki and the Maidens performed a "special" number they'd nearly burned the place down, though the incident inspired the flaming cocktail that Louie entered into the regionals.

"How much damage can they do in a week?" Sophie wondered.

"Don't even go there." Em saw Louie waving her over to the table and waved back.

"I've got this," Sophie said. "Go join Louie. The show's about to start."

"You sure?"

"Go. Your dinner is probably cold by now."

"No worries. Kimo's macadamia nut-crusted seared *ahi* is perfect hot or cold."

Em left the bar and threaded her way across the room to a table right in front of the stage. Her uncle was holding court wearing a pile of lei from well-wishers. They were so thick around his neck they nearly reached his chin.

Completely oblivious of the humidity, he looked as dashing and debonair as ever in one of the colorful silk aloha shirts from his vast collection of originals made in the forties. Loose white linen pants completed his outfit. His thick white hair and golden tan accentuated his deep blue eyes. Six foot two and in great shape, Louie could command a room with his megawatt smile.

"Here she is." He rose and pulled out Em's chair with a flourish and remained standing until she was seated. "Em, you know everyone, don't you?"

She smiled at the people gathered the table and nodded.

"Of course. Thank you all for coming."

"Are you kidding me?" Jack Robbins, the part-timer from New York, had to yell to be heard over the din. The crowd nearly drowned out the Tiki Tones, the three-pieced combo playing old retro Hawaiian tunes on stage. "We're delighted to be here!" Jack pounded Louie on the back with one hand and fanned himself with a dessert menu with the other. "Louie and Irene were the first people we ever met when we bought our condo here thirty years ago. Never saw two people as full of aloha, that's for sure."

"They were quite a team," Em agreed.

A life-sized portrait of Louie's deceased wife, Irene Kakaul-anipuakaulani Hickam Marshall graced the wall above the stage. Irene appeared to be smiling her regal Hawaiian smile down on the revelers. Each evening Louie wrapped up the nightly entertainment with a song he had written especially for Irene, his Tiki Goddess. All the old timers, the *kama'aina*, and the newcomers, *malihini*, joined in to help Louie salute the one true love of his life.

Em took a bite of her *ahi*. It was so delicious she stifled a moan of delight. Kimo, their chef, was Kiki's husband. He had outdone himself tonight. The thick fillet of *ahi* was seared to perfection. His aioli sauce to die for, and the *ahi* was nestled on a creamy bed of whipped purple sweet potatoes.

"Aren't you having a Great Ball of Fire?" Annette Robbins, Jack's wife, was a blonde. She was seated across from Em. She held up her glass for a toast.

"I'm fine with water." Em figured it best to stay clearheaded while the Hula Maidens were on stage. She picked up her water glass. "Plenty of time for a drink later. Cheers, though."

Just then Brandon, one of the Tiki Tones, executed a drumroll, and the leader of the band Danny Cook slipped into MC mode.

"A-looo-ha!" he shouted.

"A-looo-ha!" The crowd called back. Cheering and whistling commenced. Danny waited until the audience died down then said, "You all know why we're here."

"Eo!" someone yelled in Hawaiian.

"Well, just in case you maybe stumbled in here off the cruise ship and have no idea whazzup, we're here to give Uncle Louie Marshall, owner of the Tiki Goddess, a big send off. As most of you know, tomorrow he's going to Oahu to do us all proud at the Western Regionals of the National Cocktail Shake Off competition."

Brandon hit a drumroll again. The crowd roared. Beaming from ear to ear, Louie got to his feet and waved to the assemblage. He stepped on stage, his eyes suspiciously bright when he took the mic. He let his gaze roam the room before he spoke.

Em knew Louie loved nothing more than packing the place full of people from all walks of life to share a few hours of fun. He truly was the ambassador of aloha and good times.

"Thank you all for being here tonight to celebrate with us. I'm so thankful for all of your support and aloha. I'm really looking forward to heading to the contest even though I'm never anxious to leave Kauai. As you all know, Kauai *no ka 'oi.* Kauai is da best!"

He waited for the thunderous applause and wolf whistles to die down.

"I'm excited that my niece, Em, is accompanying me to Waikiki. She's been such a big help that she deserves a little *holoholo* too." He paused and chuckled. "For those of you who don't know, *holoholo* means to take a pleasurable trip. Hopefully, it'll be really pleasurable, and I'll be bringing home a trophy to share with all of you."

Louie opened his arms to include the whole room and made a gracious bow before he turned the mic back over to Danny.

Danny glanced toward the small alcove between the ladies' room and the bar where Kiki and the others waited just out of sight.

"The Hula Maidens are anxious to perform for you tonight, so without further ado, here's their leader, Kiki Godwin!"

A hush fell over the room. Fans of the reality television series *Trouble in Paradise* knew Kiki was the outspoken leader of the troupe of aging dancers. The minute she appeared the crowd went wild. Cameras and cell phones came out, and people jockeyed to get a better shot of her in her full performance regalia.

Her faux-leopard, off-the-shoulder full length sarong was so tight it forced her to take mincing steps. When she reached the stage, Danny offered his hand. She smiled at the crowd, shrugged, winked, and hiked up her skirt in order to manage the steps.

Her hair was swept into a tight bun on the crown of her head and held in place with a pair of long ebony chopsticks. Small golden tikis dangled from the ends. Kohl eyeliner swept almost all the way to her temple to give her an exotic Asian look. Her false eyelashes were so thick they looked like fans flapping up and down when she blinked. Her lips were bright crimson outlined in deep magenta.

She waited in silence, drinking in the applause while the crowd cheered and continued to snap photos. Kiki turned left and right, striking poses that would have been sexy if she were thirty years younger. Now they were just odd. With her heavy lashes flapping and golden tikis bobbing, she was a sight to behold, and she milked every minute.

Finally Danny waved his arms and motioned for everyone to sit. As people settled back into their chairs, Kiki blew into the mic to test it.

In a low, seductive voice she began, "You've all seen the movie *South Pacific*, haven't you?"

There was scattered applause, and some folks even answered back.

"Well, if you haven't, you should. It was filmed right here on Kauai in 1957, back when folks on the mainland were working hard to buy their first homes and nice cars in the suburbs. But every once in a while some of those hardworking folks dared to dream of traveling somewhere that was still primitive, somewhere forbidden, somewhere that spoke to the savage in all of them.

"So they gathered around barbecues in their backyards, mixed up cocktails with exotic names like Mai Tais and Singapore Slings, and after couple of sips they were dreaming of hot tropic nights, trade winds, and palm trees. They dreamed of tearing off their neckties and aprons and sailing away to distant shores where they could dance to the beat of native drums and either chase pagan goddesses or become one."

She paused and took a long, slow breath and let the crowd imagine.

Then in just above a whisper she said, "Tonight we will present what we call our Dance of the Pagan Goddesses just for you. This dance is dedicated to Uncle Louie, and we sincerely hope it brings him luck at the Shake Off. So now, without further ado, the Hula Maidens are proud to present our rendition of 'Bali Hai,' from the movie *South Pacific.*"

3

KIKI SLOWLY TURNED and mermaid-walked off the stage. Everyone in the room waited in breathless anticipation.

Danny stepped up to the mic holding a conch shell in his hands. Brandon began a slow and steady drumbeat. Em glanced over at Louie who was as mesmerized as the rest of the crowd. She wished she could relax, but there was no telling what Kiki and the others had cooked up. All she could do was pray it wasn't dangerous.

The Maidens filed on stage more or less (mostly less) moving in time to Brandon's steady drumbeat. Eventually there were seven of them crowded on stage: Kiki, of course, and then came Flora Carillo, trinket shop owner. There was Suzi Matamoto, a successful North Shore realtor, Big Estelle Huntington, a retiree so named because of her Amazonian height and also to distinguish her from Little Estelle, her ninety-two-year-old mother who was also named Estelle. They were joined by Trish Oakley, a professional photographer, as well as Lillian Smith, a recent Iowa transplant, and Precious Cottrell, a hairdresser who was a little person and the newest member of the troupe.

All of the Maidens were dressed in ultra-tight, off-the-shoulder leopard print sarongs just like Kiki's. In her leopard print with her top knot speared with chopsticks, Precious reminded Em of Pebbles on *The Flintstones*. She had taken to dancing with the group like a duck to water.

Watching Precious's short legs tackle the low steps to the stage, Em tapped Louie on the shoulder.

When he leaned toward her she asked, "Do you think we should build a ramp for Precious?"

Louie leaned closer to Em's ear and whispered, "If we build a ramp then Little Estelle can ride that motorized sit-down contraption onto the stage. We'd never get her off."

"You're right. Bad idea."

Little Estelle got into enough trouble *off* stage. Supposedly a former Rockette, she sped around on a Gadabout, a powered scooter equipped with an irritating horn. She attended every Hula Maiden meeting and performance with her daughter.

Little Estelle had been a bit down ever since her break up with Lars, the twenty-year-old boy toy she'd hooked up with through iLoveCougars.com. She bemoaned the fact that after she made the mistake of telling him if he ever left her she'd have him neutered by one of the local pig hunters, Lars escaped and fled back to Finland, or Iceland, or somewhere in Scandinavia.

At the moment Little Estelle was parked as close to the front door as she could get and still see the show. The tray on the front of her Gadabout was already lined with empty cocktail glasses.

"Bali Hai will call you . . ."

The band started the haunting melody and lyrics in fits and starts. The Hula Maidens began to dance, and things were a bit uneven until finally they were all sort of moving as one. The crowd went wild with applause. The din nearly drowned out the band.

Louie leaned close again and yelled in Em's ear. "Where's Pat Boggs?"

Em glanced around, afraid to take her gaze off the stage. She didn't see the Maidens' Sergeant-at-Arms anywhere.

She shrugged at Louie and mouthed, "I don't know. She should be around."

The number went on and on, repeating the verses and the chorus until everyone in the room was bellowing, "Baaaaliiiii Haiiiii will call you," along with the band until there was a collective gasp. The single strap holding up Precious's sarong had suddenly snapped, and it dipped low, exposing her left breast.

Trying to avoid a complete wardrobe malfunction, she grabbed the strap and clamped it between her teeth. The move saved her from further exposure, but she lost her timing just as the Maidens were nearing their big finale.

The women were whirling their arms like windmills when Precious fell out of step. She moved left when she should have gone right and crashed into Big Estelle who rammed into Flora. Flora whipped around, and her wrist ended up slapping Lillian smack in the mouth. Precious ricocheted off of Big Estelle and rolled off the stage then bounced down the steps.

Lillian burst into tears. Em expected her to run off the stage, but to her credit, Lil kept dancing until the final strains of "Bali Hai" drifted away. Then, covering her injured lip with her hand, Lillian ran down the steps and stumbled over Precious, who had just managed to get to her feet. Thankfully there were so many people jammed around the stage Lillian wasn't launched across the room. She then crashed into a male tourist wearing an "I Love Kauai" T-shirt. He grabbed her and kept her from toppling over.

"So far this is not as bad as last time," Louie said.

"What happened last time?" Annette from New York wanted to know.

"See the woman with the pink hair who just ran off stage?" He nodded toward Lillian.

"Yes?"

"Last time they performed a special number she set her hair on fire."

"Oh no!" Annette stared at Lil.

"Thankfully it was a wig," Em added.

"Still, it was pretty darned memorable," Louie said.

On stage, Kiki had the mic in her hand again. She turned to her squad.

"Maidens, please stay in place for the presentation," she said.

"Uh oh." Louie looked at Em. "What's up?"

"I have no idea," she whispered.

"Probably giving me a going away gift." Louie straightened in his chair and looked up expectantly.

Precious had dusted herself off and was back on stage. Lillian was still sniffling, but no one was paying any attention. The tourist who had caught her patted her on the back until her husband MyBob took over. When Kiki shot a glare in their direction, Lillian pulled herself together and sulked back up to the stage to join the others.

Kiki slowly surveyed the crowd, waiting for everyone to settle down. The Maidens, lined up in very wide faux-leopard behind her, smiled and waved at the audience.

"Drumroll, please Brandon," Kiki urged.

Brandon hit the drum. Pat Boggs, Kiki's second in command, appeared around the back of the bar carrying a large manila envelope. She wore a casual shirt made of leopard print, blue jeans, and cowboy boots.

"He looks like a woman," Jack Robbins said.

"You mean she looks like a man," Annette corrected.

"That's Pat," Uncle Louie informed them. "Pat keeps the Maidens in line for Kiki. Used to be a sergeant in the Army or a Marine or something bad-assed."

Pat waved at the crowd as she bounded onto the stage.

"The ahhhn-velope please." A ripple of laughter followed Kiki's dramatics.

Pat handed it over. Kiki looked at Louie.

"We love you *so* much, Uncle Louie. We're *so proud* that you've entered the Shake Off Regional competition. We just know you'll win."

Her gaze shifted as she took in the crowd. "What an *exciting* time for the Goddess and everyone here on Kauai, to think one of our very own is going to be in the spotlight."

"Did she forget you all starred in that TV show?" Annette asked Em.

Em shrugged. Not knowing what Kiki had conjured up had her holding her breath. She reminded herself to breathe.

Kiki was still at the mic. "Louie, we pictured you in Waikiki *all* alone, and we could hardly bear it."

"All alone?" Em mumbled. "What am I? Chopped liver?"

Kiki held a long dramatic pause and let her gaze roam the audience before she turned to the other Maidens and yelled into the mic. "One, two, three!"

"We're going with you!" the Maidens yelled, and then they started clapping and jumping up and down.

Tears streamed down Lillian's face. It flushed as pink as her hair. Her upper lip was swelling. Kiki's eyes were suspiciously bright, though probably from the martinis she'd downed earlier and not actual tears.

In shock, Em glanced at her uncle. Louie's smile faltered for a nanosecond, but he quickly recovered his suave demeanor. On stage, the Maidens were still clapping and hugging each other. Still parked by the door at the other side of the bar, Little Estelle passed out. Her head flopped forward onto her scooter horn, and the constant shrill beep added to the din. Finally someone gently nudged her head off the horn.

Kiki held up the large manila envelope. "This contains our tickets to Oahu. Not only were we able to raise enough money for new costumes, but by some complete miracle, all of us were able to get on the same flight with Louie and Em. We'll meet you at Lihue airport tomorrow morning, and away we go!"

Louie elbowed Em and winked. "Smile. Like you mean it."

"Did you know?" she asked.

"Of course not. Did you?"

"Do you think I'd have let things get this far if I'd known?"

When the ruckus finally died down, Kiki managed to talk someone out of a chair and dragged it over to join them at the front table. Suzi, Trish, and Big Estelle were still dancing. Lillian was sniveling in the corner. MyBob awkwardly patted her shoulder.

Someone had hoisted Precious onto a tiki barstool where she was intent on downing a Great Ball of Fire while Sophie pinned up her gown. Little Estelle was still face down on the scooter tray.

Kiki leaned toward Louie. "Are you surprised? Did anyone let the cat out of the bag?"

"No, they didn't, and yes, I'm surprised."

"Shocked is more like it," Em said.

"You won't have to worry about us at all," Kiki went on. "We rented an extra-long van. I researched all the tiki bars on Oahu and managed to book the girls some gigs almost every night. We'll start at the Hau Tree Bar on the beach at the Hilton. Flora's cousin works there, and she got us great rates. We won't miss a minute of the Shake Off, and we'll all be together!"

"Whoohoo." Em picked up her empty glass and set it down again.

"Exactly. Nothing like taking the show on the road."

"What about Little Estelle?" Em asked.

"She's coming, of course."

"Of course."

"Big Estelle found a place to rent her mother a scooter. Precious even cancelled all her salon clients for the week."

Em noticed Precious was still perched on the barstool and now surrounded by people.

"That gal could be a stand-up comic, you know?" Kiki said.

"What are you thinking?" Em caught the gleam in Kiki's eye.

"Maybe we can work Precious into the hula show. Let her have the mic once in a while to tell jokes."

Em glanced over at Louie. He'd already lost interest and was talking to Jack again.

"Don't forget the real focus is on Uncle Louie this week," Em reminded Kiki.

Kiki turned and stared at Em and then fluttered her lashes. "Why, of course it is. What did you mean by that?"

Em shrugged. "Just that trouble seems to follow the Hula Maidens like big stink on poo."

Kiki threw back her head and roared. "Stink on poo?" Still chuckling, she carefully pressed her false eyelash back into place. "Don't worry, Em. What harm could we possibly do on Oahu?"

4

EM HAD JUST started walking across the parking lot toward the beach house she shared with her uncle when she passed Sophie leaving in her clunker Honda. Em waved as Sophie drove out of the driveway. Louie had been on hyperdrive with excitement when he left the bar. As she walked through the balmy night air, Em heard David Letterman squawking, "Nightcap! Nightcap! David wants a nightcap!"

She hoped Sophie was up to the parrot-sitting challenge.

Tires crunched on the gravel behind her as an unmarked Kauai Police Department cruiser crept into the lot. The utilitarian vehicle wouldn't fool anyone. It had no hubcaps, just black wheel rims, and it already looked beat to death despite being a newer model.

When Detective Roland Sharpe parked and stepped out of the vehicle, Em's pulse jumped a notch. She watched him walk across the lot until he paused a couple of feet away and looked down at her.

"Ms. Johnson."

Apparently he was in one of his official cop moods.

"Detective." She liked calling him detective. It made her feel like a character on a cops and bad guys show on TV.

"Beach?" He nodded in the direction of the ocean.

She really should be inside checking her suitcase for the last time and printing out boarding passes.

"Sure." As if any woman would turn him down.

They walked side by side across the lawn in front of Louie's beach cottage. When they reached the edge where grass became sand, she stepped out of her slippers and left them behind.

"Were you out detecting tonight?" She raised her voice over the sound of the waves rushing over the coral reef.

"Not sure you could call it that. A 911 came in from some folks out in Haena staying in a vacation rental. A guy was yelling something about being trapped in the house. Lots of screaming in the background before the call was dropped. The dispatcher thought it was a home invasion robbery."

"Has there ever been one here?"

"No, but it's not impossible."

"I heard a lot of sirens earlier."

"Yeah. Five car alert. We pulled in units all the way from Lihue." He sighed.

"No invasion?"

"Bull."

"I can see how you'd feel that way."

"Huh?"

"Like it was a bunch of bull."

Roland shook his head. "Actually, it was a bull. Walked right down the middle of their cul-de-sac and stopped outside the front lanai and started munching all the *ti* plants. Wiped out most of the landscaping. The thing had three-foot horns, and the tourists were afraid to go out and shoo it away."

"So how many officers did it take to round up one bull?" She hid a smile.

He shrugged. "I have to admit it was a big, ugly dude. Nobody wanted to go near it, so the guys went door to door up and down the highway. It didn't take long to find the owner. A little old Japanese lady came toddling down the road in a cotton bathrobe and curlers in her hair, carrying a piece of rope. Walked right up to the bull, slipped the rope around his neck, and led him away."

"Another major crisis averted."

"KPD to the rescue again." He stared out at the waves. The foam riding the surf was illuminated blue-white by a bright sliver of moonlight. He turned back to Em. "How was Louie's send-off party?"

It was her turn to sigh.

"What happened?" he asked. "No, don't tell me. The Hula Maidens pulled one of their stunts?"

Em nodded.

"Another fire?"

"Not this time. They're restricted from using fire. Besides, that we could put out. In a way this is worse. They surprised Louie by announcing they are all going with us to Oahu to support him at the Shake Off."

"All of them?"

"Right down to Little Estelle and Precious."

"Maybe I should issue an APB to the Chief on Oahu. Warn the HPD to be on the lookout. Have some riot gear ready."

"Call Hawaii 5-0. I'd rather run into that cute McGarrett guy."

"He's not real, you know."

"They might be filming at our hotel."

"I'm sure your neighbor could tell you. Isn't he working over there right now?"

"Nat? Yeah. Working on his new show. They're filming eleven episodes. Said he's slammed with work."

"Good. Then he'll be too busy to see you."

"Are you jealous, Detective?"

He took a step closer. "No need. Maybe Nat Clark can write television scripts, but can he fire dance?"

Em tried to picture their part-time next door neighbor, the successful prime time television writer, fire dancing in his Tommy Bahama shorts and tortoise shell glasses. He was smart, good looking, and interested in her, but he didn't hold a candle to Roland's flaming sword.

"When are you coming back?" Roland asked.

"Next Monday. Early flight."

"Long time."

"Six nights."

Without warning he leaned close enough to kiss her. Em held her breath. Her toes curled into the cool sand. The kiss was short but sweet.

"Stay out of trouble," he said as they walked back toward the lawn. "Don't let those women drive you crazy."

"I plan to book a massage at the hotel spa. That should help."

"If you're lucky the place has an in-house shrink."

5

LIHUE AIRPORT WAS a far cry from LAX or even Honolulu. The Hawaiian Air check-in desks were located in the long open air lobby that stretched from one end of the three-block structure to the other. Em had printed out their boarding passes last night, but since Louie had bags to check, they had to line up for a ticket agent rather than go straight to security.

"Go with the flow" had been her mantra since they left the house before dawn to catch the eight a.m. flight. She didn't like the notion that she was a control freak, but she was having a hard time squelching the urge to organize her eccentric traveling companions.

Louie had filled an assortment of 1950s luggage covered in decals from various exotic ports of call that he'd seen before he married and settled down on Kauai. He'd barely been able to close the largest suitcase after carefully wrapping and depositing his favorite cocktail shakers, drink umbrellas, swizzle sticks, and a couple of his favorite tiki mugs inside. The clasp looked perilously close to snapping.

Dressed in a crimson aloha shirt covered with images of papayas, pineapples, and bananas, he looked like an oversized fruit bowl.

They were surrounded by a gaggle of women in matching "Yes, we are THE Hula Maidens" T-shirts and traditional purple *pau* hula skirts. With four yards of fabric gathered around their waists they looked like a school of beached puffer fish. Fake silk flower arrangements were pinned in above their left ears. The cement floor around them was covered with rolling bags, cardboard boxes, oversized straw purses, and even a one-hundred-and-fifty quart cooler closed with duct tape.

Nearby TSA agents in powder blue uniform shirts covered in official embroidered patches and badges grimly waited for the onslaught to begin beside the luggage x-ray conveyor belt.

The queue inched closer to the Hawaiian Air check-in counter. Em rolled her single carry-on beside her. Everything she needed for the four-night, five-day trip was inside. Her attention drifted to her uncle's suitcases again, and her "go with the flow" drifted away on the trade wind breeze.

"Uncle Louie, did you ever take your Booze Bible into the business center to get it copied?"

Louie's Booze Bible was a handwritten ring binder containing every cocktail recipe and accompanying legend he'd written since before he had opened the Goddess.

He patted the battered leather briefcase hanging from an over-the-shoulder strap.

"I've got it. Don't worry. I'm not letting this briefcase out of my sight."

"But . . ."

He frowned behind his aviator sunglasses. "I'm worried about leaving Letterman."

"He and Sophie looked perfectly happy when we drove off."

"He was squawking his head off. He's not used to being fed with three-foot barbecue tongs."

"It's not safe for her to get any closer."

"He won't get to go outside and sit on his perch in the shade until I get back."

"She'll follow your instructions to the letter. She's not going to risk having him outside. He'll be fine." The macaw was older than Em, in great health, and would probably outlive them both. She was about to reassure Louie again when she was jostled from behind.

"Oops. Sorry," Kiki said before she glanced over her shoulder. "Settle down, Flora. You just shoved me into Em."

The heavyset woman behind Kiki waved her hand as if shooing a fly. The long row of gold Hawaiian Heritage bangle bracelets on her arm clanked together.

"*Kala mai*, Kiki, but I gotta move away from Lillian. She's been givin' me stink eye since last night."

It was hard to miss Lillian's pink bouffant hairdo. The woman was a few yards away with realtor Suzi Matamoto, and she was indeed giving Flora stink eye. Photographer Trish Oakley was snapping away with her camera, documenting every move the group made.

Kiki turned to Em. "Lillian thinks Flora slapped her in the mouth on purpose during the performance. She's still upset. I think she's probably just nervous because she never goes anywhere without MyBob."

"Do you think they'll actually come to blows?" Em said softly.

"No way." Kiki didn't sound really certain.

Go with the flow, Em reminded herself. Go with the flow.

There was a scraping sound behind them as Big Estelle shoved the ice chest across the floor. The cooler was big enough to bury Precious in.

"What's in there?" Em was almost afraid to know.

"The usual. Flowers and *maile* for lei, frozen *akule*, and twenty pounds of Hanalei poi." Kiki thought a minute and added, "Also a box of malasadas stuffed with whipped cream."

In what universe was this normal stuff? Em wondered.

"I really can't believe we're all here." Kiki smiled as she scanned her troupe. "It's so wonderful to have the girls all together, not to mention the fact that we're going to support Louie." She clasped her hands over her heart and sighed. "Well, life just doesn't get any better, does it?"

Em couldn't comment on that since she'd just spotted Little Estelle chatting with the good looking Hawaiian Air employee who was assigned to her wheelchair. She was outfitted in the Maiden's official travel T-shirt, but instead of a *pau* skirt, she had on purple capri pants and a white visor on her head that sported a huge "I'm Looking for Love" pin with three-dimensional eyes that bugged out.

A woman waiting in the line beside them reached over the rope swag and tapped Em on the shoulder.

"Do y'all live here?" she asked.

"What was your first clue? The ice chest or the outfits?" Em laughed.

"Are you part of some Hawaiian circus?"

Em followed the woman's gaze. Down the line, Precious was rubbing the back of her head and kicking the shin of a surfer wielding a long surfboard wrapped in a padded bag.

Kiki leaned around Em to address the woman.

"I'm surprised you don't recognize us," Kiki smiled. "We're the Hula Maidens. Stars of the reality show *Trouble in Paradise.* Maybe you missed it?"

"The only reality show I watch is *Honey Boo Boo.*"

Kiki looked her up and down. "That figures."

"The line is moving, Kiki," Em said, hoping to avoid a fight. "Time to roll."

Somehow they made it through ticketing and checked their bags with the TSA agents, but not before the agents insisted Big Estelle cut the tape on the cooler so they could look inside. Em saw the men exchange glances as they checked out the neat packages of frozen fish and Hanalei poi. Em wondered if the girls would ever see the cooler again, but the agents let them tape it up again before it disappeared into the x-ray machine.

"Let's get fried rice," Suzi Matamoto suggested. "This is the best of any place in town, and you can only get it once you get through security."

"Louie?" Em turned to her uncle. "You want to get fried rice?"

"Sure. Best on the island. I just hope they're not out of it already. It's already going on seven a.m. you know."

"Probably best if we stick together," Em said before she noticed Kiki wasn't with them. "Trish," she called out to one of the sanest members of the troupe. "Where's Kiki?"

"At the bar," Trish called as the automatic door to the cafeteria swooshed open.

"It's not even open yet." As the group surged forward, Em was pushed into the cafeteria on the crest of a Hula Maiden wave.

"She likes to stand outside and look in the window," Flora said. "She says a girl can dream."

Just then the cafeteria door opened and Kiki leaned in. "The Pali Boys are setting up out here in the lobby to play for the tourists. Forget the rice. We've got time for a couple of dances!"

Em and Louie barely got out of the way as the Maidens all dropped their carry-ons, purses, and backpacks at the nearest table and stampeded back out the door.

6

INSIDE THE BOARDING area at Gate 6, Em clung to her go-with-the-flow attitude and paged through the latest edition of the *Garden Island* news. The all caps banner headline screamed "Activists Claim GMO Corn Causes Zombies." Her mind wasn't on the story but kept drifting to Phillip. She wondered if her ex had changed at all and wished she hadn't agreed to meet with him.

The Maidens had just filed in. Too late to get seats together, they were scattered around the room chatting about their successful appearance in the lobby and how they'd left travelers cheering for more. The plane had arrived and was waiting in view at the end of the jet way.

Flora wedged into the seat beside Em and was fanning herself with a *lau hala* fan. She leaned over and said, "One tourist came up to me and said he *nevah* saw anything like us in his life."

"I'm sure," Em said. Before she could add anything, their flight number was announced. All around the room passengers began pulling out their boarding passes and grabbing their belongings.

Big Estelle came bustling over to Em. "No one has seen Mother." She glanced into the Gate 5 waiting area on the other side of the long, narrow room.

Em took one look at the straw bags and heavy leather pack Big Estelle was wrestling with and said, "Let me run out to the lobby and look for her."

Big Estelle sighed. "Sorry, Em. That would be great. You can go a lot faster than I can."

"Watch my stuff for me." Em hurried out into the open air corridor outside the boarding gate. She headed along the cement walk to the lobby where passengers could not only enjoy the cafeteria or the bar and live Hawaiian music, but could also grab a bottle of water, gum, candy, or a newspaper from one of the smaller stores but also that last minute flower lei to take with them.

Em's sandals slapped against her heels as she ran through the lobby, ducked into the cafeteria and then the bar. Not even Kiki was there. She even looked behind turning display racks in both the sundry and flower shops, but didn't see Little Estelle.

How could they have lost an old lady in a wheelchair? Em figured Little Estelle must have rolled off on her own while the others were dancing.

Airport security lines fed into the lobby. Em walked up to the glass dividers and watched travelers grab their bags and belongings out of plastic bins rolling off the conveyer belt. Uniformed TSA agents were eyeballing every move. A gray-haired Hawaiian man in uniform manned a podium at the exit.

"Did an elderly woman in a wheelchair go by?" Em asked him.

He looked her up and down with an expression reserved for crazy *haoles*. He nodded toward the area marked off for more thorough screenings. Em spotted Little Estelle standing beside her wheelchair, one arm outstretched, one hand braced on a countertop for balance, as a handsome young man waved a wand over her Hula Maiden T-shirt. She had a smile as wide as a Hawaiian rainbow on her face.

"I don't suppose there's any way I can go over there," Em asked the security guard.

"Nope."

"They're going to start boarding our plane," she tried.

"Sorry."

She cupped her mouth and called, "Estelle! Little Estelle, you're going to miss the plane!"

Little Estelle glanced over. "It'll be worth it, honey!"

"Sir? You with the wand," Em yelled. A family trooped past her lugging their baggage and cutting off her view. When they moved on she saw the young TSA agent looking her way.

"Her plane is about to leave," she yelled.

He motioned for Little Estelle to sit down. She hesitated until he took her arm and helped lower her into the wheelchair. The young agent walked over to Em.

"What's going on here?" she asked him.

"May I see your boarding pass?"

Luckily Em had it in her pocket. She pulled it out and handed it to him. The dark-eyed man who looked to be in his late twenties looked it over carefully and handed it back.

"If you're finished with her I can take her to the gate," Em said.

By now they were at the miniscule area set off for more thorough screenings.

"I'd be happy to hand her over, but Auntie is insisting she's feeling a little terroristic. Said she was afraid someone slipped something dangerous into her underwear and we should check it out."

Little Estelle poked him in the ribs with her index finger. "I'm not your 'auntie,' gorgeous, and there's something very dangerous in my underwear." He had referred to Estelle as auntie, not out of disrespect, but as most locals did when speaking to an older woman, related or not.

"Why isn't a female agent patting her down?" Em wanted to know.

"Hey, butt out. Don't spoil the fun," Estelle said.

"You're going to miss the plane, Estelle. Is that what you want?" Em heard an announcement that their flight to Honolulu was now boarding at Gate 6.

"What I want," Estelle said, "is Mr. Hunk's phone number, but he won't give it to me."

"Please," Em appealed to the TSA agent. "Can she go now? Her daughter already hauled her carry-ons to the gate." Since she was behind Estelle's wheelchair, she raised her index finger to her temple and rolled it around in circles.

The young officer immediately put down the wand and told Little Estelle she was free to go.

Em didn't give her a chance to protest as she backed the chair out of the small booth and shoved it through the security line exit, across the lobby, and down the walkway to the gate. Em's cell phone went off, and she pulled it out of her capri pocket as she bustled along.

"We're in the jet way," Louie said. "Where are you?"

"We're on the way. Don't let them leave."

"Ha. Fat chance. This is the on-time airline. If you aren't here in a second they'll lock the door, and we'll be wheels up without you."

Em shoved the phone into her pocket and barreled down the inclined walkway.

"Yee-haw! Now we're moving." Little Estelle flapped her arms as if flying.

Em wheeled her through the automatic doors to the gate. Thankfully the room had emptied, and there were only a few passengers left to board. The aisle between the rows of chairs was clear. Em rushed Little Estelle to the front of the line and caught her breath after they made it on with only two passengers left ahead of them.

By the time Little Estelle was settled in a bulkhead seat and chatting away to the man beside her, Em was able to make her way to her own seat beside Louie. She passed Big Estelle in an aisle seat, and a few rows back she saw Trish, also on the aisle. Louie had to get up to let Em slide into her window seat. She dropped into it and looked around. He'd already tucked her purse under the seat in front of her.

"You made it. I knew you would," he said.

"I didn't." Em let go a sigh of relief. "I feel like we've been away for two weeks already, and we haven't even left the airport." She was afraid to look around. "Did everyone get on? Is Kiki here?"

"They're all here. Big Estelle said she didn't care if her mother made it or not when she handed me your stuff. They're spread out all over the plane. Kiki said they all managed to get aisle seats. She was pretty stoked about that. Guess it was too late for them to get seats together."

"Just as well." Em imagined the Maidens talking nonstop all the way.

"It's only a twenty-five minute flight," Louie reminded her as they taxied down the runway.

The flight attendant was showing them how to put on a life vest and blow into a tube on the shoulder if it didn't inflate automatically.

"Fat chance," Louie said as he watched the pretty young thing pretend to puff into the tube. "If we're gonna need a life vest we might as well bend over and kiss our sweet *okoles* goodbye."

Em looked out the window as the tarmac sank below them and they were airborne. Within seconds they banked over the turquoise waters of the Pacific, and the lush green mountains of Kauai grew smaller behind them as they climbed into the clear blue sky, headed across Ka'ie'ie Waho Channel toward Oahu.

Em reached for an inflight magazine just as the flight attendant stopped in the aisle and asked if she wanted any POG, the passion-orange-guava juice that was complimentary. Em declined. Louie asked for two of the little plastic cups sealed with foil.

As soon as the attendant moved on he pulled out a 50 ml mini of rum.

"How'd you get that on board?" Em asked.

"Kiki bought it for me at the sundries shop." He opened the top and dumped it into the POG cup. "Want some? I have plenty."

Before she could say no thanks, the song "Beautiful Kauai" came blaring over the speaker system, and up and down the aisle, the Hula Maidens were suddenly climbing out of their seats and dancing the hula.

"Look, a flash mob, Mommy." A little boy in the row across from Em and Louie clapped his hands.

"Flash mob hula. A-looo-ha!" someone else called out.

"Look, Bill," the woman seated behind Em said. "It's those dancers from the *Trouble in Paradise* show."

"They sure looked a lot younger on TV," said a man beside her.

Em opened her magazine and held it in front of her face. If the rest of them were pulled off the plane and arrested when they reached Honolulu, she planned to deny knowing them.

All around people held up their phone to snap photos of the flash mob hula.

Thankfully the song was short. When it ended, passengers whistled, clapped, and applauded. One by one the Maidens buckled themselves into their seats.

Em heard a click over the speakers.

"Here we go," she whispered to Louie. "They're going to announce TSA and the police will be waiting at the gate."

Louie drained the last drop out of his second cup of POG and rum and smiled. "You worry too much. Chillax."

The captain's voice filled the cabin. "A big mahalo to some very special ladies flying with us today. I'm sure most of you recognized the Hula Maidens from the show *Trouble in Paradise*. On behalf of Hawaiian Air we'd like to say mahalo to the Hula Maidens for sharing their aloha with us."

The passengers burst into applause again.

"So much for getting arrested." Louie passed his empty cups and mini bottles to the attendant in the aisle with a plastic bag.

With the possibility of a night in jail evaporating, Em's stomach was tap dancing with anxiety over being face-to-face with Phillip again tomorrow.

"I can't wait to see what happens next," Louie said.

"I can." Em closed her eyes and shook her head.

7

KIKI COLLAPSED INTO a faux wicker chair at one of the four tables the Maidens had pushed together at the Hau Tree Bar between the Rainbow Tower, the beach, and the Super Pool at the Hilton Hawaiian Village. She grabbed a drink menu and fanned herself.

"How long until the rooms are ready?" Trish Oakley pulled out a chair next to Kiki and sat down. Except for when she flash danced, her camera hadn't left her hands throughout the trip from Kauai. Now Trish started snapping away at scenes on the Waikiki shore.

"I think they said forty-five minutes." Suzi Matamoto took a seat and signaled a young waiter in uniform.

"Lucky they aren't making us wait until three o'clock check in," Trish said.

"Lucky we even got to book our rooms here so late. The place is packed with those women attending the Mindy's Miracle Makeover Cream Convention."

"I saw some of them over by Benihana," Trish said. "They're all wearing lavender and more makeup than a Kabuki dancer. Did you see the glimmer eye shadow?"

"I saw them," Trish said. "I'll bet they brought enough hair spray to blow this hotel sky high."

Kiki laughed. "A couple of them passed me on my way down here. They tried to talk me into a free makeover. Can you imagine? As if I need one."

She gazed toward the Super Pool, ten thousand square feet of splashing fun, according to the Hilton website. It was surrounded by lava rocks, tropical flowers of all colors, and the obligatory faux waterfalls that tourists expected. Her hands were itching to start purloining greenery for hair adornments.

"What'll it be, ladies?" A handsome young twenty-something waiter drew their attention. He added, "We're not open for lunch yet."

"I'll have a martini. Three olives," Kiki said. "That is lunch."

The others had ordered when Flora came huffing up to join them.

"Your face has gone red," Kiki told her. "Better sit down and catch your breath."

Flora managed to wheeze out, "Mai tai," to the waiter. "Double fisted."

"What took you so long?" Big Estelle was seated at the far end of the table arrangement. Her mother was parked next to her on a rented scooter contentedly scanning all the male sunbathers scattered around on chaise lounges.

"I was on the phone with the airlines," Flora said. "How you think they lost twenty pounds of *poi*, eh? Not to mention all the other stuffs. My ice chest didn't get here."

Kiki shook her head in disbelief. "How dare somebody steal our *poi*? And what about all the frozen *akule* Kimo sent along?"

"It's not stolen," Suzi chimed in. "It probably didn't get on the right plane from Kauai. When it arrives in Honolulu somebody will bring it over here from the airport."

"Fat chance," Little Estelle sniffed. "All that *poi* is gonna end up at some luau. Mark my words. We'll get an empty cooler back."

Kiki thought it best to change the subject. "Our flash mob dance was great. We'll have to do it again on the way home."

"They asked us not to, remember?" Suzi wagged her finger at Kiki. "They said once was enough."

"No worries. It'll be a different flight crew," Big Estelle said.

"Maybe they made a note on our paperwork."

"What paperwork?" Kiki wanted to know.

"The flight list or something."

Flora turned on her. "What? You think they're going to send us to hula jail or something?"

Kiki barked out a laugh. "Hula jail? I'm glad there's no such thing, or we'd be serving life sentences by now."

Lillian came rushing up. She scanned the bar area before she grabbed one of the last remaining chairs and dragged it over to the table. Her lip was still swollen, and she'd barely spoken all morning. She only spoke loud enough for them to hear over the kids hollering in the nearby *keiki* pool.

"Tell me if you see any of those Mindy's Miracle Cream gals coming."

"Why?" Kiki asked her.

"Because back in Iowa, I used to be one of them. I was even named one of the top Miracle Makers for selling the most product three years running. If any of them recognizes me, I'll be called out for not living up to the Mindy Promise."

"The Mindy Promise?" Flora said. By now all the Maidens were staring at Lil.

She raised her hand as if being sworn in. "I promise to apply Mindy's Miracle Cream nightly. I promise to apply Mindy's Miracle Makeup the minute I wake up in the morning and never, ever go to bed until I've used Mindy's Miracle Makeup Remover and then moisturize with Mindy's Miracle Makeup Moisturizer."

They all joined in when she said Mindy's Miracle Makeup Moisturizer.

"Look at me," Lil cried. "I barely have on any foundation, and my eyeliner keeps melting and smearing."

Just as the waiter returned to the table and began passing out their drinks, a woman on the other side of the bar in a red straw hat and a flowing accordion-pleat caftan shouted, "It's them!"

She waved at the Hula Maidens, grabbed her husband's arm, and started pulling him toward the table.

"It's them, Fred. It's the Hula Maidens." The tourist filled out her Moroccan print caftan. "You're the Hula Maidens." She was staring down at the assembled group.

"We know." Kiki reached for her martini.

The woman dug a pen out of her purse and grabbed a cocktail napkin off the table.

"May I have your autographs?" Her hands shook as she handed Kiki the napkin first. "I can't believe it. I thought you'd be on that other island. Cow-eye, right?"

"Kauai," Suzi, a stickler for Hawaiian pronunciation, said distinctly.

"Whatever. We heard a rumor going around the lobby that you were here. We just have to see you dance before we head home for Nebraska tomorrow. Is there any chance at *all*?"

By now guests seated around the bar and Super Pool area were watching the exchange.

Kiki paused and patted her hair into place. "We're going to be on Oahu for five nights for the big cocktail Shake Off. Tonight we're going to be dancing right here at the Hau Tree Bar."

The waiter had just set Little Estelle's drink on the tray of her scooter. He turned to Kiki.

"You are?" His smooth brow was suddenly furrowed with lines. "Dancing out here? We've never had dancing out here. There's barely room to move."

The Maidens were all watching her expectantly. Kiki cleared her throat.

"We're dancing here around seven."

The woman in the caftan grabbed her husband's arm again and started dragging him toward the Ali'i Tower. "Come on, Fred. We've got time for a last shopping spree before we come back to get a seat in the bar." She turned around and waved at the group. "Ta, ta, Maidens. Mahalo!"

They waved back.

"Wow, Kiki. Thanks for booking us some gigs. This is going to be great," Trish said.

Kiki smiled, drained her martini, and signaled the waiter.

8

"WHAT AM I GOING to do, Em?" Louie actually hung his head in his hands and moaned. "I'm ruined without my recipes."

Em reached for her cell. "No problem. I'll call Sophie and tell her to FedEx your copy over. It'll be here tomorrow." She started to enter the number for the Goddess but heard him mumble.

"Did you say something?"

"There is no copy," he said.

"What?" Em realized he'd never definitively answered her when she'd asked about making a copy of his recipes at the Lihue airport.

Her uncle sank into a chair, rested his elbows on the desk, and cradled his head in his hands.

"I never had a copy made." He gazed up at her, looking sheepish. "I was afraid to take it to the business center. I thought someone might steal my recipes now that we're all so famous."

"And now they have. The whole notebook." The large, battered, three-ring binder was full of handwritten legends and cocktail recipes. There were even doodled illustrations. There was no file on a computer, no back up.

"Who would do such a thing?" he moaned.

"Your competition for one."

"You think so? I haven't even gone to the contest registration area yet. How would they know I'm here?"

"Well, there *was* that minor ruckus in the lobby when we checked in."

Naturally hotel guests in the reception area recognized the Maidens, which didn't deter Kiki from yelling, "Do you *know* who we are?" at the reception clerks when their block of rooms wasn't quite ready.

Suddenly they had been surrounded by a crowd of autograph seekers.

"Maybe it was a crazed fan," Louie said.

"Could be. There's been plenty of press about the contest, you in particular, thanks to the show. The Booze Bible is legendary. You're a threat to the other contestants."

"If someone stole it," he sighed, "I'm toast."

Em picked up the house phone and asked for security. A recording in English and then rapid-fire Japanese asked her to please hold. Hawaiian music immediately filled her ear.

"Are you sure you packed it?" she asked.

He closed his eyes. "Of course."

"You're sure? Absolutely."

"I looked into the briefcase when I was in the airport boarding area just to make sure. Remember, you asked me about it when we were in line. So I checked when we were settled, and it was right there. You were out looking for Little Estelle. Where was she, by the way?"

"Practicing her perversion as usual. Let's focus, okay? When did you next see it?"

"We were in the van on the way here from the airport. I looked at it again just to make sure."

"Where did you stow the briefcase? In the back of the van with all the other luggage?"

"No. On my lap."

"Okay. So when we checked in, did you set it on the luggage cart with everyone's stuff?"

He frowned, remembering. "I was talking to Kiki and the girls about their rooms not being ready and about the lost ice chest."

"Where was your satchel, Uncle Louie?"

"I'm pretty sure I still had the strap over my shoulder. I never set it down."

"Then we left the Maidens and got checked in."

"Right. Then I came up here with you and put the briefcase on the desk in my room. Now it's gone."

"But the briefcase is still here."

He shook his head. "Yeah. They just took the binder."

A recording of Don Ho crooned "I Will Remember You" in Em's right ear.

"How could it just vanish? You never left the suite. Did you go to the bathroom?" she asked.

He shook his head no. His eyes widened. "I took the ice bucket and went to get ice. It's the first thing I do when I get to a hotel. Isn't that the first thing everyone does when they check into a hotel? Fill the ice bucket? I went out through the door in my room." They were sharing a suite, two rooms separated by a sitting room with an efficiency kitchen.

"Did you lock your door?"

His forehead wrinkled. "No. I used that bar thing to hold it open."

"Oh, Uncle Louie."

"Hey, the ice machine is just down the hall around the corner."

"Did you pass anyone in the hall?"

"No."

"You're sure."

He squinted as if scanning his memory.

"I passed a guy in a baseball cap."

The phone clicked, and a voice came on cutting off the Hawaiian music.

"Hilton security," a male said.

"This is suite 2042-44. Marshall and Johnson. I'm calling to report a robbery."

"You were held up at gunpoint?" The voice sounded doubtful.

"I meant burglary."

"Okay, den. Somebody will be right up." There was a click on the line. Em hung up and turned to Louie. Right about now Roland would be taking notes. She grabbed a notepad and pen off the nightstand.

"Describe the guy in the cap." *Before you forget.*

"Average weight. Medium height."

"Eyes?"

"I'm sure he had some. He had on sunglasses."

"Hair?"

"Couldn't see it under the cap."

Em sighed. "What did the cap look like?"

"Dark green I think."

She wrote down *green.*

"Or maybe black."

She wrote down *maybe black.* "Anything else?"

"I think it was a University of Hawaii cap."

She wrote down *UH.*

"He had on a jacket."

Em paused. "A sport coat?"

Louie shook his head no. "The zipper kind. Matched his pants. It must have been a jogging suit."

"Didn't that strike you as a little odd, seeing a guy in a jogging suit? It's eighty-seven degrees outside."

He shrugged. "I was thinking about ice. Maybe he can't take the air conditioning. I can't. What am I going to do, Em?"

"Let's go in the sitting room and wait."

They left her room. Louie sank onto the sofa. Someone knocked at the door.

"Sit tight," she said. "There's security."

Em opened the door and stared up at a tall local wearing a generic hotel employee sport coat. His badge identified him as security. He was holding a notebook and pen. His name tag said Kim.

"You call in a burglary?"

"Yes, we did." Em introduced herself and Louie. "We're here for the Shake Off competition. My uncle is a contestant. He went to get ice, and when he came back, his briefcase containing a notebook full of a lifetime of cocktail recipes was empty."

Kim turned to Louie. "When you went to get ice did you lock your door, sir?"

"No. I used that bar thing to prop it open."

"Safety rules are posted behind the door and inside the hotel guide on the desk in every room. Valuables should be locked in the room safe or given to the front desk where they'll be locked in a larger hotel safe. Your sliding glass doors to the balcony should be locked when you leave the room."

Em looked at the wall of windows and the slider to the balcony.

"We're on the twentieth floor," she said. "Has Spiderman gone rogue?"

"Where there's a will," Kim said.

"There's a way." Louie sounded as glum as Em had ever heard him.

She told the hotel detective Louie had seen a man in a jogging suit pass him in the hall. Kim took notes.

"You surely have hallway security cameras," she said.

"Temperamental at best," Kim said. "The salt air and humidity always short out the cameras. I'll run the video back and see if we can get a look at the guy you described."

"I didn't see his face," Louie said. "I wasn't really paying attention."

"What about the Honolulu police?" Em was thinking of Roland and the KPD. She wished he was on the case. "Should we call them?"

Kim shrugged. "Unless there's been a fortune in jewelry stolen or someone is kidnapped or murdered, hotel security pretty much deals with petty burglary. The HPD has more to worry about than a missing recipe notebook."

Louie sat slumped over on the edge of the bed, the wind clearly knocked out of his sail.

"That notebook is my *life*," he said. "My life's work is in it."

Em gave Officer Kim her cell number and walked him out into the hallway.

"Please, Mr. Kim, this means so much to my uncle. If there's anything you can do to help recover his notebook, or anything we can do to help you, please let us know."

Kim's two-way radio beeped. He clicked it on, and a garbled message echoed in the hall.

"Be right there." He clipped the radio onto his belt again and looked at Em. "We'll do what we can, ma'am, but don't get your hopes up."

9

THIRTY MINUTES before Happy Hour was due to end, the Hula
Maidens were still in their travel outfits making a beeline to the Hau Tree
beachside bar to score cheap drinks before they performed.

"Hurry, ladies," Kiki directed. She glanced back at Flora. The hefty
woman was waddling as fast as she could.

"My thighs are rubbing," Flora groused. "I'll get that chappin' thing
if I'm not careful."

Kiki made an executive decision. "We'll meet you there. Come on,
everyone. Faster."

When they reached the open air bar every seat and table was
occupied by tourists of all ages in swimsuits and resort wear as well as
locals. Judging from the number of discarded umbrella drinks still on the
tables, the bar was doing a bang up business, and the guests were feeling
no pain. Screams and splashing sounds drifted from the nearby *keiki*
pool. Kiki turned to Pat who was carrying their boom box in a black
duffle.

"Did you put in fresh batteries and bring extras in case there's no
outlet nearby?" Kiki asked.

Pat's hand shot to her temple. She saluted. "Roger, that."

"Microphone?"

"Affirmative."

The Maidens spread out. This wasn't their first rodeo. They knew
what to do. They hovered in pairs close to various tables until one was
vacated by a young couple clearly on their honeymoon—if the way they
were groping each other after a couple of rum drinks was any indication.

Trish, closest to the table, whistled and waved, and the Maidens
stampeded over to surround the small table like African wildlife
crowded around the last watering hole in the veld.

Flora came lumbering up and gasped, "We need to order."

"We need to order *now*." Suzi checked her watch. "Only twenty
minutes of happy hour left."

Trish waved Flora into one of the two open chairs. "Sit before you collapse."

Flora sat. She took a swig out of a plastic Menehune Water bottle that everyone knew contained something a lot stronger than the brand's water. Precious climbed up onto the other free chair. Kiki, Lillian, and Big Estelle flanked them. Lillian looked around furtively, afraid one of Mindy's Miracle Cream women would recognize her. Little Estelle had parked her scooter beside a table where two muscular young black men with buzz cuts and gold chains tried hard to ignore her stare. A waiter in a blue aloha shirt with hula dancers cavorting across the fabric took their orders.

"I'll have two," Kiki added.

"Sorry, we can't stack drinks," the waiter said.

"The first one won't last long," she told him.

"Sorry, Auntie. We don't want to get busted by the alcohol commissioner."

Across the way, Little Estelle suddenly laughed uproariously, farted, and tooted her horn.

"Service men, you say?" She cackled. "Perfect. You can service me."

Trish leaned in and said to Kiki, "She's doing that all the time now."

"She always goes for the young ones. Those boys are probably from one of the military bases."

"No, not the pick-up thing. The farting. She tries to cover it up by tooting her horn."

Pat hurried over to join them. "I found a plug, but it's too far away. I'm going with batteries."

Lillian scanned the crowded lanai at the edge of the sand. "Where are we supposed to dance?"

"There's no stage. There's not even a clear spot where we can line up," Big Estelle added.

"How about the beach walk?" A wide sidewalk on the other side of a low wall separated the hotel and bar area from the sand.

"Everyone spread out and find a place to dance between the tables. Right up close and personal with the audience. Try not to knock over anyone's drink," Kiki said.

"Just like we did that time on Moloka'i," Suzi added.

"I didn't go to Moloka'i," Lil whined. "Who can I follow if I'm not in line?"

Flora said, "Don't follow nobody. You should know your dances by now."

"I do, but I forget them when I get nervous."

Precious tugged on Kiki's arm. "What about me? No one will see me if we're all spread out between tables."

Pat reached down, picked Precious up, and stood her on the chair.

"There," Pat said. "Don't fall off."

"Let's do this," Kiki said.

Suzi hesitated. "Is anyone going to introduce us? We haven't even been greeted by the bar manager or anyone."

"We don't need an introduction," Kiki said. "Look around. Everyone's staring at us in expectation. Everyone who isn't watching Little Estelle paw that guy's muscles, that is."

"What about an MC at least?" Suzi suggested.

Kiki countered, "That's what Pat's for."

Pat had the boom box balanced on the chair Flora vacated. A little boy walked by dripping water in his wake. He looked up at his mother who'd obviously only been in the pool from her neck down. Her face was covered with an inch of foundation, and her hair was perfectly styled.

"What's that, Mom?" he asked.

The woman looked at Pat. "I think it's a woman." She reconsidered and said, "Maybe it's a man."

"No, Mom, that." The kid pointed at the boom box.

"It's from the olden days. It plays CDs. Looks like it's a radio, too."

The little boy stared up at Pat. "Why don't 'cha got an iPod?"

"How old are you, kid?" Pat asked the little boy.

"Eight."

"If you wanna live to see nine you'd better get movin'." Pat reached into the black duffle again and pulled out an empty plastic jug labeled TIPS. She handed it to a newlywed couple at a nearby table and said, "Hold this."

A short blond woman in navy and white striped nautical resort wear tapped Pat on the shoulder and thrust a bar menu at her.

"Aloha, Pat! I've so enjoyed you on *Trouble in Paradise*. May I *please* have your autograph?" the woman said.

Pat turned three shades of red and barked, "Hold your horses, lady. We'll be selling T-shirts later, too."

"Hit it," Kiki said.

Pat hit the play button, and "Little Grass Shack" came booming out of the portable.

The Maidens started dancing, making hitchhiking motions over their right shoulders as lyrics about going back to little grass shacks floated on the trade wind breeze.

As Kiki danced she scanned the crowd. Most of the patrons at the tables were smiling, but not all. A couple of locals got up and left. She spotted the manager as he stepped out from behind the bar and edged his way closer to where Pat hovered beside the boom box. He didn't look happy. In fact, he looked down right pissed.

When the song ended, he said something to Pat that Kiki couldn't hear. Pat stopped the CD, looked over at her, shrugged, and folded her arms.

Kiki left the lineup and walked over to Pat and the manager.

"Is there a problem?" she asked.

"He said I had to stop the music." Pat turned a mean-eyed squint on the manager. He appeared intent on ignoring her.

"Why?" Kiki batted her false lashes and tried smiling.

"No dancing out here. It's not allowed."

"But we're *the* Hula Maidens. We always dance." Kiki waved her hand toward where the others had been lined up, expecting them to still be there smiling and looking professional.

Instead, Suzi and Trish had broken rank and were signing napkins. Precious was stuck on the tabletop. Kiki watched her get on her hands and knees and ass up, she climbed down.

Lillian stared around bewildered, patting her ratted pink hair into place. Flora had already retreated to her table. She made loud sucking sounds through her Mai Tai straw. Little Estelle was still parked beside the burly young black men. They'd given up trying to ignore her. She was squeezing one of their meaty biceps.

The manager hadn't caved. "I don't care who you are. No dancing out here. We don't have a cabaret license for this area."

"You don't need a cabaret license for a hula show. Hula is considered a cultural experience for the tourists."

The young man looked stumped for a second. More tourists wielding cameras had gathered and were now taking photos and videos. People on the beach were walking up to see what was going on. As the crowd swelled, the waiters and waitresses weren't able to navigate around the tables.

"Ready?" Pat's finger was poised over the boom box.

"Wait just a minute now." The manager's frustration had escalated. His plastic smile was gone. He shoved his hand through his hair.

"Mau kau kau!" Kiki shouted the call to attention.

"A'i!" the Maidens shouted back. They all snapped to and bustled over to line up again. Precious climbed back onto the table top.

Pat hit the button, and Don Ho's recording of "Pearly Shells" started.

"Ooh!" The crowd cheered and applauded as soon as they heard Don's voice singing a recognizable song. Some of the older guests teared up. The legendary entertainer had appeared at the Hilton Hawaiian Village for years.

The Maidens started dancing. Kiki turned up the megawatts on her smile. She focused on the audience and not the manager as he started tapping on his cell.

10

EM WALKED BESIDE her uncle as they exited the Ali'i Tower, prepared to wander the grounds and decide where to have dinner.

"I'm thinking we should have something substantial. We haven't had anything healthy all day," she said. "There's a Benihana's across Rainbow Drive."

"I'm not in the mood to eat." Louie sounded lower than the sun after sunset.

"Once you see food you might change your mind. Did you get registered for the contest?"

"Yeah. It went quick. They were really organized. None of those hip young men running this thing would have been careless enough to lose a lifetime's worth of recipes."

"I'm sure you'll remember your entry recipe once you start mixing. Get a good night's sleep and tomorrow you'll . . ."

They had crossed the grounds headed toward the beach. They were approaching the beach bar when Em recognized the shrill, short *whoop-whoop* bursts of a police siren.

"What's going on? Sounds like it's coming from the beach," she said.

Louie was tall enough to see over the growing crowd. "I hate to say it, but it might be the girls." He always used the term *girls* lightly.

"Oh, no," Em groaned. "Not already."

Louie grabbed her arm and maneuvered through the crowd of swimmers, surfers, and tourists knotted around the Hau Tree Bar outdoor bar. Kiki and the Hula Maidens were seated on the ground with their arms linked together.

As Em and Louie walked up they started chanting, "We shall not be moo-oo-oved."

Pat yelled, "Louder, ladeeze!"

Apparently, Pat had opted not to join the sit in but was running things from the sideline.

If things weren't bad enough, a news crew was set up on the beach side of the bar, complete with a handheld camera. Em recognized Moanike'ala Nabarro, the KITV reporter and weather girl. She was holding a mic, conferring with the camera operator.

As much as she hated to get embroiled in the Maidens' latest fiasco, Em knew there was no way out. She walked up to Pat, whose buzzed hair was spiked and glossy with pomade. The essence of Old Spice wafted around her. Em tugged on the sleeve of Pat's bright aloha shirt until she had her attention.

"What happened?" Em asked.

"Do ya want the long or the short of it?"

"Abridged, if possible."

Pat started holding up fingers as she ticked off facts.

"One, the ladies were performing. Two, the manager tried to stop 'em. Three, he claims he don't have a cabaret license or somethin'. Four, folks started yellin' for him to leave them alone and let 'em dance. Five, Kiki said hula is a cultural experience, and ya don't need a cabaret license. Six, the manager called hotel security. Seven, hotel security was afraid of the crowd 'cause it's gettin' surly. Eight, security called 911. Nine, the beach cops rolled up on their big wheels. Ten." Pat stared at her hands. "Damn it," she said. "I'm outta fingers."

"Just go on," Em urged.

"Well, the news crew was doin' a weather spot on the Waikiki sunset at a Pineapple Upside Down Cake Contest and heard the commotion. They arrived the same time as the police pulled up. Kiki told the weather girl the Maidens have every right to perform.

She said, 'We're the Hula Maidens!'"

Pat paused to take a breath.

"And here we are," Em sighed.

She spotted a guy who had to be the bar manager. He appeared to be more flustered than the other staff. The waiters and waitresses were doing their best to accommodate the customers despite the swelling crowd. Cops were spread out around the edge of the crowd, some in uniform, some still obviously cops in aloha wear. All remained stoic, no doubt wishing they were anywhere else right now.

A voice came over the two-way radio hooked to the nearest cop's belt. "The paddy wagon is here."

Trish yelled, "Paddy wagon is an offensive slur against the Irish."

"Nowadays everything's a slur against somebody," Pat said.

"Round 'em up," the officer in charge ordered.

Pat turned on him. "Seriously? You're *seriously* going to arrest a bunch of old ladies?"

Kiki yelled, "Hey, I represent that remark, Pat."

"Stand down." The officer went toe to toe with Pat.

Uncle Louie nudged Em. "We have to do something."

Aware of the news crew, Em lowered her voice. "You can't risk getting hauled off before the contest. You've got to be at that orientation meeting tomorrow morning."

"But . . ."

She knew Louie would protest and argued, "Look, anyone familiar with the show knows you're connected to the Maidens in a big way. Take my advice and get out of here. I'll do what I can."

He looked crestfallen. "You sure?"

"Yes. Now scoot back to the edge of the crowd. Don't do anything to call attention to yourself."

Em waited until he took her advice, then she walked over to the officer in charge. He had salt and pepper hair and looked to be in his mid-fifties, no doubt stationed at Waikiki while counting down to retirement.

"Excuse me, Officer." She read the name on his badge. "Officer Young. Is there any way we can fix this?"

"Yeah. We can get these women out of here, so everyone can get back to enjoying what's left of the evening."

The crowd had begun a chant on their own and was getting louder.

"Hu-la Mai-dens! Hu-la Mai-dens!"

"Do you know these nuts?" the officer asked Em.

She swallowed. They were definitely her nuts, and she and Louie were indirectly responsible for them being on Oahu.

"I do."

"Then convince them to stop resisting arrest. I'll see what I can do after we get them outta here."

Em worked her way over to where Kiki was sitting cross-legged on the ground. Two officers followed her. She yelled to be heard over the crowd.

"Kiki, this will go a whole lot smoother if you all get up and go with the police."

"We haven't done anything."

"Look around. You've created a real mess here. Half of Honolulu will be down here in an hour if you don't comply."

Kiki's chin jutted. "Good. We can use some back up."

Em went down on one knee and leaned closer. "Stop this now

before you all spend time in jail. It's not cute or funny. If for no other reason, think of Uncle Louie. Don't ruin his place in the competition."

Kiki tried to extract her arm from Lillian's. The Iowan was sitting next to her, sobbing her eyes out. "I should have brought Bob! Who's going to bail me out?"

Precious, seated on the other side of Lillian, grabbed her hand and whispered, "Pretend we're together. We don't want to end up playmates for hard core prisoners."

Lil let out a wail that nearly drowned out the chanting crowd.

Kiki allowed a patrolman in Bermuda shorts to take her arm and hoist her to her feet. He held on, indicating Lillian should be next. She rose with Precious clinging to her. The trio was escorted to the police van waiting on the delivery drive that ended at the sand. Their supporters surrounding them fell silent.

Following Kiki's example, Suzi, Trish, and Flora went peacefully, waving to their fans as they were led through the crowd. Tourists, beach-goers, and hotel guests parted like the Red Sea to let them pass. Big Estelle brought up the rear of the line.

As they walked by Moanike'ala, the reporter, Lillian grabbed her mic. "Please, Bob, if you're watching, send bail!" she cried.

Em followed them to the van.

Big Estelle wasn't as complacent as the others. "This is your fault, Kiki!"

Kiki made a show of huffing and puffing as she grabbed the door handle to pull herself up. She disappeared inside the van.

"If they don't have a sense of humor here, how's that my fault?" Kiki's voice carried out the van door.

"You should have gotten permission," Big Estelle shot back as she grabbed the handle by the door and hefted herself inside.

"It's easier to say oops later," Kiki said.

"Now Mother will be here unsupervised while I'm in the pokey. No telling what she'll do." Big Estelle stuck her head back outside the van. "Em, will you keep an eye on Mother?"

"I'd rather keep an eye on a rabid Rottweiler," Em mumbled.

Then to Big Estelle: "I'll try," she said.

Pat had followed along, toting the duffle with the boom box.

"Get in." Young nodded toward the open van door. "You're part of this crew."

Pat threw up her free hand. "Hey, I'm just the sound tech."

"We're taking you in, too."

"Aw, come on, man," Pat said.

He signaled another officer. Pat handed the bag over to Em.

"Don't lose this. If you do, it'll be the end of us."

Officer Young turned to Em. He lowered his voice.

"Come to the Waikiki substation. It's just down Kalakaua. Give us about an hour. Between you and me, they won't be held long. The show of force is just to teach 'em a lesson and get the crowd to disperse."

As the news crew jogged past, Em heard Moanike'ala Nabarro say, "Let's get some shots outside the station."

The crowd surged toward the police van and started booing as the doors closed. Uncle Louie appeared at Em's elbow.

"If the bar manager's smart he'll offer everyone a free round of drinks before they decide to block the van's exit," Louie said.

"If he was smart he wouldn't have let this thing explode," Em said.

A surfer standing behind Louie had overheard. "Free round of drinks? I heard free round of drinks."

A stampede ensued as the crowd headed toward the bar and started claiming tables. When the paddy wagon pulled out with lights flashing, no one was paying attention.

The fate of the Hula Maidens was already yesterday's news.

11

LOUIE WAS TOO depressed to go with Em to the station. She left him in the suite muttering something about ordering room service after he lined up his cocktail making equipment.

She followed the directions the concierge gave her and drove the rental van down Kalakaua Avenue to the Waikiki substation. It wasn't much bigger than the Hanalei Post Office. The Maidens were slumped in chairs in a holding area. Em ended up at the desk of a lieutenant who had been assigned to get them out of the building.

"You sure you can handle them?" Lieutenant Chun looked skeptical. He wasn't about to turn them loose without someone taking responsibility for them.

"I'll try my darndest."

The lieutenant shook his head. "You know, my wife's not gonna believe it. If we didn't live all the way over in Pearl Ridge and traffic wasn't so bad, I'd call and tell her to come down and meet 'em. She never missed a single episode of *Trouble in Paradise*. She's a hula dancer, you know. Real kine, not like these ladies. But they're funny, eh?"

"Really funny."

"You were never on the show much," he said.

Em shrugged. "I was too boring to get much air time. I hid from the cameras a lot."

"I think I put the fear of God in 'em," he said.

If only.

Em figured a lecture from an officer of the law might work on Lillian and Precious, the newbies, but Chun was wasting his breath on Kiki and the others. The only thing Kiki was afraid of was losing a live audience.

Before she walked away from a living, breathing HPD officer, Em said, "May I ask you something, Lieutenant Chun?"

"Sure."

She explained about the theft of Louie's Booze Bible and added, "That notebook is my uncle's life. It's invaluable. I'm thinking we should give up on Hilton security and call the police. Could you take a report?"

Just then a brawl broke out in the lobby where the details of a fight at a big Samoan reunion were being sorted out. Lieutenant Chun pushed away from his desk. At six-four he towered over her.

"Lady, you bettah jus' let hotel security work it out. We got real worries here. A bunch of Medicare age hula dancers and a stolen recipe book isn't gonna ever be high on our priority list. I'd say you got better chances of recovery with Hilton security."

He left Em and went to help other officers subdue a Samoan grandmother after she tossed a skinny Chinese guy against a wall.

By the time Em had squished the Maidens into their rental van and was on the way back to the Hilton, they had already broken the law again. There were more passengers than seatbelts inside the van, and so Precious was draped over three laps in the middle row.

"Louie had better be watching out for my mother," Big Estelle yelled from the far back seat.

The last time Em had seen Little Estelle she'd been with the two muscular servicemen at the bar.

"I'm sure she's fine."

"You don't sound like she's fine. You sound like you have no clue."

12

LOUIE WAS STILL DOWN in the dumps when he woke up. Em hated to make things worse, but she decided to tell him she was going to meet her ex for lunch at a nearby hotel.

"What's he doing here? Stalking you?" Louie shook his head. "He's probably regretting letting you go and wants to get back together."

"Too late for that. Besides, I'm the one who filed for divorce," she reminded him. She told him about how Phillip had read about Louie's participation in the contest and how Phillip was going to be here on Oahu this week too, and so he invited her to lunch.

"I think it'll be a good thing. Closure. Gotta be good." She wasn't feeling real certain.

The phone in the suite rang as Em debated what to wear to lunch. It was Hilton security officer Kim calling to tell her that he had recovered the video of their hallway taken around the time they'd checked in yesterday. He asked when it would be convenient for her to meet him at the security office and view it.

"I'll be right down," she said.

The resort was already swarming like a beehive alive with guests. Em had seen at least two Starbucks coffee shops in the complex with lines of customers streaming out the doors. The body clocks of new arrivals from the mainland were still set on earlier time zones, and most of them had already been up for hours.

She passed the penguin lagoon where a couple of molting African penguins hid in the shade of a lava rock cave. They appeared to be staring forlornly at turtles lazing on faux rock islands in the middle of an odiferous pool. When she reached the security office, Mr. Kim was waiting at the desk.

"Thank you for calling me in," she told him.

"We were in luck. The camera was on yesterday. Like I said, it's quirky at best."

"The weather," she said.

"Right. Too much humidity and salt air off the ocean. Come with me."

He led her into another room, smaller, with banks of screens that showed the various locations in the hotel. He made a few strokes on a computer keyboard, and the image of a hallway appeared.

"That's the twentieth floor yesterday morning a few minutes before you checked in," he said.

As Em watched, the hall remained empty. He fast forwarded the video, and she suddenly saw herself and Louie appear at the bottom of the screen. Louie had the strap of his briefcase looped over his shoulder just as he had assured her. They walked down the hall. Louie used his card key to open the room. They went inside, and the hallway was empty again.

"Keep watching," the security officer said. "No one else walks down the hall for a few minutes."

Em watched. He kept fast forwarding to a point where Louie stepped out of the room with an ice bucket in his hand. He turned, fiddled with something, and must have been propping the door open with the latch before he walked down the hall. When he turned the corner he disappeared from view.

A few seconds later a group of five—a couple with three children of various ages—came into view. They were animated and chatting to each other as they hurried along. One of the little ones skipped ahead of the rest.

"Right there," Kim said, pointing to the screen. "See that?"

"I do." Em nodded. Someone in a dark hoodie sweatshirt, baseball cap, and pants trailed close behind the family. He was carrying what appeared to be an ABC Store shopping bag. When they passed Louie's door, the person slipped inside.

"That has to be your thief," Kim said. "Appears to be a man."

"Right."

Kim fast forwarded the video again to the point where the man in the hoodie slipped back out into the hallway and headed in the opposite direction of the camera. They had no glimpse of his face. He was still carrying the bag. Em had Kim run the video back to his entrance to the room. The bag looked considerably heavier when he walked out.

Almost immediately after the man stepped out of the door and was in the hall, Louie turned the corner and was walking toward the thief. Louie nodded genially when they passed, but the encounter lasted no more than a second. Em was surprised Louie had remembered as much detail as he had.

The man with the bag continued on to the end of the hall and turned the corner.

"There's no elevator at that end of the hall," Kim said. "He doesn't come back into view at all, so he had to have taken the emergency stairs to exit the building. My guess is he shed the outfit, probably put it in the bag, and walked out of the building."

"If he had on board shorts and a T-shirt he would blend in without ever being noticed," Em said.

"Unfortunately that's probably the case," Kim agreed. "In a city of one million it's easy to hide in plain sight. We can pretty much assume that notebook is gone for good unless you can think of someone who might have it out for your uncle."

Em frowned, thinking. "I was hoping he'd forgotten to bring it and that there was no thief. Now we're going to have to focus on who might have wanted it, which leads me to think it had to be someone who wanted to sabotage Louie's chances of winning the contest."

"One of the other contestants."

"Right. Someone probably staying here at the Hilton."

13

AT ELEVEN, EM left the Hilton and headed on foot to meet Phillip at Orchids, an upscale restaurant in the Halekulani beachfront hotel not far away. After last night's fiasco and the missing Booze Bible, she definitely wasn't looking forward to seeing her ex, but at the moment anything was better than being at the hotel waiting for the Hula Maidens' next misadventure.

Little Estelle hadn't shown up all night. Her daughter was so beside herself with worry that Kiki gave her two Valiums and put her to bed. Now Big Estelle couldn't stay awake more than ten minutes at a stretch.

In the middle of the night Little Estelle had sent a mass text message to all of the Maidens saying she was A-Okay and not to worry. Lillian was locked in her room, letting her Facebook fans and her private fan club in Iowa know that she was all right after one of them posted the KITV news clip of her arrest. The pitiful on-camera plea for help with bail was burning up the social media websites.

Uncle Louie, certain he was going to come in last in the Shake Off, was still worrying about the fate of his missing Booze Bible. Until she saw the man in the hoodie on the video, Em had convinced herself that he'd lost it somewhere between Kauai and checking into their room.

The Halekulani looked a lot closer on her map of Waikiki. By the time Em walked into the casually elegant oceanfront restaurant which appeared to be quite popular, not to mention expensive, she was beyond glowing. She was downright sweating.

As she took in the posh interior of the room complete with a baby grand piano, she hoped her ex didn't stick her with the bill. Not only had Phillip been a player during their marriage, something she found out the hard way when someone sent her a photo of him in Costa Rica with another woman, but he'd also been living the life of a high roller, assuring her that his business was doing well. In reality, he was in debt up to his *cojones*.

The host informed Em that Phillip was already seated and waiting for her. He led her through the maze of white linen covered tables and bamboo chairs toward view seats.

Em spotted Phillip immediately. The divorce and his subsequent downfall had apparently been good for him. He was tan and fit and smiling. Though he had a slightly receding hairline, he still had a head full of rich chestnut brown hair which he'd taken to combing straight back. When he saw her across the room he waved and waited beside her chair for her.

"Em." He stood back and eyed her from head to toe. "The casual look suits you. I like the ponytail."

Casual? She was wearing a new belted sundress she'd picked up at a pricy boutique in Hanalei. She'd even jettisoned her rubber flip-flops for a pair of dressy sandals. Compared to what she'd been wearing over the last year at the bar, she was in formal wear.

Phillip, in his fitted Armani shirt and white linen pants, looked every bit the wealthy tourist. He held her chair while she sat down and then took his seat across the table.

Em decided on her way here the last thing she needed was a drink, but now that she was face-to-face with the man who'd cheated, lied, and turned her entire life upside down, she smiled across the table at him and ordered a shot of Patron.

"Straight tequila, Em? That's a new twist."

"Life is full of unexpected turns."

She smiled at Phillip and pictured Uncle Louie back at the hotel with his cocktail building implements spread all over the small kitchen area in the suite and Kiki and the rest of them resting up for their next fiasco and mentally compared her new life and the people in it with the life she'd led back in Orange County.

"Never a dull moment," she added.

"So you like living in Hawaii?" He picked up what appeared to be his usual bourbon on the rocks and leaned back in his chair.

Em's gaze kept drifting to the vast stretch of turquoise water stretching toward the horizon and then to Diamond Head in the distance.

"What's not to like? It's paradise."

He didn't need the details of how she worked from nine in the morning until one a.m. closing or how she was still sharing the beach house with her uncle. He really had no business knowing that she was "kind of" dating both a successful screenwriter and a fire dancing detective.

Kind of.

"How are you doing?" she asked.

"Great, as a matter of fact. I've started my own business and turned my finances around. I found a great condo, and I'm living in Marina del Rey now. I like it a lot better than Newport. It's far more cosmopolitan, not to mention closer to LA."

By the time their divorce was finalized, they'd lost their home on exclusive Linda Isle and all of their assets in order to cover his debts. All Em had been left with was his precious Porsche, which she sold to pay her own expenses before she moved to Kauai to help Louie run the Goddess.

"I'm glad you've found your footing again." She didn't ask how many bimbos he was dating.

Her tequila arrived. She downed the shot while the waiter went on and on about the menu, and then Em ordered another.

Phillip continued to talk about himself, his new company, how he found the perfect condo, and how he was happier than he'd ever been in his life. Em threw back her second shot as soon as it hit the table and then started guzzling water. It was going to be a long day. The last thing she needed was a banging headache. Her stomach knotted when she thought he might be about to suggest they reconcile, now that he'd righted his ship, so to speak.

The waiter was hovering again, so Em ordered the Manoa salad and the olive oil poached salmon with Big Island goat cheese, pistachios, and roasted beet root entree. Phillip decided on the lobster sampler with lobster bisque, lobster salad on a bun, Hirabara greens, and chips.

When their entrees came the portions were substantially better than Em expected. She wasn't especially fond of expensive little pyramids of food that wouldn't fill a hummingbird beautifully displayed in the center of huge square plates. The Goddess was known for serving huge portions. No one ever left hungry.

"We're staying at the Moana," Phillip informed her after he'd tasted his lobster salad. "It's the hotel known as the First Lady of Waikiki. What about you?"

"We're at Hilton Hawaiian Village where the Shake Off contest is being held."

"Ah." He finished his bourbon on the rocks. "That's right. I told you how I read the article in the *LA Times*?"

"When you called a couple of days ago," she said.

He looked at her empty shot glass. "Would you like another drink?"

"No, I'm good for now."

"Since when did you start drinking straight tequila?"

Since the day you told me you'd be fishing off of Catalina with the guys, and I opened a text with a photo of you in the airport in Costa Rica with a Barbie doll hanging on your arm.

"Oh, a while back," she said. "But I rarely indulge. Not a good idea if you work in a bar."

A thought filtered through the mellow tranquility induced by the Patron. Em looked down at her empty plate, blinked, and then looked at Phillip again. "Did you say *we're* staying at the Moana?"

He signaled the waiter for another Maker's Mark, and his confidence seemed to slip a notch.

"My fiancée and I. I'm getting married."

"*Re*-married."

"Right. It's her first wedding, so it's going to be a big one. Her name is Felicity. Felicity Duncan."

The minute he made the announcement, mixed feelings of euphoria and freedom came over her on a wave of surprise.

Em smiled. "That's great. Seriously. Congratulations."

"We met at a yoga class. It was love at first sight."

"Yoga? You're into yoga?" She'd seen the young women going in and out of yoga classes. Tall, stick thin, bendable as pretzel dough.

"It's great. You should try it. Very relaxing."

So is the Patron, she thought.

"Are we having dessert?" Em waved a waiter down. "I'd like a dessert."

She ordered the Halekulani's Signature Coconut Cake and turned down another shot of tequila, though Phillip was pushing it. From where she sat Em had a side view of the entry. Phillip was going on about the benefits of stretching.

"Felicity says you're only as young as your back is flexible," he said.

"Oh, really?"

Em knew the minute she looked over and saw a taller, thinner, much younger version of herself standing in the doorway that she was looking at Felicity the Flexible. The blonde was staring at Em, clutching shopping bags that announced she'd done a fair amount of damage on Luxury Row, the haute shopping block on Kalakaua Avenue that included eight international boutiques: Bottega Veneta, Chanel, Coach, Gucci, Hugo Boss, Tiffany & Co., Tod's and Yves Saint Laurent.

"There she is now. I told her I wanted to introduce you, but I'd about given up on her showing up."

Em couldn't decide if Phillip looked more like a proud father than a man in love. He was beaming as he watched Felicity Duncan cross the room.

Felicity, who couldn't be a day over twenty-five, was sporting a perky pair of implants.

"Darling," she said as she lifted her face to give Phillip what amounted to some quick air kisses with fully enhanced lips. Then she slid into a chair and piled her shopping bags on the floor around her Gucci wedges. She adjusted the plunging neckline of her designer sundress.

Then she finally looked Em's way and gave a breathless, "Hi."

"You found some things you liked?" Phillip asked.

Felicity shrugged. "A few."

The waiter sidled up again and asked if she'd like something to drink.

"A Diva martini," Felicity smiled.

Em stared.

"Sorry, we're out of Diva at the moment." The waiter didn't bat an eye. "How about Grey Goose?"

Starting at $3800, Em wondered how many restaurant bars in Honolulu kept a bottle of Diva vodka on the top shelf.

Felicity pursed her ample lips and shrugged. "That's fine. No olives."

An awkward silence ensued. Phillip filled it with talk about the advantages of living in Marina del Rey over Newport Beach until the waiter returned with Em's dessert and Felicity's martini.

"How about lunch?" Phillip asked his fiancée before the waiter left.

"You know I don't eat lunch. Ev-ver." Felicity rolled her eyes.

Em looked down at four layers of sliced chiffon cake layered with coconut Amaretto cream, whipped cream, and shredded coconut. She picked up her fork and sectioned off a mouthful.

Once she'd swallowed, Em asked with all the syrup she could muster, "So when is the big wedding?"

Felicity looked out the window.

Em took another bite. She was more than ready to go but wasn't about to leave one morsel of her dessert.

"Two months," Phillip said. "We can't wait."

As she polished off the last of the coconut cake, Em decided Felicity looked like she could wait forever. Phillip couldn't take his eyes off of his fiancée.

Finally Em folded her napkin and sat back.

"That was a wonderful meal, Phillip. Thank you so much. I'm glad we caught up and *so* happy for the two of you." She scooted her chair back before he could stand. "Right now I'd better get back to the Hilton. Uncle Louie probably needs me."

She grabbed her purse and slipped the strap over her shoulder. Phillip stood and rested his hand on Felicity's shoulder, making sure anyone who was paying attention could tell he was with the younger of the two women.

14

WHEN EM WALKED back into their suite, Louie was still trying to recreate his contest recipe.

"How was your lunch?" he called out from across the room.

"It was okay. I'll tell you about it later."

No one was paying attention. Em was relieved none of them asked who she had lunch with.

Kiki, Suzi, and Trish were lounging in the sitting area channel surfing. Kiki's waist-length hair, whether she wore it up or down, was always artfully combed. Right now it looked like a hurricane had hit it. Not only that, but bits of leaves and flowers were scattered all over the sofa and the carpet.

Em was about to ask what happened when she heard a loud thud and a scream come from the vicinity of Louie's bathroom.

"Who *was* that?" she asked.

No one responded.

She walked across the suite into his room, knocked, and then opened the bathroom door. A small bar of hotel soap sailed past her head and she ducked. She took one quick look inside and slammed the door shut. She walked back into the sitting room.

"What is a monkey on a leash doing in the bathroom?" she wanted to know.

Suzi yawned and stretched. "He hates women."

"He tore Kiki's lei off her head and tried to rip her hair out." Trish looked over her shoulder at Em. "Did you bring home any snacks? Chips or anything? I could sure use some Pirate's Booty."

"I could use a pirate's booty, too," Suzi laughed. "Seen any around?"

"Just the pirate ship that takes tourists out."

"The contest committee is throwing a party tonight with a pirate theme. It's open to the public," Louie said.

"Excuse me, but maybe I should have asked *why* is there a monkey in the bathroom?" Em said.

Louie put down his jigger and wiped his hands on a towel.

"He's on loan," he said. "I was chatting with some of the other contestants, and one of the guys asked if I had brought my taste-testing parrot along—they had all seen Letterman on the reality show. I told him no and added that I sure wish I had. Nothing like a taste-testing parrot, I said."

"Otherwise, all he has is us." Kiki waved her hand. "But I have to pace myself."

"I'm not a fan of flaming drinks," Suzi said. "Louie says his entry is a flaming shot, but that's a secret."

"No tasting for me. My stomach's been off since we got arrested," Trish added.

"They've been no help at all," Louie said.

"About the monkey, Uncle." Em winced the minute she said it.

Louie ran his fingers through his hair. "So the guy says he has a friend who owns a monkey with a knack for knowing when a drink is absolutely great. I asked if I could maybe rent it for a few days, and he set it all up. The monkey was delivered about an hour ago."

"Is he a good taste tester?" Em asked.

"I don't know yet. He's way more temperamental than Dave. If he hates a drink, he gets pissed and throws it against the wall. He's already busted four glasses. I'm working on a flaming drink, so I can't very well set fire to it in a plastic cup."

"Melts," Kiki said.

"No doubt." Em nodded. Suddenly even dining with Phillip and Felicity seemed preferable to this insanity.

"What's its name, Louie?" Trish asked.

"I forgot to ask," Louie said.

The phone rang and Em answered. When it was the front desk for Louie, she expected someone had complained about the shrieks sporadically emanating from the bathroom. Em handed him the phone.

"Please send it up with a porter," Louie told whoever was on the line.

Kiki roused herself but didn't leave the sofa.

"We really should go. We've got to get Big Estelle on her feet before four thirty. We're dancing in the main lobby."

"If you get arrested again I'm leaving you all in jail."

"I cleared it with the hotel manager. We're dancing from four to four thirty in the main lobby area near the front desk."

"You really have permission?" Em folded her arms.

"Would I lie?" Kiki tried to pat her hair back into place with her hands.

"With or without a polygraph?" Em said.

Louie said, "There's a press conference for the contest in the lobby after the dancing."

Em asked, "Has anyone seen Little Estelle?"

"Unfortunately, yes," Suzi told her. "She won't say what she was doing or where she was last night, but she's positively radiant."

"For someone her age," Trish added.

"And she's into rap music now. Writing rap music, actually," Kiki said.

"Rap?"

Suzi put her feet up on the coffee table. "Last I saw she was on her scooter headed to the sundry shop for a notebook and some pens."

Trish walked over and looked at the snack basket on top of the mini bar. "She was singing 'Swing that wood. Swing that wood' over and over. I thought maybe she'd met a baseball player, but she winked at me, and she wasn't talking about a wooden bat or wood from a tree. She winked and said, 'You know, like when a guy gets a *woody*.'"

Em rubbed her temples.

There was a knock on the door. Before Louie answered, he whispered not to mention the monkey. He opened the door to the porter holding a manila envelope. Louie thanked the young man, and Em quickly scrambled to get him a tip before Louie closed the door again.

"Must be from the contest committee." Louie started opening it.

Something crashed in the bathroom.

"Maybe someone should check on the monkey," Em suggested.

Kiki held up both hands and shook her head. "Not me. He almost scalped me. He's *really* pissed off."

Louie pulled two sheets of paper out of the envelope, perused them, lost all color in his face, and sat down at the dining table.

"What is it?" Em rushed over.

"A ransom note."

"Ransom?" Suzi hollered. "Who got kidnapped?"

"The Booze Bible," Em said.

Kiki threw her hands in the air and yelled, "Louie's recipes have been kidnapped? Armageddon!"

The women were on their feet and crowded around Louie so they could read over his shoulder.

"I have twenty-four hours to come up with one hundred thousand dollars before they destroy it. If we go to the police, they'll destroy it." His hand shook as he held up the second page. The paper was yellowed, and it had three holes along the left side.

"This is page one. The first recipe I ever mixed. I named it 'The Panty Dropper.' One sip, and panties start dropping."

Kiki laughed. "I remember Irene always turned three shades of red after you put that one on the menu. Everyone wanted to hear how you came up with the name."

"It started out as a private joke between us." Louie's eyes would glisten whenever he spoke of his late wife, Irene Kakaulanipuakaulani Hickam Marshall, co-founder of the bar and his very own Tiki Goddess. "After one drink she dropped her drawers."

"Maybe you should use that for the contest," Em suggested.

Louie got up and handed her a fruit basket that was on the coffee table.

"Feed the monkey, would you? All he's had so far is Kiki's lei."

"Not to mention some of my hair and scalp." Kiki sniffed.

"Where are you going?" Em noticed Louie was headed for the door.

"To the bank to see about a loan. I'm going to put the Goddess up as collateral."

Em set the fruit basket down and hurried after him.

"You can't do that. The Goddess is free and clear, and it's all you have. It would take forever to pay off a hundred thousand dollars. Now we have some evidence the notebook was actually stolen. We can take it to the police."

"We can't go to the police," he protested. "The letter says that if we do, the Booze Bible will be destroyed. They've already torn out the first page."

Kiki said, "Now that we know it's been stolen, we can all start hunting for the thief. We've called the airlines every two hours since we landed, and our cooler full of *poi* and flowers and stuff is still missing. Maybe the notebook was stolen by the same creep. Next time we call we'll ask if they found anything like it."

"Kiki, that's *not* a good idea," Em said.

"It won't hurt to ask."

"Not that. I meant all of you running around looking for the thief," Em said. "It's better if none of you say a word. Don't tell the others."

"We didn't receive a proclamation from the Mayor and a commendation from the Kauai Police Department for nothing. We're the number one volunteer crime solving squad on the island," Kiki reminded her.

"You're the only volunteer crime solving squad on the island. This isn't Kauai," Em reminded her.

"It won't hurt for us to keep our ears and eyes open," Suzi chimed in.

Kiki rubbed her head and winced. "Let's go get dressed."

"Walk between us," Suzi suggested. "If those Miracle Cream women get a load of you now you'll never shake 'em."

Kiki and the others left, and Em turned around and saw Louie sitting on the sofa staring down at the letter in his hands.

"Let me have that," she said. "You focus on mixing up a winning drink and this afternoon's press conference. I'll think about what we should do. We have twenty-four hours to come up with something. Even if we pay the ransom, there's no guarantee you'll get your notebook back at all, let alone in time for the final contest round."

Louie looked uncertain and confused. The monkey was shrieking and pounding on the bathroom door again.

"Maybe you're right. Let's think this through. Kiki and the girls might be able to help."

Em opened her mouth to protest and then snapped it shut. The last thing she wanted was to have to deal with the Maidens while they were playing detective again.

He glanced at the clock on the bedside table. "I'd like to go down to the lobby early. Chat up some of the others. Who's to say one of my competitors didn't steal it like you thought originally? I wouldn't put it past any of them."

"You might be on to something, but tread lightly. Someone crazy enough to do that could be dangerous."

"I'll be careful."

"Let me just freshen up, and I'll walk down with you."

Louie nodded. "Great. I'll be ready to go as soon as I mix the monkey a Singapore Sling. His owner said he's into classics."

15

THE SUN WAS shining, and a light mist cast a rainbow over the ocean as Em and Louie walked down the shady stone walkway toward the Tapa Bar area. Em watched as the colors of the rainbow deepened over Waikiki, but the shower quickly moved on and the colors soon faded. Within seconds there was no sign the rainbow had ever been.

Just beyond the Tapa Bar, a banner announcing the annual Shake Off kick-off party had been stretched above a planter where a tall wooden tiki faced the ocean.

7 P.M. TONIGHT! SHAKE OFF COMPETITION
PIRATE PARTY
HILTON CONVENTION CENTER BALLROOM
TICKETS AVAILABLE TO THE PUBLIC / COSTUMES
ENCOURAGED!

Em paused to read the sign.

"They gave me two tickets in my registration pack," Louie said. "With everything that's been going on, I forgot to ask if you'd like to go. The info says they serve a mean pirate's grog. How about it?"

Em started to say no when out of the blue she thought, *loose lips sink ships.* Maybe after the entrants downed multiple mugs of pirate's grog, she might be able to ferret out some information that would point to whoever had gotten his hands on Louie's Booze Bible. She'd already been seen around the resort with Louie and the Maidens, so what better way to go undercover than to don a pirate costume?

"What are you wearing?" she asked Louie.

"I brought an old bandana to tie around my head and an eye patch. That's as far as I'll go aside from saying arrrgggghhh a few times."

"I'll see if I can come up with something," Em said. She'd just found the perfect excuse to slip over to the security office again. "I'd better start looking around if I'm going to go. I'm sure with all these shops around I can come up with a costume."

The first store she passed was Louis Vuitton. *Or maybe not,* she thought.

The penguins were still looking glum as she passed their concrete lagoon. She walked into security and was relieved when she found Mr. Kim manning the security desk again.

"Ms. Johnson," he said. "Sorry to say I don't have any leads yet. We've been slammed."

"High crime at the Hilton?"

He shook his head. "Not that much. We spend most of our time rousting the obvious hookers and tossing locals out of the pools."

"I really need a favor." She smiled up at him and took a deep breath. "Someone delivered an envelope to our room earlier today, and my uncle would like to know who left it. Do you think I could take a look at the footage from the front desk area? Just to see who dropped off the envelope?"

"You know, Ms. Johnson, the Hilton staff is here to serve you with aloha, but you can't expect us to show you video feeds whenever you get a whim. The stolen binder or whatever is one thing, but now you need to see the feed so that you can write somebody a thank you note?"

She was a nanosecond from telling him about the ransom demand, but she thought of how upset Louie would be if she did anything to jeopardize the Booze Bible.

"I know it sounds ridiculous," she said. "How about a bribe? We've got twenty pounds of Hanalei *poi* on its way over from Kauai," she said.

"No bribes. I'll even forget you offered." He shook his head, but he was smiling. "Even if I could take the time to run the playback for you right now, the whole system is down at the moment. We've got a tech team on the way. Looks like you're out of luck."

16

KIKI SURVEYED THE open air reception lobby like a general weighing her options before battle. The Maidens, outfitted in casual floral sheath dresses with faux white gardenia hairpieces, were gathered in an alcove by the ladies' room.

As yet there was no sign of Pat. Though no one had actually worked up the courage to approach them, people were staring and whispering in anticipation. *Trouble in Paradise* fans were well aware that whenever the Maidens gathered, catastrophe was just around the corner.

Little Estelle was parked off in an out of the way spot. Wearing earbuds, she was frenetically writing on a yellow legal pad, her head bobbing to whatever streamed through her iPod.

Back toward the Tapa Bar, the Shake Off conference coordinators had set up a press conference area where they were offering free Mai Tais to anyone over twenty-one as well as selling an array of official Waikiki Western Regional Shake Off T-shirts, visors, and beer cozies. Kiki was thrilled about the press conference, giddy with all the possibilities that might come of it. Aside from hula, there was nothing she liked better than notoriety.

A potbellied man dressed like an oversized pirate's cabin boy walked up with an armload of flyers.

"Arrrggghhh!" he yelled.

"Arrrggghhh!" Kiki yelled back.

"That's the spirit." He tried to hand her a flyer. "How about coming to our Shake Off pirate party tonight? Only sixty dollars for dinner, all the grog you can drink, live music, and fun."

She waved away the flyer. "We make our own fun. Move along, buddy."

She finally relaxed when she spotted Pat toting the boom box, weaving her way through the gathering crowd.

"Did you hear about the pirate party tonight?" Pat asked.

"Yeah, I heard, but we're not going."

"It sounds kinda fun."

"We're all going bar crawling down Kalakaua. We'll have a drink in every hotel bar. Depending on what entertainment they have going, we might have a chance to dance."

"Sounds okay, but I'd love to dress up like a pirate." Pat surveyed the area. "Where do ya want me to plug in?"

"We'll be dancing between those two columns flanked by potted palms," Kiki said. That put them smack in the middle of the reception area. "We'll have to go with batteries."

"I'll see if there's a plug behind one of those big cement pots. We could get lucky." Pat walked off.

A couple of tourists spotted her and yelled, "Hey Pat! Is that really you?"

"Who the heck you think I am? A Pat Boggs impersonator?" Pat snorted a laugh and said, "Catch ya'all later. We'll be sellin' T-shirts right after some dancin'."

The tourists made the okay sign and walked off to sample free Mai Tais.

When Kiki thought she heard masculine voices speaking thick Pidgin English, she turned around and saw five older Hawaiian men who had just piled out of a van parked at the curb. They started pulling guitar and ukulele cases out of the vehicle. They were wearing matching aloha shirts, kukui nut necklaces, and white pants.

The balding, heavyset man apparently leading the pack reminded her of her husband, Kimo. He headed straight toward her with a huge smile on his face while carrying a guitar case and music stand in his beefy hands.

"You're Kiki, the leader of the Hula Maidens, yeah?"

"For sure," she smiled back. "I'm Kiki."

"I'm Byron. We're the Kamakanis. We saw you folks on the news last night and thought we'd come down and help you out while you're here."

"Help us out?"

"Play music for you. We know pretty much all the songs you dance."

By now the other four musicians had joined them.

"I seen all your shows on TV," one of them said.

"You ladies got it goin' *on*," the eldest of them added.

Kiki was so beside herself she clapped her hands. "Live music! I can't believe it."

Byron laughed. "Far as I know we're still alive. So it's okay we play for you?"

"Okay? Of course it's okay. Better than okay. We're dancing in about five minutes." She motioned Pat over from where she'd been keeping an open space between the palms and columns.

"Three minutes and forty-five seconds," Pat said.

"We bettah go tune up," Byron winked.

"Show these gentlemen where to set up," Kiki told Pat.

Pat hollered at a porter watching from the bellman's podium. "How 'bout some foldin' chairs for these boys?" She clapped her hands twice and added, "*Wikiwiki.*"

Kiki gathered the dancers and lined them up so they'd be ready to walk in with some semblance of order and decorum. The crowd began to swell in the reception area. New arrivals waiting to check into their rooms were forced to line up off to one side of the reception desk or the other.

A thirty-something guy wearing a T-shirt with a tiki mug surrounded by the words Official Shake Off Official on it, a goatee, and a black fedora walked up to Kiki. "Excuse me, ma'am," he said.

"Kiki. It's Kiki." Not far away, a cooler had mysteriously appeared beside the Kamakanis, and the guys were apparently tuning up with beers.

"Kiki, how long is your show?" He scanned the crowd. Phones and cameras were snapping. "We've got a press conference scheduled for half an hour from now."

"No worries," Kiki tried to assure him. "We'll be done by then."

"I caught you on the news last night and heard about what happened at the Hau Tree Bar. We don't want our press party delayed or interrupted."

Kiki tossed her hair over her shoulder and smiled what she hoped was her most winning smile. "Of course not. We'll finish on time."

As the hipster started to walk away, Kiki added under her breath, "Unless the crowd goes wild and we're forced to keep dancing."

17

"UNBELIEVABLE." EM raised her voice so Louie could hear her over the quintet of older Hawaiians singing and playing ukes and guitars. She'd just re-joined her uncle near the lobby.

"What's that?" he asked.

"Kiki managed to find some musicians."

Kiki and the Maidens were spread out across the huge open reception area in front of the driveway where cabs and vans pulled into the Hilton. Miraculously, there was no sign of trouble. No security rushed in to stop them. There was no police presence to speak of.

Em wished she felt more relieved.

"Kiki gets what Kiki wants." Louie was distracted by his own problem. He barely gave the Maidens a glance as he headed for the competition press area. He was wearing his official entrant's lanyard and badge, but there was little need for her uncle to identify himself. With his thick silver hair, deep bronze tan, not to mention his height and classic aloha shirt, he was easy to spot.

Em watched as fans of the cancelled reality show stopped him and asked for his autograph. He was every bit as famous as the Hula Maidens but oblivious to his notoriety at the moment. He had bigger fish to fry.

She considered herself lucky. Of average height, wearing a nondescript blond ponytail and sunglasses, she wasn't as recognizable as Louie and the Maidens. Not only that, but during the *Trouble in Paradise* shoots she stayed off camera as much as possible. If people looked twice at her in public now they thought she looked familiar, but most of the time didn't make the connection.

"Looks like the Maidens decided to take their show on the road."

Em turned when she recognized Nat Clark's voice. Her part-time next door neighbor was standing right behind her. She was so glad to see someone sane that she hugged him without thinking.

"Hey, Nat. I'm so glad to see you. How's it? You're not filming this afternoon?"

"Early wrap," he said. "I've got to fly to California tomorrow after shooting. If I'd have known I'd get that kind of a reception, I'd have shown up earlier."

"I'm glad you found me. I just came down from the room. Louie has a press conference in about thirty minutes."

Nat had on sunglasses, but he wasn't wearing them just to look cool or anonymous. His prescription tortoiseshell glasses somehow added to his easygoing charm, in a Clark Kent sort of way.

"Do the Maidens have anything to do with that warm welcome? Are they driving you nuts already?" He glanced over at the dancers. "I didn't know they were coming."

"Louie and I didn't know either until the night before we left. Did you catch the news last night?"

He shook his head no. "We had a late call time."

"You're the writer. Do you really have to be there?"

"Until this thing really gets off the ground, I like to be on the set in case they need any last minute re-writes."

"We were only here a few hours when the girls were hauled off to jail."

"Why am I not surprised?" His gaze strayed back over to the performance. "You want to stay and watch this? Or would you like to get away for a few minutes? I'm starving."

"Are you kidding? I can see them dance every night. I'd like to be back for the Shake Off press conference, though."

"Then let's go to CJ's. It's a New York style deli right here in the hotel."

"Lead the way," Em said.

Once they were seated Nat changed his glasses and leaned back. "Better?" He handed Em a menu.

"Much. Nothing to eat though, thanks. I'd love an iced tea."

Nat ordered two iced teas and a kalua pig Reuben sandwich with grilled onions and barbecue sauce. When the waiter walked away, Nat gave Em his full attention.

"So aside from the crazy makers showing up, howzit going? Is Louie excited?"

"I'm afraid the Maidens aren't our only problem. We weren't here an hour when Louie announced his Booze Bible had been stolen."

"That's terrible. I know what that notebook means to Louie. I've always thought he should have it published. Are you sure it's not misplaced?"

Em nodded. "I thought maybe that was the case. I hoped maybe he left it on Kauai, but less than an hour ago he received a ransom note. Whoever has his Booze Bible wants one hundred thousand dollars for its safe return."

"Are you kidding?"

"I wish."

"When was the notebook stolen?"

"Right after we checked in. Louie left his room for some ice and left the door propped open."

"Have you gone to the police?"

"The extortionist said if we do that he'll destroy the notebook. An HPD officer basically told me they have bigger crimes to solve, and they can't be worrying about a missing notebook that belongs to an old *haole* from North Shore Kauai."

Nat was appalled. "He said that?"

"He didn't come right out and say it, but I got the drift. The Hilton security officer I've dealt with let me watch the video recorded by our hallway camera yesterday. I saw the thief go into Louie's room and walk back out before Louie got back. In fact, they passed each other in the hallway. The guy was in a hoodie and had a bag in his hand the whole time, so the Booze Bible was probably in it when he left."

"What about the extortion note? Did someone slip it under the door? Maybe he's on the hallway video again."

"No. A porter delivered it from the front desk." Em sipped some tea.

"Was it mailed?"

"No, there was no postage. Just Louie's name on the front of the envelope."

"They must have surveillance in the reception area. Whoever dropped it off there might be on video."

"*If* the camera recorded it. They're having trouble with playback on that one. I already stopped by."

"I think an extortion note would get HPD's attention. A hundred thousand is serious stuff."

"Louie's terrified that the thief will destroy the notebook."

"Do you think you're safe?"

"From pretty much everyone but the monkey."

Nat spit ice tea down his shirtfront. "What monkey?"

"The one locked in Louie's bathroom. He didn't bring Letterman. Someone rented him a Capuchin monkey that is a cocktail taste-tester. Trouble is, the thing gets furious if it hates a drink, and it's pretty much disliked everything Louie's given it. It also hates women. It tried to snatch Kiki bald. When we left the suite it had smeared complimentary shampoo and conditioner all over the bathroom and was guzzling mouthwash."

"You're not thinking of paying the ransom, are you?"

"Louie is. I've talked him out of it for now. I'm not paying any extortionist, but we have to do something. He gave us twenty-four hours. You're a mystery writer. Any ideas?"

"If I'd written a treatment of this scenario no one would approve it."

Em sighed and gazed around the open air lobby. Four young women, obviously out for the evening, were checking out Nat, and Em realized, not for the first time, that he *was* good looking. Not only that, but he was available, a great conversationalist, and level-headed. He had a successful career in a business where most people never made it, not to mention he owned homes in LA, Honolulu, and on Kauai.

"Ask about the video playback in the reception area when you get back. Maybe they're working. In fact, I'll go with you if you want," he offered.

"I'm a big girl. I can handle it," she assured him. "I'll ask on my own."

She hated to admit that hotel security staff might think she was just another ditzy blonde considering the company she kept.

"It's almost four thirty." He checked his watch and signaled the waitress.

They walked back into the hotel grounds together.

"Looks like the Maidens have finished without any mishaps," Em told Nat.

"Either that, or they've been rounded up again."

"Please." Em held up her hand. "Don't even go there."

They spotted the women seated with musicians at tables at the Tapa Bar and skirted behind some high-end stores without being noticed as they headed for the main lobby area. Louie must have been chosen to be featured at the Shake Off press conference. He and the conference organizers were seated behind microphones at a long table answering questions and talking about the event.

"Louie looks pretty calm," Nat said.

"He's always at ease behind a mic. The free Mai Tais help, too. He's worried sick about his notebook and afraid to mention the theft to anyone."

"For good reason. His Booze Bible is being held hostage. The thief might rip out another page for spite."

Em sighed. "Dismantling it bit by bit seems pretty sadistic."

"I'm glad it's just a notebook and not a person," Nat said. "Otherwise you'd be getting packages with fingers in them."

"That's a visual I don't want to think about." She watched Louie for a moment and then said, "Listen, I can check in at security on my own. You don't need to stay."

"You're sure? I really don't mind."

"I'm sure." She smiled. "Thanks for getting me out of here for a while. I really appreciate it."

He leaned close and kissed the corner of her lips. "Always a pleasure."

Em watched him walk away before she headed over to security again.

Mr. Kim wasn't there. An older man was in charge of the desk.

When she asked if the reception area video playback was fixed and if so, could she view it, he said no.

"The tech team is in there right now. Even if it was fixed, we're short-handed tonight. Can't take the time to help you. With the press conference for the Shake Off thing going on, the Miracle Cream ladies leaving, and the Shriners set to check in tomorrow, not to mention those *pupule* hula dancers that were arrested Tuesday night, most of our officers are out patrolling the grounds. We've got twenty-two acres and thirty-five hundred rooms here, you know."

He studied Em for a moment.

She sensed the moment he recognized her.

"Aren't you with that bunch? The old ladies who dance on the television?" he asked.

"The *pupule* dancers? I am. I'm also here with my uncle. He's in the Shake Off. It's very important that I find out who dropped off an envelope for him earlier today."

The security office remained adamant. "The equipment's still not working right now. The weather wrecks it."

"So I've heard," Em said.

The officer leaned back and called toward the video room, "Hey, Elwin, is the system still broke?"

"Still broke, uncle. Fix 'em bumbye."

"See?" He shrugged. "Nu'ting I can do."

Em gave up and went back to the press conference where most of the reporters were directing their questions to Louie.

She watched with interest and finally when Louie was finished, she waved him over.

"That was great," she told him. "A couple of those guys weren't very happy sharing the spotlight with you."

He looked back at the tables set up for the Shake Off promotion.

"I'm not part of the in-crowd." He frowned. "What they don't get is I'm the real deal. I'm the true tropical concoctionist they're all trying to be. I have a past. I have a story. I was around when tiki bars and exotica were invented."

Em studied the young men gathered across the outdoor lobby. They were decked out in vintage bark cloth aloha shirts and Rat Pack hipster fedoras reminiscent of Sinatra. They were even wearing black and white spectator wing tips. Didn't they have a clue? No self-respecting tiki bar owner would wear hard shoes and socks in the tropics.

"They're probably all jealous of you." She noticed one of the young guys was staring over at Louie while talking to one of his cohorts. "Most of the press was directing questions to you, I noticed."

He shrugged. "I know a few of these local reporters. The rest already know me through the show. I tried to share the spotlight. Believe me. I tried to get the press to ask more about Lamar dePesto. He's the founder of this whole national contest. He started it about eight or nine years ago. Can I help it if I'm a celebrity?"

Louie nodded toward a group of mixologists. "See the short guy in the mostly yellow shirt? His name is dePesto. He's won the Western Regionals every year. He's from San Diego. He hooked me up with the guy who rented me the monkey."

"How about telling them to pick up that monkey and that you want your money back? We could get rid of it tonight."

"I don't want to insult him."

"No way you could insult that monkey."

"The owner. I don't want to insult his owner. Or dePesto." Louie had missed the joke altogether.

She pictured the monkey smeared with conditioner. "Just say it didn't work out."

"What are you thinking? You're frowning." He followed her gaze.

Em tried to relax her expression. "Maybe dePesto is afraid you'll take the crown."

"They don't give out crowns. They give out golden swizzle sticks."

"Maybe he wants to win desperately enough to steal the Booze Bible," she said.

"You think?"

"Who else would know how valuable it is?"

If Louie wasn't so tan he'd have lost all color in his face.

"Maybe he's already copied all my recipes." Louie looked glum for a minute. "Did you find a costume?"

"Not yet, but I found out there's a costume shop within a short walk. It's on Ala Moana in the Ilikai Hotel. They rent and sell. I'm going to walk on over and check them out."

"Great. Hope you find something."

"If I'm not back by seven, go ahead and leave without me. It may take a while for me to get back and changed. Just leave the ticket on the dresser in my room."

Louie hoisted his drink. "Arrrgggghhh. Aye, aye, matie."

18

IT WAS CLOSE TO six by the time Em walked into the costume store in the Ilikai Hotel within walking distance from the Hilton.

Just inside the front door, the shelves to her right were lined with various lengths and colors of wigs on Styrofoam heads. The opposite wall was covered with accessories from hats to masks to capes, swords, whips, feather dusters, and handcuffs. The rest of the room was filled with costumes on hangers, and there were mannequins dressed in various costumes standing around.

She checked out the handcuffs and pictured herself taking down the Booze Bible extortionist. She thought of her promise to Roland. No more Nancy Drew.

"Aloha." The clerk was a tall, thin young man with his hair pulled up into a knot and held in place with a chopstick. "How may I help you?"

She walked over to where he stood across the counter. Up close she could see that he was wearing false eyelashes. His lower lids were lined with kohl.

"I need a wig," she said, starting at the top.

"Lime green and blue are major hot sellers right now."

"I was thinking of something a little more subtle. Black would be great."

He squinted at her. "I see you in a Cleopatra cut."

"Actually, I need a pirate costume."

"For the Shake Off party?"

"Right. I guess you've had a rush on pirate wear."

"We have, but mostly guys. I've got just the thing for you, honey." He walked over to a tall rounder, sifted through the hangers, and finally pulled out a long, clear plastic garment bag and walked back.

"Here you go. This one's called 'Pussy in Boots.' It's for the perfect pirate wench. Try it on. You'll love it."

"Pussy in Boots?"

"The boots rent separately, though." He looked her feet. "What are you? A seven?"

She nodded. He handed over the bag and went to get the boots. Em studied the photo on the label on the bag. She blushed just looking at it.

He came back with a pair of black stiletto boots as long as her legs.

"These are thigh high." He draped them across the counter.

"What do you wear under this thing?" Em pointed to the photo of the costume.

"As little as possible."

"No, seriously."

"It's all in there, crinoline and all. I guess you could shove a pretty piece of lace in the bodice if you're uncomfortable." He glanced at a clock on the back wall. "It's past closing time. You want to rent the costume or not?"

"What about a wig?"

"Oh, yeah." He walked over to the line of Styrofoam heads and slipped a black Cleopatra-cut off of one of them. From the accessory wall he grabbed a tricorn hat in black edged with black lace.

"You'll need this, too."

"How about an eye patch?" The hat would help to hide her face, but would that be enough of a disguise?

He snapped his fingers and hurried back to the accessory wall.

"Here you go." He brought her a black satin eye mask decorated with sequins.

"Great." She doubted even Louie would recognize her in this get up. She realized she had no idea what all this would cost.

"So how much is the rental fee on this?"

"Two hundred nine dollars and eleven cents."

Em started to say she'd changed her mind but quickly decided two hundred nine dollars was a heck of a lot less than a hundred thousand. If she could unmask the extortionist decked out as "Pussy in Boots," the rental fee was worth twice the price.

Before she changed her mind, she pulled out her credit card and handed it over.

19

LOUIE HAD ALREADY left by the time Em wrestled all the bags and boxes back up the elevator to the suite. She hurried into her bedroom and locked the connecting door in case he came back. She really wanted to see if he could recognize her or not at the party. The less he knew about her plan the better.

She zipped open the garment bag and laid out the costume pieces: fishnet stockings, a short red full skirt, and black crinoline to wear beneath it along with a black leather bodice that laced up over a low-cut red peasant blouse. She stepped out of her comfortable capri pants and knit top and started by pulling on the fishnets. When she had the outfit on, she sat on the bed and pulled on the stiletto boots. They were far more comfortable than they looked and slid on like butter on hot toast. She pinned her hair up and tugged on the wig before she finally looked in the mirror.

Cleopatra goes pirate.

She put on hot red lipstick, black eye shadow, and brushed on a light bronzer, all of which the shop clerk had talked her into at the last minute. When she slipped on the black satin eye mask, she didn't even recognize herself.

Em left the suite and took the elevator down to the Ali'i Tower lobby. She hadn't worn stilettos for so long she was a bit wobbly. The uneven stone walkways that threaded through and around the resort didn't help. She took her time, ignored the stares and wolf whistles, but secretly smiled to herself as she walked to the Hilton Convention Center.

Carrying her ticket in one hand and a small woven purse in the other, Em entered the building and followed the music. It was the same kind of music Louie loved, mid-50s exotica at its best—pure South Pacific meets Asia. A piano and stand-up bass player were joined by musicians on a vibraphone, bongos, a conga, gongs, and bells. They let out occasional high-pitched shrieks mixed with bird calls, inspiring jungle fantasies.

A huge banner was draped above the entrance to the ballroom warning that guests should PREPARE TO BE BOARDED! Em handed her ticket to the pirate at the door, a short bald man in a blue and white striped shirt who looked like Disney's version of Mr. Smee in *Peter Pan.*

"Ah, my fine wench! Careful, or you'll be taken captive and held for ransom!"

"Ransom?" Em stared at him for a moment then realized he was making a joke.

"Right you are! Arrrggghh! Be sure to grab a mug of grog. You can keep the mug." He indicated a table behind him covered with brown ceramic barrel mugs. Shake Off Waikiki 2014 was emblazoned across the front. "You can bet those will be hot ticket items on eBay under Tiki Mugs and Collectibles after the conference."

Em picked up her grog. Obviously the other partygoers had weighed anchor an hour ago, and most of them were three sheets to the wind already.

She wasn't two feet into the room when a tall man—made even taller by a black tricorn hat with a skull and crossbones on it—walked up to her.

"Tell me now, wench, what's a fine beauty like yourself doin' wanderin' on her own among these landlubbers?"

She wanted to suggest he stick a sword in his *okokle* but figured she had to play the pirate game and make nice if she wanted to get close to someone on the committee.

"I'm meeting someone, captain, or I'd shiver your timbers." She lifted her mug, toasted him, took a swill of grog, and coughed. The beverage consisted of plenty of extremely spicy dark rum, a trace of unrecognizable fruit juice, and not much else.

As Captain Hook wandered away, Em checked out the huge room. Tables covered in white linen cloths were scattered around the room, but not many of the attendees were seated. Thick rope was draped along the walls, and fake parrots hung from the ceiling on swing perches. The band was set up on a stage decorated to look like a main deck. A raised quarter deck, complete with a rail and mounted ship's wheel, was at one end of the stage.

A bar was set up on the floor in the opposite corner, stacked wooden barrels that held a long wide plank. Behind it, Hilton bartenders had bandanas tied around their heads and were outfitted in white open-throated shirts with billowing sleeves. A skull and crossbones flag was draped above the liquor shelves behind the bar. A mile long buffet table stretched along another wall.

She took a step toward the bar but stopped when she spotted Louie across the room in deep conversation with a man dressed like a British sea captain. Then taking a deep breath, she made a point of walking right past them and even smiled Louie's way. He smiled back but didn't recognize her. If her uncle couldn't see past the costume, her two hundred and nine dollars and eleven cents had been well spent.

She spotted Lamar dePesto, contest founder, standing with his committee chairmen and cohorts at one end of the long plank bar. She took a few more swigs of grog to muster her courage.

She almost made it to the edge of the group when someone bumped into her and actually copped a feel of her behind.

"If 'ye are free tonight I'd be 'appy to show you me longboat." A smiling, bald, suntanned man nudged her with his elbow and winked. He reached for her again.

"Hey, matie, no fair." The stilettos gave her a good three inches over him. She slapped his hand away.

"'ave pity on a poor castaway, lass." He reeled closer. She stepped back and checked out his outfit—cut-off raggedy shorts, a ripped and faded aloha shirt, and a very real sunburn beneath a fake shaggy beard. "I been all alone on a deserted island for three years, pinin' away for someone like you to wash up on the beach."

He listed forward, fell against Em, and almost toppled her. She navigated the stilettos better than she thought she could and quickly regained her balance. When she reached up to shove him away, she accidentally sloshed nearly all of her barrel of grog down the front of his shirt.

"Listen, Robinson Caruso, how about you sail off and find another port?"

"Sheesh, what a poor sport," he mumbled as he walked away.

Finally Em reached the group near the bar. All four men standing together in a knot turned to stare, apparently rendered brain-dead by the sight of deep cleavage. If she'd walked by as herself, they wouldn't have given her more than a casual look, but "Pussy in Boots" had them all salivating.

"What can I do for you, my lovely?" DePesto separated himself from the others.

Em held up her mug with a smile. "I'm out of grog."

"Can't let a buxom wench like you go thirsty. Not around here."

"Do you have anything other than grog? Like tequila?" She scanned the back of the bar. All she saw was rum and gallons of juice.

"I like your style, but sorry. We're keeping it simple tonight. Only premix."

He slid her mug across the bar and yelled, "More grog for the pretty lady."

She laughed and had to raise her voice to be heard over the music and pirate banter in the room.

"Too many bartenders in one place?"

"Something like that. We didn't want anyone grandstanding tonight. This party is purely for pleasure. May I say the same about you?" He reached for her refilled mug and handed it to her.

"What's that?" She took a small sip. Even more rum this round.

"That you're purely for pleasure too."

Oh puh-lease. Em fought to keep her smile pasted on. Did dePesto think she was one of the hookers walking up and down Kalakaua?

She took a step closer. "Tell me all about this Shake Off. I've never heard of one before."

He told her way more than she wanted to know, not only about the Shake Off but how he had founded the event nine years ago and managed to win, at least the Western Regionals every year. Then he went on to assure her that he'd rounded up some of the toughest judges in the business, and *no way* were they biased.

She wondered if the idea of a conflict of interest ever entered his mind. He was probably surrounded by yes men who spent a lot of time telling him how groovy he was. The heels made them just about the same height. Em noticed he had leaned forward to look down the front of her low-cut red blouse until Mr. Smee crashed past them chasing a plump matron in a silk period costume that looked like something Marie Antoinette would have worn in a smaller size.

Smee, waving a rubber sword, yelled, "When I get a hold of you, my beauty, I'm going to keelhaul you over my yardarm! Blow me down if I don't!"

DePesto watched them tumble over a table and shook his head in disgust.

"I'm thinking of a new theme for next year. This pirate thing is getting old."

"Any ideas yet?" Em took another sip. Flirting would be far easier if she had a buzz going.

"Zombies. They're still popular."

"Zombies are popular? Not much personality though. A lot of growling and shuffling."

"Tiki Zombies or Zombie Tikis? Which do you like better?"

"I'll have to think about that one." She thought about batting her lashes at him, but they kept sticking to the eye holes in the mask. She fingered his official badge covered with small replicas of the golden swizzle stick award.

"Lamar dePesto. Is that your real name?"

"Do you *think* it's my real name?" He cocked his eyebrow and waited.

"Do you *want* me to think it's your real name?"

"Catchy, huh?"

She nodded yes and didn't add that it made her think of an oily green sauce.

She thought she might be getting somewhere when suddenly her uncle joined them. Em held her breath. All Louie said was, "Nice boobs."

Nice boobs? Her uncle complimenting her boobs was disgusting.

Before she could say anything, Louie asked, "Where did you get them?"

"My boobs?"

"No." Louie's face turned very, very red. "Your *boots*. I was just thinking my niece might like a pair."

"Oh, she probably wouldn't," Em said a bit too quickly. She cleared her throat and lowered her voice. "You'd hate for her to break her ankle or something." She buried her face in her mug until Louie picked up a fresh drink and wandered off.

Lamar dePesto waited until Louie walked away.

"Some of these guys would do anything to win," he said.

"What do you mean?" she asked.

"Take that guy. Some old dude who had a reality show on cable. Everyone is touting him as an original, like Don the Beachcomber or Trader Vic. The press is calling him the front runner."

"Not only that, but there's something secretive going on with him," he went on. "He's been lurking around the lobby looking bummed. I think he might be worried he won't be able to pull off an upset. I know personally that he's so worried about his recipe he's rented a taste-tester." DePesto didn't add that the tester was a monkey.

"Isn't that against the rules?"

He shook his head. "Not if you use this particular taste-tester."

"Wow. I guess some of these guys would do anything to win."

"You're right about that."

"How far would you go, Lamar?"

"All the way, baby. Whatever it takes," he said.

Em felt like she'd just fired a cannonball and made a direct hit.

"Hey, I have some tequila in my luxury suite. It's one of the huge perks of being the founder of the Shake Off and booking the contest here. Wanna run up for a quickie?"

"Sure, why not."

"You would? I mean, hey, that's great."

She couldn't figure out why he was acting like he'd just won the lotto. He waited for her to turn toward the entrance before he rested his hand at the small of her back.

"Maybe I'll try my contest entry on you. How does that sound?"

"Arrrggghhh! Time to set sail. Let's go."

She figured she had as much expertise as a monkey.

20

LAMAR DEPESTO'S SUITE was on the top floor of the Ali'i Tower with a three hundred sixty degree view of the Pacific and Waikiki. He ushered Em inside and headed straight for the wet bar lined with top shelf liquor. She walked out on the balcony to enjoy the view and took a deep breath of fresh air.

"Would you like me to make you a margarita? The real deal? Or maybe a tequini? How do you like your tequila?" he asked.

After swilling a mug of pirate's grog, switching to tequila sounded terrifying.

"Straight, with a water back up." She smiled and sauntered, as well as she could in the stilettos, back into the room.

"May I use the bathroom?"

"Of course." He paused with a bottle of Hornitos in hand and nodded in the direction of a short hallway. "Help yourself."

Em locked the bathroom door behind her and set her little woven handbag on the counter top. *If* dePesto had stolen the Booze Bible and *if* he'd hidden it in the bathroom, the only place big enough would be on one of the shelves under the sink. It was a place to start.

The shelves were lined with towels and various items emptied out of his toiletry bag.

She knelt down and ran her hand around under the pile of folded towels. No ring binder. In the process she knocked her tricorn hat on the counter top. It slipped back, nearly pulling her wig off. She straightened the hat, smoothed down the wig, and opened her purse. She reapplied the hot red lipstick. Then Em took a deep breath and walked back into the living area.

Lamar was holding an ice bucket in one hand and a tumbler in the other. The tumbler had a good three fingers of tequila in it.

"There you go." He smiled.

Em smiled back. Lamar waited.

With no other recourse, she knocked the shot back. Her eyes watered, but she didn't cough.

She said, "Yum. What about you? Aren't you having one?"

"I'm gonna go for some ice. I'll be right back," he said.

"Great." *Definitely great. Go.* She'd see what she could find in the bedroom.

"Tequila's on the bar."

"I'll wait for you to pour me another."

Before he went through the door he paused. "I hoped you were in there taking off the mask."

She pursed her very red lips. "I thought it would be fun to keep the mystery going."

"Aye, aye!" He was out the door in a flash.

Em ran back down the hall into the bedroom as fast as her stiletto boots could carry her. She tore through the dresser drawers, opening and closing them, running her hand under his piles of T-shirts and underwear. No Booze Bible. She knelt on the floor, looked under the bed, ran her hands between the mattress and the box springs, opened the closet, and tried to reach the top shelf.

She ran over to grab a desk chair to climb on. There was a lap top as well as a portable printer and reams of paper on the desk. Em was about to drag the chair over to the closet when she suddenly recognized the manila envelope lying on top of a pile of contest information. It looked just like the one Louie had received from the extortionist.

Her hands were shaking as she tried to work the clasp and finally succeeded. She pulled two pages out of the envelope and scanned it. The first page was indeed written by the extortionist. Whoever had stolen the Booze Bible was offering to sell a copy of Louie Marshall's famous Booze Bible for twenty-five thousand dollars.

Em's heart sank when she looked at the second page. The handwriting was Louie's. It was his recipe for his "Tiger Shark Attack," a drink he'd concocted after nearly being chomped by a shark off of Kauai. The extortionist had torn out another page of the notebook.

Em's mind was reeling. Was dePesto the recipient of the letter or the one sending it? If so, the Booze Bible had to be in the suite somewhere. Was he sending the letter going to one of the other contestants? Someone desperate enough to buy a *copy*?

"What are you doing?"

At the sound of dePesto's voice, Em whipped around and almost toppled off her heels. She dropped the envelope and the papers on the desk. The recipe floated to the floor.

"I . . . I'm . . . I was just looking for an . . . um . . . a private place to make a call."

He was staring at the dresser. She had left the top drawer wide open.

"Were you going through my drawers?"

"Maybe the maid left it open?"

"I don't think so. This room was cleaned hours ago."

"Maybe you left it open."

"I would remember. What were you doing with that letter?"

"What letter?"

"The one you had in your hand when I walked in. I *saw* you drop it."

She shrugged and tried to smile.

"I'm calling security," Lamar said.

Em had imbibed in enough grog for the shot of tequila to put her over the top. She was invincible. She threw her shoulders back and raised her chin—a move that unfortunately emphasized her cleavage. DePesto's eyes bugged. She hunched her shoulders.

"Go ahead and call them," she dared him. "Call them, and I'll tell them you're an extortionist. I'll tell them you stole my uncle's recipes and you're holding them for ransom."

DePesto shook his head. "What in the hell are you talking about? What uncle? What recipes?"

"I'm Louie Marshall's niece. His Booze Bible was stolen the day we arrived. Today he received an extortion letter demanding money. A letter just like that one." She pointed to the desk. "In an envelope just like that." She pointed again. "That someone tore out one of his recipes to prove he had the notebook. Just like the recipe on the floor. That's another page of the Booze Bible." She took a step toward him. "I think that someone is *you*, Mr. dePesto. A few minutes ago you admitted you'd go all the way and do whatever it takes to win the Shake Off."

"Get real. I don't have to cheat."

"Then explain that letter."

"Someone left it at the front desk for me."

"Ha!"

"Why didn't Marshall tell me his recipes were stolen?"

"Because he thought *you* or one of the others may have taken them. I think his notebook is somewhere in this suite." She pulled open the desk drawer and then slammed it shut. Then she marched over to the closet and pulled out his suitcase. It was the hard-sided kind a gorilla could jump on and couldn't break. Em tugged the case out. Ignoring dePesto, she stepped on it to reach the closet shelf.

"Hey, get off my suitcase. Stop that. I'm calling security," he yelled.

Em spied an extra pillow on the shelf. No better place to hide something big than a pillowcase. She grabbed it and started to tug when one of her heels suddenly punctured the suitcase. Her boot sank through the case all the way to the top of the heel. She tumbled backward. Her booty hit the floor, and her tricorn hat fell off and pulled her wig off with it.

"They don't make suitcases like they used to." Em laid there spread-eagled and watched the ceiling begin to whirl.

Lamar disappeared into the living room area. Em struggled to sit up and pulled her boot heel out of the suitcase. She was on her hands and knees trying to stand when dePesto appeared in the doorway.

"Is that a *knife?*" Em's breath caught. She looked around, thinking she might be able to whack him in the head with a lamp, if she could get to one.

"No, it is *not* a knife. It's a citrus saw." He looked at the tiny lime green plastic saw no bigger than a paring knife. "But it's sharp."

He kept the saw pointed at her as he picked up the phone and punched one of the Lucite buttons.

"Yes. This is Mr. dePesto, founder of the Shake Off. Lamar dePesto in the Presidential suite. I'd like to report an intruder. Yes, I'll hold but . . ."

Her head started spinning as Em watched helpless from the floor. The odious taste of bad pirate swill filled her mouth. Her real hair was stuck to her head. A loose bobby pin dangled near her temple. The black tricorn lay on the floor beside her; the skull emblazoned on the front grinned up at her. Her wig was sticking out of the hat. She grabbed the wig and shoved it back on.

If she was going down, she wasn't going down with hat hair.

21

TWO PLAINCLOTHES Hilton security officers in aloha shirts and Bermuda shorts drove Em down to the Waikiki substation. Shaken and tipsy, she tottered along on her high heels. The one she'd rammed into dePesto's suitcase wobbled.

The Hilton cops escorted her into the waiting area filled with the flotsam and jetsam of the nightlife on Kalakaua Avenue. Three hookers in heels higher than Em's were squished together on two chairs on the far side of the room. They were tall, lean, beautiful, and no doubt expensive. All wore the same tired, bored expressions. They'd been here before. One of them popped chewing gum in time to the beat a kid in a hoodie was tapping out as he slapped his palms against his thighs. He didn't appear to be a stranger to the Waikiki substation facility either.

A panhandler with his face and hands covered in gold paint wearing a gold Statue of Liberty robe and foam rubber crown was handcuffed to the arm of a chair.

One officer at a desk near the door kept watch.

At least she was the only "Puss in Boots" in the room.

Em whimpered, but it wasn't because of her situation. Her head banged as if ten Taiko drummers were trapped inside. The Hilton security officers pointed her to a chair.

"Sit," one of them said. He handed over her tricorn.

Her other escort walked over to the officer at the desk and handed him the shopping bag that contained Em's purse and mask.

Em sat. Until then she hadn't noticed the rip in her right fishnet stocking. She tried to calculate what that was going to cost, but her head wasn't working right with all the drumming going on.

She rubbed the spot between her brows with both thumbs, but the banging continued. A door opened, and she recognized Lieutenant Chun when he strode into the main room and sized up the crowd. He signaled the hotel cops, and one of them walked over. They chatted for a minute or two while Chun nodded and glanced her way now and then. Finally the Hilton officers walked out. Chun wagged his hand at her, indicating she should cross the room.

Em rose slowly so as not to stir up her headache any worse. As she started toward Chun one of the hookers yelled, "Hey, she just got here. We been here a good forty minutes. You're wasting our time, Chunnie."

Chun shot her a dark glare. The hooker shut up. The girl beside her went right on popping her gum. The Statue of Liberty had either passed out or fallen asleep.

"I thought you were the sane one," Chun said as he ushered Em into his office. "Where's the rest of your gang?"

"Drinking their way down Kalakaua."

"Shoots." He wagged his head. "Probably going to end up bookin' them too."

Em sank into the chair in front of his desk. "Booking? You're going to book me? I'm innocent."

"Hilton security says you broke into some guy's room and were caught in the act of rifling through his stuff."

"I did not break in. I was invited."

"To steal stuff?"

"I didn't steal anything. I was pillaging. Plundering. That's what self-respecting pirates do." She started to smile. A hiccup slipped out.

"You t'ink dis is funny?" He leaned back in his chair. *He* definitely didn't think so. Em tried to sober up. "I was searching for my uncle Louie's stolen notebook."

"The missing recipe book again," he sighed.

"I think Lamar dePesto took it."

"De Presto? What is he? A magician or something?"

"De*Pesto.* Like the sauce. He's the founder of the Shake Off cocktail competition."

"Really."

"He's won the contest the last eight or nine years. He even admitted to me that he'd do anything to win." Rum and tequila were having a tug of war with her brain cells. For a second she saw two Chuns.

"When was the last time you arrested a pirate?" She leaned her elbows on the desk and propped her chin in her hands. Her hat slid off her lap and onto the floor.

Chin wasn't smiling. "Actually, when they were filming the last Pirates of the Caribbean movie here. How about you go on with the story, eh?"

"Earlier today my uncle received an extortion letter asking for one hundred thousand dollars for the Booze Bible."

"So how come you didn't call the police?"

"The letter said not to or else. Besides, *you* thought our case would be a waste of the HPD's time."

"So you decided to get caught ransacking some guy's room looking for it yourself."

"I didn't ransack anything. I was just looking."

"Speaking of looking, you look better as a blonde." He stared at her wig for a minute before he turned his attention to her face again. "So did you find anything incriminating?"

She nodded yes and immediately wished she hadn't moved her head so fast.

"There was a letter on his desk just like the one my uncle received. Only the letter in dePesto's room asked for twenty-five thousand for a measly *copy* of the Booze Bible."

"So he's not the guy."

"But he could be. Maybe he's the one who sent us the letter. He has laptop and a portable printer hooked up on his desk. Maybe he plans to sell copies of the book to anyone who will pony up twenty-five thousand."

"Kinda steep for a recipe book, yeah?"

"Maybe not to someone who knows what it's worth."

"But you didn't find the book," he said.

"I didn't have time to conduct a thorough search before he walked in and caught me going through his things."

"What did he say about the letter? You ask him about it?"

"Of course. He said he didn't know where it came from. Says he received it this afternoon, just like we did," she said.

Chun sighed.

Em sighed too. "You believe me, don't you?"

"I'm probably *pupule*, but I believe you. I just don't know what to do with you."

"How about you call me a cab, and I'll go back to the Hilton and never plunder or pillage anywhere ever again?"

"It's not that simple. You were caught rifling through a man's room without permission, which is a lot like an act of burglary. How's it gonna look if I let you go?"

"Like I'm innocent. Which I am."

"That's what everybody out in the waiting room is gonna tell me, too. Only innocent people on this island."

"He invited me in for a drink," she said.

"An' you obviously had a couple."

She held up her index finger and waved it at him. "I only one shot of tequila while I was there. O-n-e. I'll admit I had some grog at the pirate party."

"Which explains the outfit," he said.

She looked down at her blouse and tried yanking up the plunging neckline but gave up after a couple of tries.

"I was working undercover." She shrugged. "This is a disguise."

"Did you meet this dePresto before the party?"

"No. But he may have seen me standing around with Louie, but my uncle didn't even recognize me."

"Did he know your uncle's book was missing?"

"Not unless he stole it. We haven't spread the word around."

"Well, unfortunately, Ms. Johnson, you got caught in the act of rifling through his stuff." Chun drummed his thick fingers on the desk.

"Don't I get one phone call?" She'd already decided she couldn't call and upset Uncle Louie. Kiki and the Maidens were out of the question. There was only one person on Oahu she could rely on right now.

"Hold on a minute." Chun got up and walked out of the room. When he came back he handed her the shopping bag with her purse inside. "Okay, make a call."

"And say what?" She pulled out her purse and dug around for her phone.

"That you need to be picked up. I'm going to let you go on your own recognizance and whoever picks you up, be sure it's someone responsible. I want your word that you'll stop looking for the damn recipe book."

"Booze Bible."

"Whatevah. Go down to the main precinct and talk to a real detective. Maybe you can identify whoever dropped off the letter on the hotel's video surveillance of the lobby area."

What was she? A hamster on a wheel? She was back to the video playback.

"I tried that. Their system is out."

"Okay, so time to phone a friend," he said.

She looked down at the small *lauhala* bag she used on Kauai. Sophie had found it at the Humane Society Thrift Shop and got it for her. It was so familiar, so *not* Pussy in Boots, she got tears in her eyes.

The time on the phone read twelve thirty-five a.m. She hated to do it, but she called Nat.

22

EM'S CELL PHONE jolted her out of a stupor the next morning. For a second she had no idea where she was, then realized she was in bed at the Hilton. She rolled over and fumbled around, patting the carpet until she found her phone on the floor.

She glanced at the caller ID and groaned. Not only was it six forty in the morning, but the caller was Roland.

She cleared her throat and tried to sound lucid. "Detective." Her voice sounded like she'd smoked a boatload of cigarettes.

"Hi." Roland was a man of few words. Any other time it would have been so good to hear his voice. After last night's caper, she was afraid she was going to burst into tears. But she was made of sterner stuff.

"Hi yourself."

"Howzit?" he said.

"Okay. Not great."

Suddenly she wanted to dump on him, tell him how much she wished she'd stayed on Kauai. Then again, how would Louie have coped without her?

Just then there was a knock on the door of the suite.

"Hang on a sec." Em swung her feet over the side of the bed and wondered if her legs would hold her. Her knees shook harder than a Tahitian dancer's hips. With her phone pressed to her ear she exited her bedroom and walked to the door in the living room/kitchen area of the suite. Naturally the peephole was an inch too high for her to peer through.

"Who is it?" She spoke as loud as she dared without waking Louie in the other room. She pictured a gaggle of Hula Maidens in the hallway. She hadn't laid eyes on them since they left the hotel to go bar hopping with the Kamakanis. Hopefully they'd made it back and were sleeping it off their rooms.

"It's me," Roland said.

"Somebody just knocked on the door," she said into the phone. The *Taiko* drummers were back.

"It's *me*," he said again.

"No, really, somebody just—"

He cut her off. "I'm outside. Open the door, Em."

She flipped the lock but left the safety guard on and cracked the door far enough to peek out. Sure enough, there he was.

"Roland?"

He still had his phone against his ear, too. "Yeah?"

She shook her head and ended the call. She whispered, "You're nuts. What are you doing here?"

He glanced over his shoulder. "You gonna make me stand out here? Somebody might call security." He was holding a small duffle bag.

She shushed him and started to open the door until she realized she was still in torn fishnet stockings. Somehow she'd changed into a long black Tiki Goddess tank top that hit her mid-thigh. She had no idea when or how she got it on.

"I'm not dressed."

"You have on a T-shirt," he noticed. "Probably covers more than your swimsuit."

She shoved her hair back out of her eyes and pulled out a hair pin. He walked in and looked around. "Where's your uncle?"

"Shh. He's in his room asleep." She motioned for him to follow as she tiptoed back to her bedroom. She closed the door behind them.

"I thought it would be harder than this," he said.

"What?"

"Getting into your bedroom." His gaze swept the space carefully.

She followed his gaze and wanted to crawl back under the covers and hide. The fluffy black crinoline adorned the lampshade on a bedside table lamp. Her peasant blouse and skirt were on the floor, and the leather bodice was draped over the television. One of her boots was spread out across the dresser, the other nowhere to be seen.

The room looked bad enough. Panicked, Em walked over to the mirror over the dresser and almost screamed. Her hair was matted and shoved off to one side of her head. Crimson lipstick smeared not only her lips but her chin. The kohl liner around her eyes made her look like a panda. Her skin was as pale yellow as macaroni-potato salad. She swallowed a gag.

"Excuse me a minute." She didn't wait for a response. She fled into her bathroom.

Em closed the door, downed three glasses of water as fast as she could, and then held her breath. The water stayed down. She wet a washcloth and scrubbed off the lipstick until she was afraid she was peeling off skin. Her chin was still pink. She grabbed some eye cream and erased the panda rings. Then she brushed her teeth and drank another glass of water.

When she walked back into the bedroom Roland was leaning against the desk, staring at the bed.

"Did you get a pet?"

"No, why?"

He pointed at something black and hairy that was curled up on her pillow. Em stared at it a second then shrugged.

"That's my wig."

"And this?" He held out his hand. The black mask dangled from his finger.

"I went to a costume party. What are you doing here, Roland?"

"Nat called me. Said you needed help."

"Nat? He did?" Officer Chun had been impressed when Nat Clark walked in to vouch for her, and Em had introduced him as the creator and head writer of the latest major network cop show being filmed in Hawaii.

"Hey, put my name in for a cop part," Chun had said. "I worked an episode of *Hawaii Five-0* a couple weeks ago. They used a bunch of real cops in an officer's funeral scene."

Nat took Chun's name and number and promised to keep Em out of trouble before he hustled her out of the station.

Roland tossed the mask on the bed and studied Em carefully. "Nat didn't say what kind of trouble you were in, but looking at you and the condition of this room, I'd say things are a lot worse than he let on."

"You flew over just because I needed help? What if all I wanted were directions to Pearl Harbor?"

"Nat sounded like it was a lot more than that. Obviously it was something he couldn't handle."

"He's flying to LA today."

"Looking at this room I'd say you need an intervention. Are you working Kalakaua now?"

"I'm sorry he bothered you, and I'm *really* sorry he didn't explain. It's nothing Louie and I can't handle."

"He didn't have a chance to tell me, actually. When he said you needed help, I said okay and hung up."

"But what about work?"

"I had some vacation time coming. Changed my shifts around. Got a flight out on a medical emergency flight headed over at four thirty this morning. Here I am."

"Wow."

"Only one problem, though." He set his backpack on the floor. "I couldn't get a room."

Em crossed her arms over her breasts.

"In all of Waikiki? Not one room?"

He arched his brow. "Not here anyway. I didn't waste time with the rest of Waikiki."

"There are thirty-five hundred rooms here."

"I was in a hurry." He shrugged. "Just say thanks."

"Thanks, of course."

A loud crash came from the direction of Louie's room. Roland's hand automatically went to his hip, but he wasn't carrying a gun.

"It's all right. That's just the monkey," she said.

"The monkey?"

"Yeah. Someone thought it would be the answer to our problem. It's locked in Louie's bathroom."

"If a monkey is the answer to your problem, why am I here?"

"I have no idea." She finally smiled. "But I'm sure happy to see you."

23

BY THE TIME EM showered and dressed, Roland was sitting on the balcony overlooking the beach, sipping coffee he'd prepared in their efficiency kitchen.

Self-conscious, she smoothed her hair back and smiled.

"The *lua* in my room is free," she said. "No sense risking a run-in with the monkey."

"I'm good." Roland walked over to the kitchen and poured a second cup of coffee and handed it to her. "Looks like you need this," he said.

"Still that bad?" She glanced at her reflection in a mirror near the bar counter.

He moved closer. "You still look tired."

"I thought this was going to be a relaxing getaway," she mumbled. "I'm more worried about Louie than I am tired."

"Fat chance of relaxing with the Maidens along."

When they heard Louie stirring, Roland headed back to the kitchen counter to pick up his coffee cup.

Em said, "I'll call room service. Would you like a full breakfast, or I can order a continental breakfast basket we can share?"

"Continental is fine."

Louie appeared in the doorway.

"Hi, Roland." Louie said it as casually as if he woke up to find Roland around every morning and seeing him here on Oahu was no different. He nodded to Em. "Continental basket sounds good to me, too. Be sure to order some bananas. A *lot* of bananas."

"For the monkey," Roland said.

"You got it." Louie nodded. He scratched his head, yawned, and headed for Em's bathroom. "Last night he ate my tube of toothpaste. I'll have to borrow yours."

Louie disappeared into her bathroom. While they waited for room service, Em filled Roland in on almost everything that had happened except her foray into snooping through dePesto's room and near arrest.

She showed him the ransom note.

"So someone really did steal the notebook, and they're holding it hostage," she said.

Roland studied the page and the envelope. "When was this delivered?"

"I'm not sure. The front desk called us early yesterday afternoon. It could have been sitting there for hours."

"You notified hotel security?"

She nodded. "We did. We spoke to a security officer named Kim when the Booze Bible went missing. He said he'd check the video camera in the hall."

"And?"

"I finally got to see it myself, and sure enough, there was a man in a hoodie who slipped into Louie's room and back out again right after we checked in. He was carrying a plastic shopping bag from the ABC Store. Everyone down at hotel security is as nice as can be, but we haven't had a chance to view the main desk video to see who dropped off the letter. The playback isn't working. I spoke to a Lieutenant Chun at the Waikiki substation . . ." She paused a minute and then quickly added, "when the Maidens were arrested and . . ."

"Arrested?"

"They were hauled in, but not booked," she said.

"I'm not even going to ask."

"I take it you missed the news a couple nights ago."

Before Roland could answer there was a knock at the door, and room service was delivered. Em eyed the assortment of sweet bread choices and poured them some juice.

Louie walked back in. "Yeah, they were arrested. It wasn't much. Just a little riot down at the beach bar. Dancing without a permit. Failure to cease and desist. I'm surprised the police didn't throw in resisting arrest."

Roland pulled a bran muffin the size of a cantaloupe out of a napkin-lined basket.

Em broke off a piece of Danish and popped it into her mouth.

Louie grabbed a croissant, a cup of coffee, and a couple of bananas. "I'll eat this in my room. Gotta be down at the conference hall before the day's competition starts."

"What's happening today?" Roland asked.

"The judges are quizzing us about our garnishes, choices of glassware, and when and why we choose traditional shakers over blenders. All the interview points will be added to our final scores."

"You'll do great, Uncle Louie." Em finished her last sip of coffee.

"Mahalo, Em, for that vote of confidence, but most of these guys and gals are professionals. They enter these things all the time. Heck, I'm just an old timer."

"You've been a mixologist longer than most of them have been alive," she said.

Louie disappeared into his room. Roland polished off his bran muffin and leaned back in the chair. Em tried to convince herself that now was the perfect time to tell him about last night and how she'd ended up at the substation.

"We should head down to the hotel security office and view the surveillance video. If we're lucky, maybe I have a calabash cousin on staff," he said.

Em promised herself she'd tell him about her own trip to the substation as soon as they had hopefully seen the video.

As it turned out, there was no calabash cousin manning the hotel security office, but that didn't matter because Varla, the gal in uniform behind the counter, was eyeing Roland the way Em salivated over the Orchids' signature coconut cake yesterday. When he flashed his KPD badge, Varla was more than willing to make points with him.

Varla had just come back from checking out the video control room. She ignored Em, speaking directly to Roland.

"You're in luck. The tech team's almost finished. Hopefully in a few minutes we'll be able to run the recordings of the front desk for the last twenty-four hours. You might catch a glimpse of whoever dropped off the envelope for Mr. Marshall."

Roland didn't give her details about the contents of the manila envelope. He only explained that they needed to find out who dropped it off.

"We'd like to look through the videos together." Roland nodded toward Em.

He'd no sooner spoken when Em's cell went off. She glanced at the screen and saw that it was Trish Reynolds. Since Trish was usually so level-headed and rarely called her, she told him, "I'd better take this. Sorry."

She stepped out of the security office onto one of the pathways that wound through the myriad pools and gardens of the resort, hoping all the Maidens were all right.

"Em, we've got an emergency on our hands."

"What now?" Em wished she'd ignored the call.

"Suzi took a tumble off of the stage at the Beach Bar behind the Moana last night. Luckily it was after we finished dancing. Her sandal caught on something, and I think she may have broken her big toe. Maybe even her whole foot. It's all *kapakahi*, and she can't walk."

"Where is she?" Em pictured the diminutive realtor lying under the stage near the banyan tree behind the Moana Hotel.

"We managed to get her back here late last night. She was feeling no pain then, but now she's in her room and pretty miserable. I've never seen her like this. She hasn't even checked her emails about pending escrows yet this morning."

"Did you call the hotel doctor?"

"Not yet. She iced it and thought it would be better by now, but her foot's looking pretty gnarly. I think she needs to go to emergency. Will you go up and talk some sense into her? We're all in the Tapa Tower on the tenth floor. I'll go with you."

"Where are you now?"

"Look through the bushes to your left."

Em could make out Trish's tall slender form and strawberry blond hair behind some palm fronds not far away.

"Why don't you just walk over here?"

"No. Please, just hurry."

"I'll be right there." Em walked back into the security office and found Roland waiting at the counter, still chatting up Officer Varla.

"Would you mind looking through the videos alone? Suzi took a tumble, and they need me," Em said.

"Sure. Is she all right?"

"She may have a broken toe."

Em left the security office and headed in the direction she'd last seen Trish. She found her slinking around the edge of the lava rock planter.

"Hey, Trish," Em said. Trish was so startled she jumped and let out a squeak. "What's going on?" Em asked.

They'd started walking toward the Tapa Tower. Trish leaned close and whispered, "I have enough oxycodone in my pocket to fell an elephant, that's what. When I saw you with Roland, I panicked."

"He's not a drug-sniffing German Shepard."

"What's he doing here?"

Em got a warm feeling all the way to her toes. "He flew over to help us find Louie's Booze Bible. Where did you get the drugs?"

"Kiki's got a full-on pharmacy in her cosmetic case. She collects leftover prescription meds from her neighbors."

"Why?"

"Don't ask me. She's convinced them it's against the law to flush leftovers down the toilet into their septic tanks. She hoards them in case of emergencies. She actually made me sign for the two pills she counted out for Suzi."

They stepped out of the elevator on the tenth floor where Big Estelle, Lillian, Precious, and Pat were in the hallway outside of Trish's door. The boom box was going, the three dancers practicing a new hula number. Suzi's door was open.

Em looked in and saw Suzi lying on the pull-out sofa. Her foot was propped on a pillow. A woman with a nimbus of frizzy black curls was moving her palms over Suzi's injured foot without touching it.

Em couldn't help but notice her shimmering purple eye shadow and long thick lashes. The woman had her eyes closed and was rocking back and forth with her hands hovering over Suzi's toes.

"Who is that?" Em asked Trish.

Trish whispered, "One of the Miracle Cream ladies from Japan. She's a witch."

"A Japanese witch." *Could this trip get any weirder?* Em wondered. "Except for the eye shadow, she doesn't look like one of the Miracle Cream crowd," Em said.

"She does when her hair is up and sprayed and she's in a power suit and full makeup."

The nimbus of dark hair quivered as the woman shook her head back and forth muttering, "Not good. Not good."

Em finally took a good look at Suzi's toe. It was sticking out at a perpendicular angle. She didn't have to be a witch to know it was not good.

Trish stepped into the room and Em followed.

"I got the pain pills from Kiki," Trish announced. "Oxycodone."

"No. Heaven's no. I don't want it." Suzi stuck out her tongue. "Big Estelle has been in a walking coma since she took whatever Kiki gave her."

"I heard that," Big Estelle sang out over the music in the hall. "I'm awake now."

"What am I supposed to do with it?" Trish was wide-eyed with worry.

"Give it back to Kiki," Suzi suggested.

"Where is Kiki?" Em asked.

"In her room working on choreography," Lillian said.

Trish dug around in her pocket. Em stared at Suzi's toe. Not only was it sticking off the side of her foot, but the area around it was black and blue.

"I think you need to go to emergency quick," Em said.

The Miracle Cream witch began nodding. "Yes. Yes. Emerlencee. Click. Vely click."

"Fine, but I can't walk." Suzi tried to sit up and fell back onto her pillow.

By now Pat had killed the boom box. She, Big Estelle, Precious, and Lillian were crowded in the doorway.

"You can use Little Estelle's scooter," Trish suggested.

"Impossible," Big Estelle said. "I dozed off, and she got away from me early this morning. The valet captain said she had him call a handicapped equipped taxi van with a lift, and they loaded up the scooter."

"Dozed off?" Precious snorted. "You weren't in your room. You were knocked out and shackin' up with Byron."

"Where did Little Estelle go?" Em *so* wished she'd ignored Trish's call.

Big Estelle shrugged. "Some recording studio. She finished her rap song and wanted to get it recorded before we left the island. I tried to stop her, but you know how sneaky Mother is when she gets an idea in her head. She ran off with my credit card, too. God only knows how much it cost to rent a sound studio for an hour."

"How does it sound?"

"The rap? How should I know?" Big Estelle looked peeved. "It's top secret."

"I'll call the front desk and see if they rent wheelchairs," Trish said. She turned to Em. "Will you go with us?"

"Roland took time off to fly over and help recover Louie's notebook. I really should stay."

"Roland's a professional. He'll call you if and when he finds something," Suzi said. "I trust you more than anyone to get me to emergency with as little drama as possible, Em."

Suzi looked up pitifully from her pillow. Her gaze surreptitiously slid to the Japanese witch. She looked at Em again and whispered, "Please?"

24

THEY TOOK SUZI to the emergency room at Straub Hospital on King Street in Honolulu. Not exactly right next door to the hotel. Remarkably quickly, Suzi's foot was x-rayed, her toe put in place and bound. As it turned out she'd broken various small bones in her foot, but she was able to limp along with a crutch and her foot encased in a navy blue boot with Velcro straps.

The others were helping her out to the curb when Em's cell phone went off. Thinking it was Roland, she answered without looking at caller ID and quickly discovered she was talking to a Honolulu PD detective. She expected him to tell her they had a lead on Louie's notebook.

Instead he said, "Mrs. Johnson, you're Phillip Johnson's next of kin?"

The question took her completely by surprise. "I'm his ex-wife. What's happened? Did he tell you to call me?"

"We found your name on an emergency card in his wallet."

"In his wallet?" A chill ran through her. "Where's Phillip?"

"It would be better if I explained in person." He gave her an address and asked her to meet him there.

Her mind racing, Em immediately thought of the extortion letter. This caller could be part of the scam. Not about to go running into a trap, she asked him for his name and badge number.

Em's hands shook as she dialed the main station and received confirmation that Lieutenant Detective Justin Bardon was indeed who he said he was. She handed the rental van keys and the Maidens over to Trish and called Roland once she was in a cab. She told him about the phone call and gave him the address.

"I'll meet you there," Roland said.

As the cab wound its way through the congested Honolulu streets, Em realized she forgot to ask if he'd viewed the front desk security videos.

When the cab driver turned onto a street lined with run-down apartment buildings, Em wondered if he was lost and felt a moment of concern until she noticed four white squad cars and a white van parked up ahead.

Cops stood around in the sun in twos and threes chatting. The street was lined with wood-framed houses sandwiched between two- and three-story apartments. Balconies were lined with clotheslines full of clothing. Piles of belongings oozed out of the apartments and were stacked along upper walkways.

Em's stomach flopped when the driver stopped in front of a pale stucco, two-story apartment building with the name Lokelani above a courtyard entry. Yellow plastic crime tape was stretched across it. A sign near the entry advertised Apartments by Day-Week-Month.

She fished around in her bag, opened her wallet, grabbed a bill, and handed it to the driver without looking.

"Keep the change." She hoped she'd paid enough.

"Wow. T'anks, lady."

A plainclothes officer approached in a navy polo shirt and black pants. He was a heavy set, barrel-chested *haole* with close-cropped blond hair and black-rimmed Ray-Ban sunglasses. She had no doubt he was a detective. His nametag identified him as the one who called her. His unreadable expression was the same as the one Roland had perfected.

"Mrs. Johnson?"

Em wasn't used to answering to "Mrs." No one had called her that for over a year.

"It's Ms." She tightened her grip on the handles of her straw purse, attempting to get her hands to stop shaking.

"Let's go into the courtyard."

They ducked under the crime tape. In the far corner of the courtyard there was a small vegetable garden plot, something she'd never expected to see in the middle of the city. A few valiant tomato plants were staked beside bushy kale, eggplant, and red peppers. The second floor balcony was lined with numbered doors. Uniformed officers were stationed outside an open door on the shady side of the building.

A feeling of dread settled over Em. It had taken a good twenty minutes for her to cross the city. An emergency ambulance would have come and gone already if Phillip was merely injured.

The detective stopped in the shade of the building near the stairs to the second floor.

"There's no easy way to say this, ma'am." Bardon looked away. "Your husband is dead."

"My ex-husband," she whispered.

"We found a card with your name and address in his wallet. He still has you listed as his next of kin."

He extracted a small spiral notebook from his back pocket.

Just like Roland, she thought before her mind jumped. *Phillip is dead?*

"What happened?"

"The manager went up to take him a spare key this morning a little after eight. He knocked, but no one answered, so he was going to leave it on the table inside. He found your husband's body on the floor."

She thought of all the stress Phillip had been under with the divorce, the loss of his business, and starting over. She pictured his fiancée with her armload of shopping bags from lux shops and then looked around the shabby apartment complex. Nothing was adding up.

"Did he have a heart attack or something?"

"No, ma'am. He was shot through the heart at close range."

25

EM REALIZED SHE must have passed out when she woke up and saw Roland leaning over her. Someone had stretched her out on a yellowing plastic lawn chair. A uniformed officer walked up with a bottle of water and handed it to Detective Bardon who handed it off to Roland.

Roland twisted off the cap and held it out to Em. She sloshed water on herself before she managed to take a sip and hand it back.

"Phillip's dead," she said, not really believing it.

"Your ex?" Roland offered the water again.

"Someone shot him."

Detective Bardon said, "The neighbors saw him having a big beef with a guy named Damian Bautista when he moved in yesterday."

Em looked around. "There must be some mistake. Phillip wasn't staying here." She looked up at Detective Bardon. "He lives in California. He was on vacation at the Moana with his fiancée."

"He rented this place yesterday late in the afternoon." Bardon made a note on his little notepad. "Said he was alone. Are you from California, too?"

"No. Not anymore. I live on Kauai with my uncle."

"Did you come to Oahu to meet your husband?"

"My *ex*. No." She shook her head. "Not at all."

"So you haven't seen him?"

"I have seen him. We had lunch together yesterday." Em felt Roland's intense stare without looking at him. She wished she'd told him she was going to have lunch with her ex before she left Kauai. Would he think she was hiding it from him?

"Her uncle is Louie Marshall," Roland explained. "He owns the Tiki Goddess Bar up on the North Shore of Kauai. There was a reality series shot there last year called *Trouble in Paradise*."

The detective studied Em carefully. "I thought you looked familiar, but then I thought, naw, couldn't be her."

"That's what everyone says," she mumbled.

"Feeling better?" Roland was still hunkered down beside her.

"A little." She tried to sit up. Another wave of dizziness hit her.

"Did you find the murder weapon?" Roland asked the other detective.

Bardon nodded. "A Springfield PC9111."

"Did anyone hear shots fired?"

"Hard to say. There's an old lady who lives on one side of that room. Has her television volume cranked up night and day. Hard to hear anything else, or so the neighbors say. If anyone heard gunfire they'd probably deny it anyway. It's that kind of neighborhood. People pretty much keep their heads down and their guard up."

He turned to Em. "Did your husband own a hand gun?"

"Not when we were married. Not that I know of anyway."

"So if you didn't come to see your husband, why are you on Oahu?"

She didn't correct him when he referred to Phillip as her husband again.

"I'm here with my uncle, Louie Marshall. He's in a cocktail mixing contest. A group of women, the Hula Maidens, are traveling with us. They were featured on the TV show."

She never thought she'd have to use the cable show as a credibility reference.

Bardon remained impassive but turned his attention to Roland. "Wasn't that show cancelled after somebody was murdered in the restaurant?"

Roland answered slowly, as if choosing his words carefully. "The murder had nothing to do with the location. The vic was at the wrong place at the wrong time."

"What brings you to Oahu, Officer Sharpe?"

"Detective Sharpe," Roland said. "Someone is trying to extort Em, and her uncle and I'm trying to find out who that is."

Bardon looked at Em. "Extortion?"

"Someone stole my uncle's notebook full of drink recipes, one he's been working on most of his life. Yesterday someone delivered a letter demanding a hundred thousand dollars to the hotel. A friend of ours called Roland and told him we needed help, so he flew over from Kauai."

"Why didn't you come to us?" Bardon asked.

Em sighed. "Somebody told me the HPD was too busy for something so insignificant and said I should let Hilton security take care of it."

A uniformed office came walking over and said something to

Bardon that Em couldn't hear. She shivered. This was real. Phillip was dead.

Detective Bardon stood. "It'll still be a few minutes," he told Em, "but I'll need you to identify your husband. The Crime Analysis Unit is almost *pau*. If you could stay put until they bring him down, I'd appreciate it."

"Me?" Em's voice cracked.

"Can't she do the ID at the morgue?" Roland asked.

Bardon shrugged. "It shouldn't take long to bag, tag, and load him in the van."

Em suspected Bardon was gauging her reaction to his insensitive remark. She was too numb to feel anything.

"You don't have to stay, Em," Roland said. "We can go to the morgue."

"I don't mind. I'd rather . . . I'd rather get this over with," she said.

Em slid over to the edge of the chaise and put her feet on the ground.

"May I have some more water?" She waited for Roland to hand her the bottle. Her mouth was dry, and her hands still shook.

Bardon asked, "You saw your ex yesterday? When and where?"

"For lunch at the Halekulani. He called me at the Goddess before I left and said he'd read about the Regional Shake Off in the *LA Times* and said he'd be here at the same time, wanted to know if I was coming over with my uncle. He asked me to meet him for lunch. I thought it would be good to have some closure. Things had gotten pretty messy by the end of our divorce."

"Did you ever think about getting back together?"

She shook her head. "Never. Ever."

Bardon excused himself and walked away, scribbling as he went.

Roland had been listening so intently he made her nervous. Neighbors were gathered in knots around the apartment building's inner courtyard. Two older women in faded cotton muumuus and a Japanese man with a hoe were sneaking glances at them. A couple of pre-teen girls who should have been in school stared and whispered with their heads together.

A short, potbellied *haole* man in a ball cap and T-shirt that said MANAGER hurried up the stairs in front of a gurney being hauled to the second floor. He carried a huge key ring.

"Maybe it's not Phillip." Em said to Roland. "I just can't see him staying here for any reason. What if someone stole his wallet?"

He shrugged. "Anything's possible."

He didn't sound convinced.

Em clung to the possibility that it was a case of mistaken identity.

"Phillip is probably sitting in some upscale restaurant about to order lunch with his fiancée right now. Someone stole his wallet. That's why the police contacted me. My name was still on his emergency ID."

The gurney appeared on the balcony again and was hauled down the stairs and out to the coroner's wagon. Detective Bardon was headed their way.

"You could be right," Roland said. "For your sake I hope so."

The HPD detective asked them to follow him out to the van where the medical examiner zipped the body bag down far enough to reveal the victim's head and shoulders.

Em clung to Roland's arm. The dead man was indeed Phillip. His face was gray and waxy. All she could see was the collar, but she thought he was wearing the same shirt he'd had on at Orchids yesterday.

Her mouth couldn't form the words. She took a deep breath.

"That's him. That's my ex-husband."

"Phillip Johnson," Detective Bardon said.

Em nodded. "Yes."

"You've made a point of referring to him as your *ex* at least three or four times, Mrs. Johnson. Was yours a contentious divorce?"

Em blinked. What was he asking, and *why* was he asking it?

"I told you it got messy at the end. That's no secret."

Roland held onto her arm and faced her away from the gurney.

"What are you getting at, Detective Bardon?" Roland sounded pissed.

"Just clarifying things. I did overhear Mrs. Johnson say things were pretty messy at the end."

Em was shaken, but not enough to let Bardon intimidate her, especially in front of Roland.

"*Ms.* not Mrs. It *was* an ugly divorce, Detective. It was an ugly marriage, but I had no idea how ugly until it was too late. I ended up with nothing, and so did he. Is that what you wanted to hear?" She hated airing her dirty laundry in front of Roland, hated sharing something she thought was behind her.

"We're done here, aren't we?" Roland asked the other detective.

"Just a couple more questions."

"Am I a suspect?" Em asked point blank.

"Until we can narrow it down, everyone is a suspect. We're looking to question Damian Bautista, the neighbor he had an altercation with. He rents the apartment next to the one your husband rented, but no one's seen him since the argument out front. You mentioned your husband had a fiancée. Do you know her name?"

"Felicity. Felicity something . . . I just met her yesterday."

"How'd that go?"

"Excuse me?" Em frowned.

"When you met her? How did it go?"

Em was fed up with his insinuations *and* his scribbling.

"It went great after I tackled her across the table at Orchids at the Halekulani and managed to pull out most of her hair. Which reminds me, her last name was Duncan. Felicity Duncan. As in donuts."

Em heard Roland snort. She glanced up at him. His expression was impassive.

"If I were you, Detective Bardon, I'd be looking for Ms. Duncan. They were staying at the Moana, or at least that's what Phillip told me. I can't see the woman I met staying here," Em said.

"Just out of curiosity, where were you from the time you left Orchids yesterday afternoon until this morning, Ms. Johnson?"

"At the Hilton first, then I went to rent a costume at the Ilikai, then I went back to the hotel and attended a party. I spent the night in my room. This morning I was with Roland until I went with a friend to the emergency room at Straub. That's where I was when you called me."

"Time of death was sometime between midnight and three a.m.," Bardon said.

"You're barking up the wrong tree, Detective," Roland said. "Besides, you know time of death is only an estimated window, especially in the tropics."

"Gotta go at this from every angle, you know that." Bardon scribbled more notes. "You're staying at the Hilton, correct?"

"Yes," Em said. "We both are."

"Together?" Bardon didn't look at Roland.

"No," Roland said.

"How long?"

"Until Monday morning," Em said.

He turned to Roland. "And you, Sharpe?"

"I'm not sure." Roland put his hand on Em's shoulder. "Is that all, Detective?"

"For now. You take care."

"Yeah," Roland said. "Mahalo."

The coroner's wagon pulled out, and Detective Bardon told them they could go and that he'd be in touch. By the time Em slid into Roland's rental car, she was trembling so badly he had to reach over and fasten her seat belt.

She lowered her head toward her knees.

"Should I pull over?" Roland asked.

"I'll be all right in a second."

Em took a couple of deep breaths before she slowly sat up and watched the cityscape slip past the car window. The tropical blue sky and puffy white clouds so contrasted with the image of Phillip lying in a body bag that everything seemed surreal.

Roland easily navigated the maze of one-way streets and crowded intersections.

"For a guy from Kauai you sure know where you're going."

He shrugged. "I lived here every summer with some cousins when I was a kid. This is where I learned fire dancing."

An unasked question hovered between them.

Em took a deep breath and started to answer it.

"Look, I didn't tell you I was meeting Phillip because—"

"It's not my business."

"But . . ."

"Really, Em. It's not."

"You don't think I killed him, do you? Bardon does."

"Of course not. Besides, you were playing pirate all night."

Em turned away and stared out the passenger side window.

"I wasn't at the party all night," she said.

They were passing Kapiolani Park. Roland pulled into a vacant parking space, rolled down the windows, and turned off the motor.

"What's up, Em? What else haven't you told me?"

"I was at the Waikiki substation last night. Nat had to pick me up. That's why he called you."

"You were *arrested*?"

"No. I was freed on my own recognizance and Nat's word he'd make sure I stayed out of trouble."

"You got sucked into one of the Hula Maiden capers?"

"No, they weren't there."

"What did you do?"

"Nice of you to assume I'm not innocent."

"I know better. Let me guess. You were snooping where you didn't belong."

"Bingo. Hilton security took me in for burglary, but I wasn't burgling. I was looking for Uncle Louie's missing Booze Bible."

"Dressed as a pirate's ho?"

"I prefer wench."

"You were in a costume playing detective again. None of the nut jobs were arrested with you?"

"None. They were on a bar crawl down Kalakaua. Don't forget those old nut jobs are my friends."

He rested his elbow over the open window and watched some kids chase a soccer ball across the grass. Em saw the muscle in his jaw twitch.

"You're pissed," she said.

"I'm disappointed." Somehow disappointment sounded much worse than anger.

"I'm sorry, Roland." There wasn't much more she could say. "But . . ."

"But you can't help yourself."

"It seemed like such a great idea at the time. My uncle and I suspected one of the contest entrants may have stolen his notebook, so I decided to mingle and see if I could uncover anything. The costume party was the perfect venue. I wore a mask and wig, and no one recognized me. In fact, Louie talked to me at the party and didn't even know who I was. Naturally, for his own good, I didn't tell him about my plan."

"Naturally."

She went on to tell him her suspicions about dePesto.

"I found another extortion letter in his suite along with a printer and computer before he caught me sleuthing."

"You mean snooping, not sleuthing."

"Speaking of the letter, did you get to watch the video feed?"

"The technicians still weren't finished when you called. It should be repaired and cued up when we get back."

"By Varla."

"Varla. Very cooperative."

"I'll bet," she said.

"Not telling *me* about last night is one thing, Em, but Bardon is going to find out. When he does, it's not going to look good. Why didn't you tell him?"

"I hadn't told you yet. Besides, I knew it wouldn't look good. Maybe he'll catch the real killer right away, and I'll never have to tell him. I don't have to worry, do I? I didn't kill Phillip."

"I know that," he said.

"You sure?"

"Of course."

"Well, that's a relief."

"Yeah, but that's only because I know you. Besides, I'm pretty sure that if you ever did try to kill somebody, you'd mess it up somehow."

She didn't speak to him the rest of the way back to the Hilton. As they walked in, Em noticed the absence of all of the Mindy's Miracle Cream conference attendees. Apparently the ladies in lavender had packed up their makeup kits and disappeared, only to be replaced by a host of Shriners in bright double XX aloha shirts and red fezzes with tassels. The male conventioneers were everywhere, posing for photos beside bronze sculptures of hula dancers, lounging on chaises around the pool, yucking it up at the Tapa Bar.

As Em and Roland passed the huge tiki standing in the planter near the bar, Em noticed the Pirate Party banner was gone, replaced by one that read Welcome Shriners. Now even the tiki was wearing a huge red plastic fez. Before they reached the security office, Roland stopped outside one of the two Starbucks on the premises.

"Want anything?" he asked.

"No thanks. My stomach is still queasy." She didn't think she'd ever eat again.

He ducked inside and left Em waiting for him on the walk. She watched two Shriners and their wives pass by. They were all carrying inflatable floats and beach towels. The scent of coconut tanning lotion wafted around them.

Roland walked back out of the shop just as another herd of Shriners in swim trunks passed by.

"Do you think they'll wear those fezzes in the water?" she asked him.

"Maybe they get fined for taking them off."

Em noted the tall lidded coffee cup and white bakery sack in Roland's hands.

"For Varla," he said.

"Bribes?"

"Whatever works."

When they walked into the hotel security office, Varla was all smiles until she noticed Em. Roland tried to sweeten her up with the blueberry scone and a latte, which appeared to help.

"I have the morning tape all cued up for you, Detective." She smiled up at him and blinked her green eyes. "Come on back and view it."

Roland motioned for Em to follow. She started to until Varla abruptly turned around. The look she gave Em made her want to shrink down to the size of a cockroach and scurry through a crack in the wall.

"The screening area's pretty small." Varla stared pointedly at Em. "You might want to wait out here."

Em opened her mouth to inform Varla that she was in no mood to be messed with, that she had a hangover, her ex-husband had just been murdered, and she was one of the number one suspects. Instead, she took a step closer to Roland and poked him in the ribs.

"I need her to ID someone," he told Varla.

After a three second standoff, Varla finally caved. "Okay. Whatevah."

Em declined a chair and stood at Roland's elbow, leaning over his shoulder to see the screen. While Varla sipped latte and nibbled on the scone, Roland fast forwarded through guests coming and going at the reception area. There was more than one reception clerk and sometimes up to four of them to watch. Roland kept pausing then pushing play and fast forward until Em was nauseous. She was about to tell him she needed a break when something flashed on the screen that caught her eye.

"Stop!" She tapped his arm. "Envelopes."

He hit pause. "I saw them too."

At the fourth desk on the right, a tall man in a baseball cap and glasses handed what appeared to be two large envelopes to the clerk. He had on an overly large aloha shirt covered in pineapples.

"Can you zoom in?" Em had an extremely eerie feeling in the pit of her stomach.

The image grew a bit fuzzy as it enlarged until there was no doubt in her mind.

"Oh, no," she mumbled.

"What?" Roland said.

"That's Phillip." Luckily there was an empty chair next to Roland. She sat down hard and stared at the image on the video monitor.

"Are you sure?"

She nodded, pointing at the screen. "I'm sure. See that watch?"

"Hard to miss. Can you print this frame along with the one before and after it?" he asked Varla.

"For you Roland? Sure thing."

Roland? Em managed to get to her feet, excused herself, and told Roland she'd meet him outside. She was feeling woozy again, in need of fresh air.

Her thoughts were jumbled. Numbly she watched a Japanese bride in a traditional white wedding gown and a groom in a black tux pose for photos in front of the hotel's wedding gazebo. The structure perched on lava boulders above a waterfall-fed lagoon below the Ocean Crystal chapel. Em didn't even hear Roland walk up until he spoke beside her.

"Are you all right?"

"I can't seem to think straight right now, and not just because of last night's grog fest. I can't believe Phillip not only stole Uncle Louie's Booze Bible, but he tried to bilk us into paying for its return."

"How would he even have known about it?"

"The same reason he called to see if I'd be here this week. He read all about Uncle Louie in a story about the Shake Off in the *LA Times*. Louie was featured and the Booze Bible was mentioned."

"Why did he expect to get you to pay for it?"

"Louie was quoted as saying the notebook contained all his recipes and was his life's work. It was invaluable to him." She paused for a minute thinking. "If the time on the video camera is correct, then Phillip delivered those envelopes right before he and I met for lunch. I can't imagine the nerve that must have taken. That wasn't the shirt he wore to lunch later. He normally wouldn't be caught dead in such a gaudy shirt or the baseball cap."

"He probably tossed them after he left here and walked over to meet you at the Halekulani. It's not very far," he said.

"He had the nerve to sit there and tell me how well he was doing and how he'd turned his life around when all the time he knew that letter was being delivered to my uncle. Thank goodness it got stalled at the front desk until I got back. I'm so glad Louie wasn't there alone. He'd have mortgaged the Goddess if I hadn't stopped him."

A thought came to her and she added, "If Phillip stole the Booze Bible, then it must be in that seedy apartment. We've got to go back."

"To the murder scene? Not a good idea."

"Why not?"

"Let me call Bardon and fill him in first. He may have already found the notebook among Phillip's things. Not only that, but if he looked you up, he may have found out that you omitted telling him about your trip to the Waikiki substation last night."

"Okay, but we need . . ."

"We *need* to think about this. If Phillip had the notebook in his possession, that gives you an even bigger motive for murder than getting revenge over a messy divorce."

"I didn't want *revenge*. I didn't want anything from him. Until just now, I didn't know he was the thief."

"That's not what I'm saying. I'm just telling you what Bardon is probably going to think."

"What do we do now?"

"I'll call Bardon and tell him Phillip Johnson was at the very least an extortionist, and I'll tell him about your little escapade last night."

"Don't forget to ask if they found Louie's Booze Bible in the apartment and if they haven't, they have to please search for it. Louie needs it right away."

"It's evidence in a murder case. They're not going to hand it over."

"Oh, Roland, they have to. Louie is lost without it. Please, call Bardon and do whatever you can. I'll buy you coffee and scones if that works."

"Don't get your hopes up." He paused a moment, watched the over-animated photographer pose the Japanese couple in the gazebo. "What does it look like anyway?"

She described the three ring binder filled with pages and pages of handwritten legends and recipes inside. Some had doodles around the margins. There were fruit juice spatters on some of the pages.

"You're forgetting one thing, Em," he said.

"No doubt. I damaged more than a few brain cells last night."

"Someone killed your ex. It definitely wasn't you. If it wasn't Bautista, there's only one other obvious suspect."

"Louie? Oh no. He was at the party. Everyone saw him there. This morning you saw him before he left for the contest. He was in the suite. Louie had no idea where Phillip was staying. Nor could he have found him at that apartment."

"Not Louie," he said. "Someone else."

When she realized who he was talking about, they both said the same thing at the same time—

"The fiancée."

26

ROLAND SUGGESTED Em find a seat in the atrium near the Tapa Bar and wait while he called Bardon. He would meet her after the call. The place was packed with Shriners, and all the seats in the bar were occupied, so she found a spot on a low planter wall where she could sit and watch the men cavort. Apparently they were living up to the "fun and fellowship" motto emblazoned on the banner near the registration area.

It was a little past noon, and they already had the "fun" requirement pretty well covered.

Em heard a very recognizable horn beep, turned, and saw Little Estelle roll up on her rented Gadabout. With so many other things to worry about, Em had all but forgotten Little Estelle had gone AWOL.

Em couldn't ignore the fact that Little Estelle was not only wearing a trucker style ball cap sideways, but also a big gold medallion on a heavy gold chain around her ninety-year-old, pencil-thin neck.

"Look at all the Shriners!" Little Estelle waved toward the bar. "This must be my lucky day. I *love* Shriners!"

"Have you told Big Estelle you're back? She's worried about you."

"That stick in the mud? If I hadn't seen her pop outta me seventy years ago, I'd never know she was mine. She's always worried about something. I'm a big girl, you know."

"Where'd you get the necklace?" Em asked.

Little Estelle lifted the medallion and stared at it for a second.

"My new bling? My producer gave it to me for a job well done." She winked.

Em wasn't about to ask for details. "How was your recording session?"

"Sweet. Got my first track laid down in a couple of takes." She was obviously distracted by all the Shriners in the bar. "I was First Lady once." She spoke with a faraway look in her eyes.

"First Lady?" Em reached for her cell. Time to call in Big Estelle and let her know her mom was definitely losing it.

Little Estelle nodded. "One of my husbands, maybe my second, was a Shriner. He rose through the ranks, eventually became the Grand High Poobah. Actually, it's called the Imperial Potentate."

"Seriously?"

"You bet'cha. We used to travel all over going to these conventions, raising money for children's hospitals. You might not think so by looking at these guys, but they're dedicated to philanthropic work. Well, that and partying. They've been at it since 1872."

"So why the fezzes?"

Little Estelle let out a cackle. "Why not? You haven't lived until you've been to bed with a man in a fez, honey. Not that I've ever needed an excuse to go wild."

Em decided no one else could keep her mind off of what Detective Bardon might be telling Roland as well as Little Estelle could.

"So, what's the title of your rap?" she asked the former first lady.

"'Motorized Love.' Wanna hear the first verse?"

Before Em could say no, Little Estelle started tapping her handlebars and making beat box sounds.

"Pooh, cheechee, pooh, cheechee, pooh, cheechee, pooh." She kept tapping as she launched into the lyrics.

"I got it goin' on, goin' on, goin' on.

All night long, all night long, all night long.

I got it goin' on, to the lef', to the right, back n' forth, all damn night.

Got it goin' on, goin' on, goin' on.

Goin' on like its galvanized, polarized, super-sized.

Motorized *luv*!

Pooh, cheechee, pooh, cheechee, pooh, cheechee, pooh."

She smiled at Em, waiting for her to say something.

"Wow."

"I know, huh? I had no idea I could do that until I tried." Little Estelle smiled.

"I'm sure it's a rare talent."

"You bet. It's a gift. My rap name is Elenee. Stands for L and E, Little Estelle, get it? Like Eminem is MnM. I'll get you and Roland front row seats at the first stop on my concert tour."

"That'll be great. When and where do you open?"

"Still working out the details. Oh my stars and garters, I *know* that guy." She pointed toward the ground in front of the bar where a hefty Shriner was doing one-handed pushups. The tassel on his fez was slapping the stone floor.

"Charlie! Charlie Watson! It's me, the former First Lady of the TajMaHaLay Temple!" She threw the Gadabout into gear and roared away.

Little Estelle had no sooner disappeared behind a phalanx of Shriners than Uncle Louie walked through the open air atrium and spotted Em. She waved in greeting as he sauntered down the walkway.

"There you are. All alone?" He looked around. "Where's Roland?"

"Making a quick phone call." She debated telling Louie about Phillip's death, but only for a nanosecond. The time wasn't right. She didn't want to ruin his day when he still needed to stay focused on the contest. Just then the Shriners let out a collective whoop, and she decided this was definitely not the place, either.

"I heard Suzi broke her toe," he said.

"Her whole foot is pretty screwed up. She'll be all right, hopefully. What are you up to?"

"We're on a lunch break. I'm looking for someone willing to help me. The Shriner who rented me the monkey is attending the convention, and he wants it back. You think Roland could coax it back into the cage? He's gotta be pretty good at locking people up by now."

"People. Not misbehaving Capuchin monkeys."

"I'll treat you two to dinner anywhere in Waikiki."

"If he can't do it I'll see if we can find someone who will."

He snapped his fingers. "Locking people up. That reminds me. DePesto cornered me and told me what happened last night. I'm sure glad you aren't in jail."

She should have known. "I'm sorry, Louie. I didn't get you tossed out of the contest, did I?"

"Fat chance. When he told me he called the police and had you hauled off, I told him I was dropping out."

"Please, tell me you didn't. I'd never forgive myself."

"He wouldn't let me. Said because of our TV series, I was a huge draw. He needs me to attract the press."

Em realized once Honolulu's latest murder victim was connected to her and Louie the press would have a field day.

"The guy is an ass." Louie rolled his eyes. "He was rambling on about you coming on to him just to get into his suite and how he caught you tossing his room."

"All of it's true except I wasn't tossing his room. I was carefully looking for the Booze Bible," she said. "I thought the costume party would be a great way to mingle with the Shake Off committee and see if I could discover who might be desperate enough to steal your notebook, so I rented a costume and went."

"When I didn't see you there I thought you found something else to do."

"You talked to me, actually."

"No way. I did?"

She nodded. "You asked me about the thigh-high stiletto boots I was wearing."

Her uncle rarely blushed, but upon hearing that he went from tan to red.

"Was that you? In that pirate wench getup?"

"Were you hitting on me?"

"Of course not. I really wanted to know about those boots. I thought you'd like some."

"I almost broke my leg trying to walk in them."

"Why did you suspect dePesto?"

"Because he said he'd do anything to win. Then when I got to his suite, I found an extortion letter just like yours along with a printer and a computer. He could have written them both, but he swore someone sent him the letter, too."

"The thief wants to sell both of us the Booze Bible?"

She shook her head. "The thief only offered to sell dePesto a copy."

"A copy? How many more offers are out there?" He glanced over at the tiki wearing the giant fez. Then he sighed. "I guess my Booze Bible is gone for good."

"Don't give up hope, Uncle Louie." She wished she could tell him more, but she'd have to tell him that the thief was her own ex-husband.

Her dead ex-husband.

"It's not worth getting thrown in jail over," he said. "In fact, I've got a new idea for my big presentation tomorrow. I'm really lucky we weren't required to turn in a recipe for approval when we mailed in our contest registration forms. In this contest it's okay to concoct something at the last minute. The only requirement is that the mix has to include a least one tropical ingredient."

He stared out toward the ocean with a faraway expression.

"You are on to something. I can see it in your eyes," Em said.

"I've got a name anyway. Now I just have to come up with a great story that goes along with the drink and sets the scene. That'll earn me a lot of points, so it's gotta be a good one."

"You're a master at legends," she said.

"So they say."

A woman in her fifties wearing a colorful sheath and an official Shake Off contestant's badge walked up to them. Louie introduced her as Fran.

"I'm headed back over to the conference center," Fran said. "What about you?"

Louie agreed to walk back with her and told Em goodbye. Before he walked away he said, "Remember to ask Roland to cage the monkey so I can return it."

"Will do." *Monkeys, murder, and mayhem. Oh my.*

After Louie left, Em took a deep breath. The idea of having a shot of tequila flitted across her mind, but the Shriners were stacked up three deep around the bar and it was too early anyway. She didn't need to compound her problems. She was impatient with waiting and ready to call Roland when she spotted him trapped behind a huge wedding party on the walkway.

An entire contingent of Japanese including six bridesmaids and six groomsmen along with assorted friends and family were headed up the path toward the Crystal Chapel. Roland stood head and shoulders above them, waiting for them to move along.

"Big business," he said when he finally reached Em.

"These hotels are like Japanese wedding factories. It's amazing," she said. "What's up with all these weddings?"

"It's cheaper to fly entire families over here from Japan than it is to hold one there, or so I hear."

"I can't imagine all the work that goes into the planning."

"One phone call, and you've got a location, photographer, rental clothing for everyone including the bride, someone to officiate, music, and a reception. They can even book high-end venues and still get off cheaper here than in Japan." He sat down beside her on the rock planter.

"How are you doing?" he asked.

Em shrugged. "Not great, but better. I think the shock is wearing off. Did they find the Booze Bible in Phillip's apartment?"

He shook his head. "No. At least not yet. I described it to Bardon and filled him in on Phillip's extortion scheme. I told him we have definitely ID'd Phillip on the surveillance video."

"Uh, oh."

"I also told him about your trip to the substation last night. He wasn't any happier than I was when he found out you'd conveniently left that little detail out of your alibi. I assured him I'd make sure you didn't go anywhere."

"Thank you."

"So don't pull any more stunts."

"Definitely not. Have they found Phillip's neighbor yet? What was his name?"

"Damian Bautista. Not yet," he said.

"Did you ask if he's got anyone looking for Felicity?"

"They do. As far as he knows, they haven't found her. She hasn't checked out of the Moana either, but she's not there, at least not in her room."

"Now what?"

He studied her carefully. "How about lunch? I'm starved."

"I don't know. I'm still kind of queasy."

"You can watch while I eat."

"Okay." She couldn't let the guy starve to death.

"Let's head up the street to the Moana. Keep an eye out for the fiancée."

"Really?" She couldn't believe it. "Are we going detecting?"

"I am. You're just my sidekick and only because I'm supposed to be keeping an eye on you and you know what Felicity looks like. If she did kill Phillip, it's a long shot that she'll stick around long."

"Maybe she just ran out of the hotels. She's probably on her way to the mainland by now," Em said. "I would be."

As they passed the Tapa Bar, Em spotted Little Estelle surrounded by a host of Shriners. Roland followed her gaze and stared.

"Tell me Little Estelle isn't trying to flash gang signs."

"I would, but that would be a lie."

"Why is she doing that?"

"Looks like she's throwing down her new rap for the Shriner's. She's Elenee now."

"Like Eminem?"

"You got it." As they walked on, Em remembered Louie's request. "I hate to ask, but would you be willing to do Louie a favor and wrangle the monkey into his cage before we leave the hotel? The owner wants him back."

"Sorry, but I don't wrangle monkeys."

"Ever? Not even for me, *Roland*?" She batted her lashes.

"I'm just not that kind of guy. Besides, we're on the job here."

"You're right." She didn't press him. She'd had enough to deal with already, and it wasn't even two in the afternoon. The fugitive monkey would just have to wait.

They headed down Rainbow Drive toward the Hilton entrance on Kalia Road.

"Now there's what I'd call some monkey wranglers," Roland said.

Em followed Roland's gaze, which unfortunately meant taking hers off of him. Kiki and the Maidens, minus Suzi, were all gussied up in neon pink ruffled muumuus posing against a lovely garden pool beside three massive bronze hula sculptures. The male dancer represented a hawk and was upright, reaching for the sky. The two female dancer sculptures would forever be performing complicated kneeling hula moves the Hula Maidens could never hope to master.

That didn't keep the Maidens from cavorting around the edges of the pond, posing on low black lava rocks or hanging on gas tiki torch poles as their fans and tourists snapped photos.

The Kamakanis sat on their beach chairs on the grassy area surrounding the pond playing a lively *hapa haole* tune that tourists loved. There was a calabash full of tips on the ground in front of Byron.

From the look of all the cameras slung around his neck, a professional Japanese photographer and Trish were in deep conversation, no doubt speaking the international language of apertures, blown highlights, and depth of field.

Kiki disengaged from one of the torch poles when she saw Em and Roland and came running over.

"I heard you were here, Roland." She momentarily ignored Em. Women only had eyes for Roland when he was around. "Have you found Louie's Booze Bible yet?"

"He just arrived this morning," Em reminded her.

"Not yet," Roland said. "Things are a little more complicated than they seem."

"Oh, what's up?" Kiki looked from Roland to Em and back. "Tell! You've got to tell me."

"We don't know anything definitive yet," he said. "We could use your help though."

Kiki puffed up like a peacock. "Of course you've got it."

"Louie needs to get the monkey back to its owner. He needs someone to put it back into the cage."

Kiki started backing away, shaking her head. "Not me. No way, no how. That thing tore my hair out by the roots." She separated her hair and showed him a scabby bald spot.

"Maybe one of the musicians will do it. They're making a lot of money off you ladies. Seems like they owe you," he said.

Kiki glanced over her shoulder. "Maybe Big Estelle can talk Byron into it. Promise a couple of favors."

"Speaking of Big Estelle, her mom's back from the recording studio. She's at Tapa Bar rapping for the Shriners," Em said.

Across the pond, Big Estelle was trying to imitate one of the massive bronze hula dancers without actually kneeling.

"Uh, oh," Kiki said. "If she pulls her back out we'll be down two dancers instead of one." She cupped her hands and hollered, "Big Estelle, knock it off!"

"Where's Pat?" Em scanned the group of Maidens.

"At the airport. They found our cooler, but it was going to take them all day to deliver it, so she went to pick it up," Kiki said.

Roland nudged Em. "We've got to go, Kiki," Em said.

"Where?"

"To grab some lunch," Roland said.

"If you could just see about caging the monkey . . ." Em hoped she sounded desperate.

"That thing hates women," Kiki told Roland.

"Maybe it will like Pat," Em suggested. "Maybe he'll think she's a man."

"Probably not," Kiki said. "I have a feeling that monkey is cagier than all of us put together."

27

KIKI SIDESTEPPED two tourists clamoring for her autograph and headed over to Big Estelle, who was signing the back of someone's T-shirt.

When she was finished she said, "Don't forget to leave a tip in that wooden bowl over there in front of our ukulele player and ma-*ha*-lo." Big Estelle waved goodbye as the delighted tourist walked away.

"Em said your mom's back safe and sound. So far anyway. She's at Tapa Bar," Kiki said.

"That's a relief. Kind of."

"Between you and me, something's going on, and Em's clammed up about it."

"You mean, between *all* of us." Lillian walked up with Precious and Flora beside her. "Em's got a secret?"

Kiki hadn't really looked at Lillian until now.

"What happened to your face?" The woman was covered in foundation makeup that ended at her jawline. It gave the impression she was wearing a mask. Her eyes were so heavily outlined with shadow and liner that she was beyond smoky-eyed. She was downright scary.

Lillian's lower lip trembled. "I ran into a couple of the Mindy's women I knew in Iowa. They took one look at me and dragged me off to an intervention and gave me a makeover before they left. They threatened to have my Miracle Maker status revoked."

"What do you care?" Kiki wondered aloud. "You aren't selling that stuff anymore."

"Well, I do have a few boxes piled up in the garage. In case anything ever happens, and the container ships can't get to the islands, I'll have enough product to go around."

Precious tugged on Kiki's muumuu to get her attention. "I've been thinking about what Em's secret might be. Maybe she and Roland are getting married, and that's why he's here."

"If I was younger I'd be tempted to go after him myself." Flora hiked up her bra straps.

"I don't think so. I think they know something about the Booze Bible, but they haven't found it yet. The competition really heats up tomorrow. Louie will be sunk without it," Kiki said.

"Is there anything we can do?" Precious fluffed the wide ruffle around the top of her muumuu.

"We've tracked down murderers before," Big Estelle said. "Seems like we ought to be able to find a three-ring binder."

"We can't do anything until we have something to go on. Then you bet your sweet *okole* we'll snap into action," Kiki assured them.

The Maidens nodded in unison. Kiki waved to Trish, who quickly said goodbye to a Japanese photographer and came walking over toting her camera gear.

"What's up?" she said.

"Em's keeping a secret," Precious filled her in. "They haven't found the Booze Bible."

"Uh, oh," Trish said.

"Em asked if we could put that rent-a-monkey back in its cage for Louie," Kiki told them.

"Dead or alive?" Big Estelle snorted.

"Us or the monkey?" Precious doubled over laughing.

"This is no laughing matter. I have the scars to prove it." Kiki flashed her scabby bald spot at anyone who would look.

She glanced over at the Kamakanis. Em was right. The wooden calabash was full of money. The musicians owed her. She motioned for the girls to follow as she headed toward Bryron.

By now there were at least forty people gathered around them on the grass at the entrance to Hilton Hawaiian Village. The bright orange double decker Waikiki Trolley had just pulled up on the corner. Spotting a crowd, disembarking passengers hurried over to see what was going on. When the crowd around them suddenly doubled in size, Kiki knew they had better get moving before the hotel management came out and got on her case again.

"Dance for us, Hula Maidens!" a woman shouted. "We came all the way from Illinois hopin' to see you dance."

Kiki sighed. "Gotta keep the fans happy," she told the others. "Line up, girls. We'll do one more number."

Lillian, Precious, Big Estelle, Flora, and Trish lined up on the grass. They left a spot in the middle open for Kiki.

"What you wanna dance?" Byron asked Kiki.

She scanned the crowd. "How about 'Lovely Hula Hands'?" Then she called out to the gathering, "We'll dance if you'll sing along!"

Everyone cheered. The Kamakanis started strumming. The Maidens started dancing. The tourists sang.

Halfway through the song, Kiki spotted two Hilton security officers on bicycles circling the edge of the crowd. Byron noticed too and picked up the tempo. By the time the officers negotiated their way through the ring of tourists, the musicians hadn't wasted any time folding up their beach chairs and closing their coolers.

"You folks are going to have to take this show somewhere else." The youngest of the two security guards was smiling as he added, "We don't want any trouble, auntie."

"No worries," Kiki said. "We don't either. We're outta here."

Byron picked up the calabash. It was full to the brim with five, tens, and twenties. Loose change clanked in the bottom of the wooden bowl.

"Pretty good tips," Bryon said.

"Stick with us." Kiki smiled and gave him a wink. "By the way, we've got real treat for you gentlemen. Have you ever seen a Capuchin monkey up close?"

28

EM AND ROLAND negotiated sidewalks jammed with tourists, a smattering of locals weaving their way through the throng, and solicitors handing out flyers for various businesses and time-share freebies. Visitors hurried along, intent on seeing, doing, and buying everything paradise had to offer.

They reached the Moana where bellmen and valets in cream-colored uniforms extended greetings of aloha to guests pouring out of cars, taxis, and limos beneath a towering porte-cochere supported by stark white Ionic columns.

"I can't go in there. I'm underdressed." Em glanced down at her white capris and black tank top, her woven purse and rubber Locals slaps, and balked. She wished she'd at least put on a sundress.

"It's a hotel. You'll see everything inside, believe me."

Skeptical, she watched another limo unload. "These people are all dressed up."

"Mainlanders. They just got here," he said. "Let's go."

She felt his hand riding the small of her back, urging her on as they walked up the sidewalk to the front steps. When Em saw the hotel's front lanai lined with rocking chairs she wanted nothing more than to sit down, watch the world go by, and forget about what happened to Phillip, at least for a few minutes.

They stepped inside the classically Hawaiian interior of the lobby with its polished *koa* wood tables, plush Oriental carpets, and two long rows of Ionic columns. There was a view from the front doors straight through to the courtyard and the sun glittering on the ocean beyond.

Roland pointed out a family of six decked out in swimwear as they trooped through the lobby. The kids toted towels and sand toys. The mother was in a lace beach cover-up that didn't cover enough.

"Told you anything goes."

Em relaxed a little and watched the beachgoers walk past another Japanese wedding party. The bride, groom, attendants, and family headed through the lobby and disappeared down a long hallway.

"See Felicity anywhere?" Roland asked.

Reminded of their mission, Em looked around as they slowly walked out to the courtyard.

"I don't see her."

"What does she look like?"

"In her late twenties, a little taller than me, porcelain skin, no sun damage, blond hair, pert nose, enhanced lips, *very* perky breasts. She'll be wearing upscale resort wear and sandals that cost more than you make in a week."

"Got it."

More rocking chairs were lined up on the wide back lanai overlooking the courtyard, pool, and the ocean. Most of them were occupied.

"Wow, this is amazing." Em didn't know how else to describe the view or the huge banyan tree that shaded the entire courtyard.

A host standing near the entrance to the Beach House restaurant overheard.

"Hey, bra," he greeted Roland one local to another. Roland nodded.

The host told Em, "That banyan tree was planted in 1825. Robert Louis Stevenson did a lot of writing under there."

"No kidding?" Em gazed up at the wide canopy of leaves and branches, the dappled sunlight streaming through. She thanked the host for the information, and when she and Roland walked by the massive trunk of the tree formed of rooted vines, she paused to touch it.

"I can't remember what he wrote," Roland said. He wasn't focused on the tree. He was scanning the poolside lounge chairs.

"Felicity won't be in the sun," Em told him. "Her lips might melt."

He turned his attention on her, and Em forgot what she'd been talking about.

"So what did Stevenson write?" he prompted.

"*Treasure Island*," she said. "I think *Dr. Jekyll and Mr. Hyde*, too."

"Saw the movie. Come on, I'm starving."

They found an empty table at the Beach Bar which was next to a low retaining wall that held back the sand. As they sat down, Em heard the call of a conch shell and turned to watch one of the crew of a huge yellow surf-riding catamaran blow the shell again. He waved swimmers away from the craft as it drifted toward the beach to offload and pick up more tourists.

While Em people watched, Roland scanned the menu. When their waitress arrived he ordered a *loco moco* and iced tea and handed Em a menu.

"You really are starving," she said.

"Those breakfast muffins wore off hours ago."

An hour ago she didn't think she'd ever have an appetite again. Looking over the menu she quickly decided on an arugula and papaya salad with orange ginger dressing and iced tea. She kept the menu to study the tropical drink offerings.

"Beach Bar," Em said. "They sure put a lot of imagination into the name."

"No matter what they call it, folks probably just say let's meet at the beach bar anyway."

"You're right."

She scanned the tropical beverages and found it typical. The hotels and resorts tried to outdo each when other naming drinks and dishes. The "Vanilla Refresh," "Hawaiian Sun," "Day at the Beach," and a host of other cocktails were all variations of liquor, fruit juices, and an occasional splash of coconut.

"These drinks don't hold a candle to Louie's. Most of his were inspired by actual events in his life. There's a legend to go with every drink he ever created." She closed the menu and pushed it away. "It's all recorded in the Booze Bible."

"There's a chance we'll still find it."

The waitress delivered ice teas and assured them their orders were on the way.

"You really think we'll get it back?"

"For your uncle's sake I sure hope so."

He leaned back and focused on the guests walking on the hotel lanai. Em figured they had as much chance of finding the notebook as spotting Felicity. She turned her gaze to the ocean and the backdrop of Diamond Head.

The gently rolling waves never stopped. Staring at them was so relaxing that eventually her breathing slowed, and a sense of tranquility washed over her. She could never dismiss the horrible truth of what had happened to Phillip, but sitting there beneath the ancient tree watching the surf and listening to its steady rhythm, she was reminded of the order of things. Just as the surf constantly rolls in and out, life goes on.

The waitress arrived with their orders. Em stared at Roland's *loco moco*: a side of ground beef molded into a patty nestled on a mound of rice and topped with grilled Maui sweet onions, a poached egg, and then the whole mountain was smothered in red wine gravy. She could tell Roland couldn't wait to dig in but was politely waiting for her, so she took a bite of her salad.

"You should have just ordered a heart attack on a plate," Em said.

"When she comes back I'll ask if they keep a defibrillator under the bar."

"So do you have a plan?" Em pushed her salad around.

"Other than the defibrillator? We get good health coverage."

She rolled her eyes. "I meant a plan to solve the murder. If the HPD can't find Felicity, what makes you think you can? What are you going to do?"

"Talk to someone at reception, make sure she really is still registered here. She may have checked out by now."

"They'll tell you that?"

"If I flash my badge at the manager."

"If she's a woman, all you have to flash is your smile."

"Mahalo." He flashed it at her.

"It still works." Suddenly she was melting from more than the heat. "Just testing."

He focused on his lunch, and when he was through he signaled for the check. Em had at least finished eating all the papaya out of the salad.

They headed for the reception area at the far end of the lobby near the elevators. Check in was at three. Since it was nearly that time, guests were queuing up. There were tourists and locals alike lined up. The Moana was a *kama'aina* favorite.

Roland asked to see the reception manager. A clerk picked up a phone, and a minute later a door opened in the wall behind the reception clerks, and a young Japanese American woman stepped out.

Roland flashed his badge and asked to speak to her in private. Em followed them into an office hidden near the reception desk. He told the young woman he needed to know if Felicity Duncan and Phillip Johnson were still registered as guests and took out his pocket-sized spiral notepad.

The manager turned to her computer screen, clicked a few buttons, and then said, "Yes." Then she paused, studied the screen before she went on. "They had a suite together until yesterday. Mr. Johnson's credit card was refused when the daily fee was automatically charged. We asked him to come down and put a valid card on file at ten a.m."

"You spoke to him at ten yesterday?" Roland glanced over at Em.

It was around ten when Phillip delivered the extortion letter to the Hilton front desk.

The manager squinted at the screen. "Actually, we texted him then. He wasn't in his room."

"When did he come in with a valid card?"

"He didn't. Ms. Duncan settled up his charges and said he was checking out, but she stayed on."

"When was that?" Roland's pen was poised over his notepad.

She glanced at the computer. "That afternoon. The change was made at four thirty. Ms. Duncan is still here as far as I know."

Em wanted to ask Roland why the HPD didn't know that, but not in front of the manager.

"Is there a pending check out date?" he asked.

"Day after tomorrow. Would you like to leave her a message?"

"No thanks. We'll get in touch with her." Roland thanked the clerk.

When they came back around the reception desk one of the bellmen greeting incoming guests walked up to Em and slipped a purple orchid lei around her neck.

"Aloha and welcome to the Moana," he said.

"Oh, I'm not a guest." Em started to take the lei off.

"No worries. Keep it." He smiled.

She thanked him and caught up with Roland, who was waiting a few feet away near the concierge desk. They walked along a few more steps.

"What now?" she asked.

"We'll hang out here in the lobby for a while if that's okay." He picked up a copy of the *Honolulu Star-Advertiser*. "Watch for Ms. Duncan to walk in."

29

ROLAND CHOSE A sofa with a view of the entire lobby and pretended to read the newspaper. Em watched as another wedding couple walked up to the photographer's desk and sat down.

She told Roland she was going to use the *lua*, got directions from the concierge, and headed down a long hall lined with stores on one side. The reception ballroom was on the other.

On her way back she paused to look in the window of the upscale Island Gallery. Her jaw dropped when she recognized Felicity admiring a bronze mermaid sculpture. A well-dressed Japanese man a foot shorter than Felicity stood beside her. He was wearing a suit.

The only other person in the room was a huge Japanese man, also in a severe black suit. He kept his distance from the pair, but his gaze continually scanned the interior of the gallery and the doorway. When he looked toward the window and noticed her, Em hurried back into the lobby area where she stopped by the baby grand piano. When Roland saw her, Em made a "curvy woman" motion with her hands. It was one of the only hula gestures the Maidens had perfected. Roland tossed the newspaper aside and headed over.

"I just saw Felicity. She's in the gallery behind me," she said.

Roland glanced down the hall. "Some of those shops open onto Kalakaua. Is she alone?" he asked.

"She's with a guy in a suit. Looks like a businessman. There's another man in there too. Huge. Really beefy. He could be with them."

Roland didn't hesitate to head for the gallery.

"Do you want me to wait here?" Em didn't want to stay behind but thought she'd better ask.

He paused a second then said, "Come on."

They walked into the shop together. Felicity and her companion were at the counter with their backs to the door. The hulk watched them but didn't move until Roland walked up to Felicity. The big man moved in. If Roland noticed, he didn't let on.

"Felicity Duncan?" Roland asked.

Felicity turned at the sound of her name and started to smile up at Roland until she recognized Em.

"Yes?" Felicity adjusted the robin's egg blue Tiffany shopping bag on her arm.

The clerk, the man beside Felicity, and the walking mountain were all listening.

"I'd like to speak to you for a moment." He reached into his pocket.

The hulk took a threatening step toward Roland. The shorter man held up his hand, and the larger man, obviously a bodyguard, stopped in his tracks. Roland pulled out his badge and flashed it discretely.

"Of course." Felicity nodded. "But if you're here to tell me that Phillip Johnson is dead, I already heard it from two HPD detectives about twenty minutes ago."

"I'd still like to ask you a couple of questions," he said.

She turned to her companion. Slowly and distinctly she said, "I need to talk to this man. Please join us." She gave a slight bow.

The Japanese gentleman bowed to Roland, to Em, and then followed Felicity out into the hall. There was an unoccupied sitting area across from the baby grand. Roland indicated they should sit. Felicity and her companion sat. She looked older today, more savvy. Felicity studied Em from head to toe and dismissed her. The bodyguard hovered a few feet away. His gaze never stopped surveying the lobby.

"I assume you're a detective." Felicity indicated Roland's casual wear, his aloha shirt, black flip-flops, and shorts.

He nodded. "From Kauai."

"So I really don't *have* to answer your questions?" Felicity leaned back.

"Not at all."

She turned to Em. "You live on Kauai, don't you?"

"That's right," Em said.

"I'm assuming this is about Phillip. Did he con you, too?" she asked Em.

"How do you mean?" Roland didn't let Em answer.

Felicity nodded toward Em.

"She should know. She was married to him. He pretended to be wealthy. He said all the right things, wore expensive watches, designer suits and clothes. He had a high-end condo on the water in Marina del Rey and drove a Lamborghini."

Em glanced over at the Asian gentleman seated beside Felicity. He looked to be in his early sixties but could have been older. His tailored black suit and starched white shirt were impeccably made. Aside from the grooms and wedding party attendants streaming through the lobby every few minutes, the gentleman and his bodyguard were the only people in the place wearing business suits. If the heat bothered them, it didn't show. Both of their expressions were closed and completely impassive.

Em turned her attention to Felicity again.

"Don't worry about him," Felicity said. "No *comprende nada*, if you get my drift."

"So you were informed of your fiancé's death by the HPD."

"About a half an hour ago, yes."

"That must have come as a shock," Roland said.

Em didn't see any evidence that Felicity had shed a tear over Phillip.

"Yes and no. But after the lengths he went to in order to misrepresent himself to me, I guess anything's possible. Who knows how many other people he's conned. He must have tried to rip off the wrong person, and his lying caught up with him. That's what I told the police anyway." She stared pointedly at Em. "He must have finally pissed off the wrong person."

"When did you find out he was not all he claimed to be?" Roland wanted to know.

She looked at Em. "Yesterday, after we had lunch with you. When we got back he admitted the hotel had been trying to contact him. They wanted him to put a different credit card on file. He asked if he could use one of mine until FedEx delivered a new one."

"So you agreed."

"Not at all. I'd had a bad feeling about things since I met you yesterday. I couldn't help but notice the way he stared at you," she told Em. "He's never looked at me that way. That, coupled with his credit suddenly going south, was enough for me. It was time to bail. I broke up with him on the spot."

"How did he take it?"

"He was upset, but not furious. He argued, pleaded, said he had a big investment deal about to close. He said when it did, he'd have plenty of money. He begged for time, begged me not to break it off. He swore he loved me."

"What did you say?"

"I said he was out of time. In fact, I told him to go back to his wife."

"Ex," Em said. "*Ex*-wife." *Thanks a lot.*

"Now he's dead," Roland said.

"Sad but true." Felicity didn't sound sad in the least. She glanced at the face of her diamond-encrusted watch.

"Did you know about his extortion scheme?" Roland asked.

"What extortion scheme?" Felicity looked up at Roland.

"He stole Ms. Johnson's uncle's recipe notebook. It's worth a lot of money to the right buyer."

"Maybe *that's* the big deal he had going." Felicity studied Em's rubber sandals for a minute. Unwilling to back down, Em met her gaze and didn't shy away when their eyes met.

"Did you ever happen to see a thick, three-ringed binder in Phillip's possession?" Em asked. "He must have had it when he was here in the hotel."

"No. Nothing like that. If he did have it, he kept it hidden."

Em had another question. "How about a laptop and a printer?"

"Laptop, but no printer," she said. "He could have used the business center here at the hotel to print something, though."

"Where were you last night?" Roland's little spiral notebook and pen had appeared in his hands.

"Last night? Is that really any of your business?"

"Phillip was killed sometime late last night or early this morning. As far as we know, Phillip Johnson knew three people in Hawaii, and one of them was you. The other two are Em and her uncle. Until his murderer is found, there's a very short list of suspects."

"Are the police so sure he was murdered? I think it was more than likely he was depressed over being found out and shot himself." Her tone was cool as ice in a rocks glass.

Em started to ask who would shoot themselves in the heart until Roland silenced her with a look.

"So again, where were you last night?" he asked.

Felicity gestured toward the man beside her.

"Mr. Hasigawa saw me sitting alone having a martini, watching the sunset. I looked so down in the dumps he asked me to join him at his son's wedding reception. He was a widower and said he felt like a third wheel."

"So he *does* speak English."

"No, his son translated for him."

"How long were you there?"

"Until the reception ended around nine thirty."

"And after that?"

She met Roland's intent stare. "After that I spent the night in Mr.

Hasigawa's suite. The whole night."

Em was certain her eyes had just bugged and hoped Felicity hadn't noticed.

"I assume Mr. Hasigawa will vouch for that?" Roland asked.

"Sure. Get an interpreter."

Em was pretty sure Mr. Hasigawa would vouch for anything if his new Barbie doll asked him to.

"We will if necessary," Roland said. "What time did you leave his suite?"

"Around ten this morning. Right after breakfast. Then we went to the Honolulu Museum of Art to view the *Erotic Art of 19th Century Japan* exhibition and have lunch. The HPD stopped us out on the sidewalk and chatted us up for a few minutes. Now here we are."

"So you've been with Mr. Hasigawa since around six thirty or seven last night?"

"Except when I was in my room changing this morning. That took me about thirty minutes before we left for the museum."

Em tried to focus on the exchange but couldn't shake the idea that Phillip was supposedly looking at her as if he was still attracted to her, as if he wanted her back.

Roland was flipping through the pages of his notebook. Apparently satisfied, he closed it and slipped it into his back pocket.

"Thank you, Ms. Duncan. You've been very helpful."

Everyone stood at once. Mr. Hasigawa bowed to all of them. Em was beginning to wonder if the man's face was paralyzed. His expression never changed.

"We didn't part amicably, but I wouldn't wish Phillip dead. The police said he died in an apartment in a run-down area of town. Is that true?"

"Yesterday afternoon he rented a day-week-monthly," Roland said.

For the first time since they'd spoken to her, Felicity appeared sad as she said, "Phillip might have been a con man, but he didn't deserve to die. I sincerely hope you find whoever did this."

"Don't worry. We will," Roland assured her.

Em wondered if jewelry repo men would be calling on Felicity soon. The woman was still wearing the huge diamond engagement ring Phillip had given her.

She and Roland had no sooner left Felicity and the Japanese gentlemen and walked out the main exit when one of the valets called out, "Hey, cuz!"

Roland stopped and exchanged a complicated handshake with one of the young valets.

"How long you been here?" he asked Roland.

Em definitely saw the family resemblance. The young man Roland introduced as Sonny Boy had the same winning smile and was just as handsome.

"Just got in. Not staying here though. I'm down at the Hilton," Roland said.

"Workin' or playin'?" Sonny Boy glanced at Em and flashed his smile.

"A little of both." Roland introduced them and then motioned for the young man to follow them a few feet from the valet stand. When they were out of earshot of anyone else, Roland described Felicity to him.

"Ms. Duncan. 'Course I noticed her. Who wouldn't?"

Roland asked him to call his cell if Felicity checked out.

They exchanged cell numbers, and Sonny Boy invited Roland and Em both to come over to his mom's place for dinner.

Roland and Em walked past the Honolulu Coffee Company in the west wing of the Moana and stepped onto Kalakaua before either of them said a word.

"What do you think?" Roland broke his silence.

"I don't know what to think. If Phillip was staring at me as if he still cared, I would have noticed. He definitely wasn't. He just seemed like the old Phillip I knew, self-centered and worried about appearances. He was all over Felicity when she joined us. Why would she think he was still interested in me? I don't get it. What do you think of her?"

"She sure moved on in the blink of an eye. Obviously she goes where the money leads her."

"True love." Em sidestepped a sidewalk solicitor handing out flyers advertising a massage parlor. "Do you think maybe she knew Mr. Hasigawa before?"

"I think they probably met just the way she said. He needed an escort, saw a beautiful woman alone, and asked her to join him at the reception. He's obviously going back to Japan soon and figured he'd hit the jackpot. She saw a meal ticket, some expensive gifts, and a diversion."

"She's got money of her own, obviously."

"For now. Ever wonder where she gets it?"

"Rich men."

"Unfortunately, Phillip's well ran dry."

"So she moved on. Poor Mr. Hasigawa," Em said.

"Don't worry about him."

"Unless he's a con man like Phillip, he's obviously wealthy and important if he's got a bodyguard. Who has a bodyguard anyway? Maybe he owns a big car company in Japan. Maybe his middle name is Toyota."

Roland was silent.

"You think?" she prodded.

"I think there's a lot more to Mr. Hasigawa than Felicity knows."

"Like what?"

"You ever heard of the Yakuza?"

"Is that a Japanese dish or a new restaurant?"

"Neither. Yakuza is the name of the organized crime syndicate in Japan. The Japanese mafia."

They walked past the Royal Hawaiian Hotel shopping complex. Roland picked up the pace to make the green light at the next corner.

"Do you think Felicity knows?" she wondered.

"No idea."

"Could she have been angry enough to have had Phillip murdered? Maybe that's the Hasigawa connection." She pictured the bodyguard and shivered despite the close heat.

"We'd have to find out if their connection goes all the way back to LA. If not, then she probably doesn't know or suspect who or what Hasigawa is and has picked up the wrong sugar daddy again."

30

IT WAS AFTER THREE by the time they made it back to the Hilton. Em returned to her suite to freshen up while Roland went to registration to see if he could get a room. She heard the Maidens laughing and talking in the suite before she even reached the open door.

"Em's back," Flora called when Em stepped inside.

The sitting room area was full. Most of the Hula Maidens were there along with the Kamakanis. The women were lounging on every available chair and the floor. Suzi had her injured foot propped up on pillows and was sprawled on the sofa. The musicians played poker at the table near the balcony slider. The TV was on, the sound muted. The place was littered with food wrappers, snack bags, crumbs, and empty Solo cups. One of the poker players was sitting on the formerly missing ice chest. Any hope of a quiet ten minute rest evaporated.

"You got your cooler back," she said to no one in particular.

"Yeah." Flora roused herself from where she was propped up on a sofa pillow on the floor. "Da poi, da flowers, da *akule*, all gone. But we got the cooler."

"Tell her what was in it." Pat was sitting on one of the bar stools at the short kitchen counter in the corner. Her hand was wrapped in so many layers of white gauze that it was almost the size of a basketball.

Flora snorted. "All our stuffs was gone. Whoever took it left a note. Mahalo for the fish and poi. They sent the cooler back with about a dozen cans of teriyaki flavored Spam. Big deal. Spam."

"What happened to your hand?" Em asked Pat.

"The gol'danged monkey is what happened to my hand. The dang thing bit me. I'm on antibiotics the size of golf balls."

"Did you cage it?"

"H-ell no. I *almost* had it stuffed in the cage, but then it bit into my hand and hung on. Like to bit my fingers off. I started screaming just as a maid walked in. She started screamin'. The monkey started screamin'. It let go of me and went for the maid. She ran out the door and so did the monkey. Once he got out in the hall he forgot all about the maid and took off."

"Where is he now?" Em asked.

"Loose in the hotel somewhere," Kiki said.

"We're *hoping* it's still in the hotel," Trish said. "If it's gone for good Louie will lose his rental deposit."

"Rental deposit?" Em looked around. Louie had failed to mention a deposit.

"Yes, and judging by Louie's reaction when we told him the monkey was missing, it was a hefty amount," Trish said.

"I hope that furry sucker is under a bus filled with a dozen six hundred pound tourists." Pat moved her arm and winced.

"Pat! How could you say that?" Lillian, her face coated in makeup, was about to cry. "That poor thing is one of God's little creatures."

"That little critter needs to be shot, stuffed, and hung on a wall or maybe skinned and made into a placemat." Pat said. "I coulda lost my whole hand. I'd like to cut his balls off, but he doesn't have any."

Em noticed Kiki staring at her.

"You look frazzled, Em. Where have you been? Did you and Roland find the Booze Bible and the creep who took it yet?" Kiki asked.

Em sank into the only available space on the corner of the sofa beside Suzi's encased foot. She glanced at the TV and noticed the early afternoon edition of the news was on.

"Where are the others?" she asked.

Kiki said, "Precious signed up for the Atlantis Submarine ride. Big Estelle is down at the bar. Last time I saw her she was hiding behind some potted plants spying on Little Estelle. Her mom met up with a bunch of Shriners she used to know, and she's been partying big time ever since."

"Last time I saw her she was performing her rap for them," Em said.

"I saw her just before I came up here," Trish said. "She had on a fez and was trying to belly dance."

"She was dancing?" Kiki couldn't believe it.

"While sitting on the Gadabout," Trish said.

Em took a deep breath and let it out and glanced over the television news. Honolulu had the lowest crime rate of any city its size, so a murder was always the lead story. It was only a matter of time before someone found out Phillip Johnson was her ex.

Em raised her voice to get their attention. "I'm glad most of you are here. There's something I need to tell you before you hear it somewhere else," she said.

One by one, the Hula Maidens fell silent. So quickly that the men at the table stopped talking to see what was up.

"There's a little more going on than just the theft of Louie's Booze Bible," she began. "Sometime between early yesterday evening and last night, my ex-husband was shot and killed."

Lillian immediately got up and rushed to Em's side and threw her arm around her shoulder. "Oh, you poor thing!"

"Are you flying to California?" Trish asked.

"He was here in Waikiki, on vacation with his fiancée."

Kiki shook her head. "Did *she* kill him? If you divorced him, he must have been a real piece of work."

"The police don't know who killed him yet, but his fiancée has an alibi." Em smoothed an escaped lock of hair behind her ear. "We did discover he's the one who stole Louie's Booze Bible."

"How did he know you were on Oahu? Did you tell him? Did you invite him up to your room? Is that when he stole it?" Kiki was on the edge of her chair.

Suzi smiled. "But now that you know where the notebook is, Louie will get it back."

"The police are still looking for it. They haven't found it yet."

"So how do you know Phillip had it?"

"The reception video tape shows him dropping off an extortion letter."

"So who killed him?" Kiki asked.

"They think maybe it was a neighbor of his. Some guy named Damian Bautista. Yesterday afternoon Phillip rented one of those no-tell day, week, month apartments and got in an argument with Bautista over a parking space out front. The neighbors saw it go down."

Flora put down her water bottle—which was full of something far more potent than water.

"Probably a case of road rage," she said. "I had that once. Went to my shrink. He gave me anger management."

"No kidding. You have a shrink?" Kiki sounded amazed.

Flora shrugged. "Yeah, sure. He tol' me to slap myself every time I opened my mouth to yell at somebody when I was driving."

"Did it work?" Em asked.

"I guess. Now I never yell at anybody. I flip 'em off, and if they don't get the message, I smack my bumper into theirs."

"So are the police looking for the neighbor?" Kiki asked.

Em said, "Yes. I have to meet Roland again in a few minutes. He's contacting the detective on the case." She didn't say any more because she didn't want Louie to find out she was a possible suspect. None of the Maidens could keep a secret very long.

"How's my uncle doing? Have you seen him?" Em asked.

Trish said, "I went over to the convention center to tell him the monkey is on the loose. He wasn't too concerned because he was elated about getting top scores on his demonstration today. He's out picking up some special ingredients and is determined to pull something fabulous together. He said he's got an idea for a whole new concoction with a brand new legend. He seemed really excited about it."

"That's great news," Em said. "He's been so down since his note-book went missing I was worried about him."

"Of course he has," Kiki said. "If I ever lost one of my hula notebooks I don't know what I'd do."

Em walked over to the efficiency kitchen, opened the refrigerator, and took out a diet soda. She found a clean Solo cup and poured the soda over ice. Liquor bottles were lined up on the countertop. Em hoped this crowd wasn't going through Louie's ingredients.

"I'd appreciate it if you all wait and let me tell Uncle Louie about Phillip," she said.

They all agreed not to bring it up until Kiki said, "What if he hears it on the news and says something to us?"

Kiki refilled her martini glass. She never traveled without it and refused to use plastic cups.

"He's been too preoccupied to watch TV. And by the way everyone, don't drink all his booze," Em said.

Kiki tasted her martini and smacked her lips. "The girls would love to see Roland tonight. We're dancing at Tiki's Grill and Bar on Kalakaua. Bring him by around seven. It's not far from the Duke Kahanamoku Statue at the other end of Waikiki."

Em knew right where Tiki's was located. Before the latest life-quake hit she had planned to stop by and see if she could pick up any ideas for the Goddess.

"I'll tell him," Em said. "But don't count on us."

She took a sip of the soda and added, "You know, Tiki's is almost across from the Waikiki police substation. If you get in trouble the police won't have to transport you. If you do get arrested again, do not call me."

She'd already seen enough of the substation and Officer Chun.

31

EM WAS ABOUT TO step into the elevator to meet Roland when he texted her and said he was waiting at Hilton's Tropic's Bar and Grill next to the beach. She made her way through the crowded walkways to the restaurant across from the Super Pool.

Happy Hour was underway, and the place was already packed. There was a waiting line out the door. People were seated on the low fire rings and planters in front waiting to be called.

She didn't see Roland in line so she looked for him inside and found him alone at a premier table for four. He was seated next to a window overlooking the pier dubbed Port Hilton where the catamaran rides launched.

"How'd you get such a great table?" She slid into the seat across from him.

He smiled. She melted.

"Oh, of course. That would do it. Did you talk to Bardon?"

"Bardon called to say he's coming to talk to us. He'll be here in five minutes."

Em's heart sank. "Should I run?"

"Hard to hide on an island."

She stared out at the rolling breakers and the horizon in the distance. "I should have stayed on Kauai."

"Your ex would have still stolen Louie's recipe book if that's what he came for. He'd have made up some excuse to talk to your uncle, conned his way into the hotel room, sent the extortion letter. If Louie was here on his own, he would have mortgaged himself to the hilt to get the book back. You're the voice of reason."

"You're right, but the voice of reason is now a murder suspect."

"What if the fiancée is good for it? We just have to disprove her alibi."

"What if she had the gangster do it for her? Or the bodyguard?"

"Possible, but doubtful. If he is Yakuza, Hasigawa will want to keep a low profile while he's here."

"We'll have to wait and see what Bardon knows," she said.

They ordered two iced teas. Em couldn't believe it when Roland ordered off the *pupu* menu a thick-cut onion ring tower with *likiko'i* Sriracha ketchup.

"You're kidding, right? We just ate a little over an hour ago."

"I'm on vacation."

"Some vacation. Did you get a room yet?"

He shook his head. "Nope. Can I hang out on your sofa?"

"Why not? The monkey moved out."

Bardon showed up just as the onion ring tower hit the table.

"Mind if I dig in? I'm starving." He set his notepad down and reached for a ring and ordered a soda.

Em watched Bardon chow down on fried onion rings, waiting to hear that she was off the suspect list. Finally he wiped his greasy fingers on a napkin and leaned back. He wasn't smiling.

"Here's what we know. Phillip Johnson was shot through the heart. He didn't kill himself. There was no powder residue on his hand. The gun was his, but wiped clean. We went through his things. After you called about the stolen binder we took the place apart again but never found it. All he had was a couple of suitcases and a briefcase. Nothing appeared to be missing. Nor did we find any extortion letters. Are you sure he was the thief?"

Em's heart sank to the pit of her stomach.

"Ninety-nine percent sure." Roland handed him the copies of the video stills. "That's Phillip Johnson delivering two large envelopes to the front desk yesterday morning. Two extortion letters were delivered in envelopes exactly like those around the same time, before Em met him for lunch. One was delivered to Em's uncle, Louie Marshall, and the other to Lamar dePesto, the founder of the Shake Off contest."

"Mr. Johnson demanded money for the return of the missing notebook?"

"Right," Em said. "One hundred thousand dollars. He left another letter offering to sell a copy of it to dePesto for a lot less."

Roland handed Bardon the extortion letter. "I've made a copy for us to keep. Here's the original delivered to Mr. Marshall."

Bardon whistled. "Good gig if you can get it." He looked at Em thoughtfully. "That must have pissed you off."

"What do you mean?" She knew exactly what he meant, but she wanted him to say it.

"Were you mad enough about the theft and extortion to kill Johnson?"

"I wouldn't have killed him even if I had known he was the thief and extortionist. We didn't see the video tape of him at the front desk until *after* we left the murder scene today. The playback cameras were down until then. I had no idea he was the thief until this afternoon. I suspected it was one of the contestants."

Bardon turned to Roland, who nodded.

"That still from the video is practically fresh out of the printer," Roland told him.

"We have no proof of what was in those envelopes Johnson dropped off or even if they were the ones delivered to your uncle and dePesto," Bardon said.

"We found Felicity Duncan," Roland said. "She let me question her. She said your men had already interviewed her."

Bardon flipped through his notebook pages until he found what he was looking for. "What'd you get?"

Roland read his own notes. "When the hotel blew the whistle on Johnson's bad credit she threw him out. That's when he must have rented the apartment. That was early afternoon, sometime after they left the Halekulai where he met and had lunch with Em. Ms. Duncan said she joined them and met Mrs. Johnson. Then last evening the fiancée met up with a hotel guest whose son was married there yesterday."

"He invited her to the reception last night," Bardon filled in.

"And ended up spending the night in his suite," Roland finished.

"She felt so bad about dumping her fiancé she just didn't want to be alone." Bardon almost smiled.

"She *said* that?" Em tried to see his notes.

"No. That was me being sarcastic," Bardon said.

"The father of the groom didn't appear to be just any guy. Did your men meet him?"

"No, they talked to her alone but they got a name. Hasigawa, a Japanese visitor."

"Right. A visitor with a bodyguard. I'm thinking they could be Yakuza."

Bardon nodded. "I didn't know about the bodyguard. We'll check it out, but for now Duncan still has a solid alibi. Hasigawa is probably here on a travel visa. We're checking."

"I don't think he'd lie for her," Roland said.

Bardon turned to Em. "Why didn't you tell me you were taken to the Waikiki substation by Hilton security last night?"

"I wasn't arrested. It was all a big mistake," she said.

"I just spoke to Chun. Attempted burglary, right?"

"I didn't burgle anything. I was looking for the stolen notebook. You can't steal something that belongs to you. He didn't book me."

Bardon pulled a folded piece of copy paper out of his pocket and slid it over to Em. "This is a copy of a letter we found in Johnson's apartment. He wrote it to you."

"Me?" Her voice broke on the word. She didn't want to touch it.

"Want me to read it to you?" Roland asked.

Though the detective knew what was in it, Em hated reading the letter with Bardon sitting there. There was no telling what Phillip had written. She picked it up, read in silence.

Dearest Em,

Seeing you today reminded me of all I lost because of my own stupidity. I am so sorry for ruining our lives, bankrupting us, and most of all, embarrassing you. Hurting you was the biggest mistake I've ever made in my life. I've done things I'm not proud of, but I am willing to change my life if you'll give me another chance. I know I broke your heart and don't deserve you, but today I got the feeling you might still love me and want to reconcile. Please, if there is any hope, just say the word.

Phillip

"*What?*" Em looked up in shock. "He's crazy. In no way did I act like I wanted to reconcile. That's the last thing on earth I'd ever want!" She handed the letter to Roland. He scanned it.

Bardon pushed the empty *pupu* plate aside and leaned forward. "You can both see how a prosecutor would have a field day with this one. Your husband admitted he ruined your life, bankrupted you, and broke your heart. Let's say you did still have feelings for him. Then you met him for lunch and saw him with a beautiful fiancée. He appeared to have money again. Furious, blinded by jealousy and revenge, you tracked him down and killed him."

Em was too livid to cry.

"*How?*" She raised her voice. Roland laid his hand on her forearm. She took a deep breath and forced herself to calm down. "How could I have tracked him down in Honolulu after he left the Moana? Come on. That's insane."

Bardon wouldn't back off. "Maybe he contacted you to tell you he'd moved out of the Moana and that his engagement was over. We'll check your cell phone records. Maybe he told you where he moved to. Besides, you're good at playing detective. I googled you and *Garden Island* archive articles came up. It seems you and your friends are always playing amateur detective. You all even received a proclamation from the mayor honoring you for helping solve a recent murder case on Kauai."

"Everyone receives a proclamation from the mayor," Roland said.

Bardon ignored him and kept badgering Em. "Maybe you thought you were so good at crime fighting that you could get away with murder."

Roland leaned across the table and got in the detective's face.

"Come on, Bardon. Back off. Are you even looking for Bautista?"

"Of course. We're just not finding him. We found his car abandoned up by Punchbowl. He didn't show up for work today."

"Where does he work?" Roland demanded.

"He's a line cook at La Mariana Sailing Club, a restaurant connected to a small marina near Sand Island," Bardon said.

Yet another stop on Em's tiki bar tour that she wasn't going to get to research while she was here.

"Do you have men watching Bautista's apartment at the Lokelani?"

"We already got a warrant. My men searched the place and said it's obvious he doesn't live there. He only uses it for a storage shed. There's not even a bed in the place. It's piled with boxes full of garage sale stuff and what they described as tourist information crap. Old books. Magazines. It's a definite hoarding situation. The neighbors confirmed he doesn't live there. Some of them never laid eyes on him until they saw him and Johnson yelling at each other in the street.

"We're trying to find out if Bautista has any family on island. No one at La Mariana knows where he lives. He pretty much goes to work, does his job, and keeps to himself. Much like you, Ms. Johnson, the folks who work with him claim Bautista's not capable of murder."

"What about Felicity Duncan?" Em knotted her fingers together below the tabletop.

"As you know, her whereabouts last night are accounted for," Bardon said.

"Her claim that Johnson misrepresented himself is certainly motive," Roland reminded him.

Bardon nodded. "So far her alibi is airtight. We can't place her at the scene."

"You can't place me there either," Em said.

"We're not going to stop looking for Bautista. Someone killed your ex-husband, Mrs. Johnson. Hopefully it won't take long to find out who. As soon as I have one shred of concrete evidence, we'll make an arrest."

"When you find the notebook, will you let us know?" Roland asked.

"Sure." Bardon folded the copy of Phillip's letter along with the printout from the security camera. "But even if we find it, we'll have to hold it as evidence."

"Understood," Roland said.

"I trust you won't let Mrs. Johnson out of your sight."

Roland assured him that he wouldn't. After the detective walked away, Roland turned to Em and slipped his arm around her shoulder in a surprising public display of affection. "This is going to be the easiest assignment I've ever had." He pulled her closer.

She found herself fighting tears. "Will you visit me in prison?"

"Sure. I know some pretty creative ways to smuggle in a key."

32

THE SUN WAS SETTING, and the tiki torches were lit when Kiki and the Maidens, along with their new sidekicks, the Kamakanis, arrived at Tiki's Grill and Bar on the second floor lanai of the Waikiki Beach Hotel.

The girls were outfitted to the hilt in matching red and white print skirts with black sleeveless tops. The Kamakanis stood around intimidating lingering tourists until they left, and the group commandeered eight tables.

Near the Diamond Head end of the strip, the restaurant overlooked both Kalakaua Avenue and the beach. Giant carved tikis greeted guests at the entrance and were scattered around the lanai and the inside dining room. Tiki masks and artifacts from all over Polynesia decorated the walls. Colorful rows of tiki mugs lined the bar.

A trio of young Hawaiians was playing contemporary rock/Hawaiian tunes on a small stage the size of a slice of *sashimi*. They weren't great, but they were loud enough that everyone had to shout to be heard. The only thing Kiki admired about them was the pattern on the fabric of their aloha shirts.

The Maidens all ordered Ocean Potions, drinks made with three kinds of rum, three liqueurs, and a splash of pineapple juice served in coconut shells. They ordered every *pupu* on the menu until their tables were littered with plates of torched *ahi*, coconut shrimp, *poisson cru*, a Tahitian version of ceviche, and prime rib *poke*.

After a couple of Ocean Potions each, the gals were cackling like a yard full of Kauai hens. Most of the newly arrived guests seated at nearby tables were tourists. They didn't even pretend not to be watching the Maidens' every move.

Feeling no pain, Kiki decided it was high time to call a Hula Maiden meeting to order. She tapped her fork against her water glass until she had the others' attention. Then she leaned in close to the table and lowered her voice. "Can everybody hear me?"

Most of them nodded. Little Estelle's scooter was parked at the end of the table. She'd spent a long day partying with the Shriners and threw a fit when Big Estelle insisted she leave the Hilton. Now she was passed out on her tray.

Precious had to kneel on her chair so that she could lean in closer.

"What's up?" Pat wanted to know.

"We have to put our heads together and help Louie," Kiki said.

"Help him what?" Big Estelle reached for a coconut shrimp and popped it into her mouth.

Kiki sipped on the straw sticking out of the coconut shell before she explained. "He has to get his Booze Bible back. Tomorrow's Saturday. We leave on Sunday. There's no time to waste."

"Do you have a plan?" Trish wanted to know.

"Of course. I had Suzi google some info about the murder while she was laid up today. So far the police haven't found the notebook. They haven't found the neighbor yet who argued with Em's ex either. The police are calling him a *person of interest*, which is police code for the sucker did it. Suzi got the address of the apartment building where it took place. I think it's time we go undercover."

"Em said not to do anything," Trish reminded her.

"When do we ever listen?"

"Sounds like good advice to me," Lillian sniffed. Her entire neck was streaked with melting foundation. No one had the heart to tell her, fearing the waterworks she'd turn on.

"We can't go undercover anymore. We're *the* Hula Maidens now." Big Estelle waved her hand around, pointing out all the people staring at them.

"Going undercover is a figure of speech. We'll get into that apartment as ourselves. We can't just sit around and let Louie down," Kiki said. "Who knows? Maybe if we help solve the case we'll get a proclamation from the mayor of Honolulu."

"Or the governor," Flora added.

"So what's the plan?" Four empty coconuts were lined up in front of Pat, who cradled her injured hand in her lap.

"You and I will pump Em for some info in the a.m., and then we'll all head over to the murder scene and see if we can come up with some clue the police overlooked." Kiki adjusted the huge faux floral hairpiece pinned near her left ear.

"We should have brought our two-way radios," Pat said.

"Who knew we'd have to fight crime on vacation?" Trish said.

"Crime never takes a vacation," Kiki said.

Lillian raised her hand. "I vote we don't do this. Em has Roland and the whole HPD here to solve the murder."

"Em's not herself. She has too much to worry about right now to be thinking straight," Kiki said. "Anyone who doesn't want to go on the reconnaissance mission tomorrow, raise your hand."

Lillian started to raise her hand until Big Estelle shot her a nasty glare, and she lowered it again.

"Great. Then we're all in agreement." Kiki ate the last coconut shrimp and looked around for the waitress. "Pat and I will get as much info out of Em as we can before we take off in the van in the morning. All of you need to be dressed and ready by nine."

Flora moaned. "Nine? In the *morning?*"

"Okay, then make it ten. Now, on to our next topic of discussion," Kiki said.

"When do we start dancing?" Flora wanted to know.

"Well . . . that's the next topic. There could be a *little* problem," Kiki began.

"Don't tell me," Trish said. "You don't have permission from management, do you?"

"No, but after casing the joint, I've decided if we leave a lookout on the corner of the balcony overlooking Kalakaua, she can give the high sign if the cops leave the substation across the street and head this way."

Kiki sent Pat over to the Kamakanis to tell them to take over the stage as soon as the rock trio took a break. Then she looked around for the waitress to order another drink. A young man wearing a black Tiki's staff shirt walked up to Kiki with a big smile on his face.

"I'd like to order one more of those coconut bowl concoctions." She batted her false lashes. "How much longer until these guys take a break?"

He glanced at his watch. "About five minutes. Are they too loud for you, ma'am?"

"Five minutes, that's great. They're not too loud, just not my style. You know what they say? If it's too loud, you're too old."

"I never heard that one, auntie," he said.

"Is your manager around? If he is, I'd like to talk to him for a minute," Kiki said.

"I'm sorry. I hope everything is all right for you tonight."

"Perfect, I just have a question."

She was happy that he didn't press her about her question. He'd no sooner walked away than an older version of the waiter came up to the table also wearing a black shirt with the Tiki Grill and Bar logo embroidered on it.

"Aren't you Kiki Godwin of *Trouble in Paradise?*" He extended his hand and introduced himself as the night manager. "I thought I recognized you ladies when you walked in. This is a real treat to have you here. What can I do to make your evening perfect?"

Kiki smiled up with the most innocent look she could muster. "We'd love to dance for you and your customers," she said.

He looked over at the postage stamp they called a stage. "We don't have a lot of room."

"We've danced in shoe boxes before," she laughed. "We'll spread out around the tables."

The trio on the stage announced they were going on break and unplugged their guitars.

"Well, that's perfect timing," Kiki said. Behind her, the Kamakanis were already on their feet heading toward the stage with their instruments. "How about a couple of numbers? Would that be all right?"

The manager looked around. Guests seated at nearby tables were hanging on Kiki's every word. They nodded encouragement.

"Let them dance," one woman encouraged. "I can't wait to tell everybody back home I saw the Hula Maidens perform live."

The manager glanced at the stage where the Kamakanis were already lining up chairs.

"A *couple* numbers would be okay. Just make sure the waitresses can get to the tables."

Kiki jumped up. "Come on, ladies. Let's give these folks a show they'll never forget."

33

EM WALKED INTO the sitting room of the suite. The air condition-ing had to be set to forty below. The drapes were drawn and the lights were low. Louie was behind the efficiency kitchen bar humming "My Tiki Goddess," the song he wrote in memory of his late wife, Irene Kakaulanipuakaulani Hickam Marshall. He sang it every evening at the Goddess at the end of the evening entertainment.

"Aloha, Em," he called out. "I haven't seen you for hours!"

"Roland and I have been busy. You sound happy." It was good to see him smiling.

"Is it too dark in here for you? I'm trying to replicate a bar mood."

"It's not too dark, just cold."

"I'm still experimenting with flaming drinks." He waved a lighter wand around, clicking the flame off and on. "Feel free to turn up the air. Or better yet, open the sliding doors, but leave the drapes closed. Where is Roland?"

"He went to Pearl City to have dinner with one of his cousins. We ran into him today when we had lunch at the Moana. He invited me too, but I thought I'd spend a quiet night in."

"And the girls?"

"They're dancing at Tiki's Grill and Bar at the other end of Kalakaua. I hope they won't get hauled off to jail tonight."

"If they do, just leave them in the clink. You know they let the monkey escape?"

"I know. I stopped by earlier. I also heard you gave the owner a big deposit."

Louie waved his hand. "I did, but I'm not worried. He'll get the monkey back. There have been plenty of sightings."

"Really?"

He nodded. "The owner thinks the monkey is probably confused by all the Shriners. So many other guys in fezzes around. So far it's having a great time on the loose, tormenting kids at the Super Pool, sneaking into a Japanese wedding reception to take advantage of all the sushi and champagne. Luckily the bride and groom got a kick out of it."

"No one's tried to catch it?"

"Security, but it's small and quick. It climbs trees, leaps from one to another and up onto balconies and slips in and out of hotel rooms."

"Food, water, drinks. That thing could live here forever," she said. "What about your deposit?"

"I saw the owner coming out of a Shriners meeting. I told him the way I see it, he should have to catch it, not me. I told him he's lucky Pat and Kiki aren't suing over their attack wounds."

"What did he say?"

"He said the monkey was in my possession when it bit Pat and attacked Kiki. He says it escaped from our suite, so it's still my problem. Its name is Alphonse, by the way."

Em wandered over to the bar and spotted an open bag of chocolate kisses, pulled one out, and unwrapped it.

"So, did you and Roland find out if dePesto wrote the extortion letter?"

"It's a little more complicated than that. In fact, it's very complicated." She popped the kiss in her mouth.

"I need those for my recipe." Louie grabbed the bag and rolled down the top. "Did I tell you I made the qualifying round with points to spare? After all the question and answer stuff we had to put together a mixed fruit juice concoction. I did something simple and it worked."

"That's wonderful. Congratulations."

"So how do you know dePesto is innocent?"

"We found out who left the extortion letters." Em braced herself. "It was my ex-husband."

"*What?* Phillip? Why would he? Sorry, but that's just crazy. You never did tell me what happened. I thought you two must have had a nice lunch. Why would he hurt us like that?"

For the first time since she walked into the suite he totally ignored his bottles and glasses and stared at her. He looked so rattled she hated to go on.

"Apparently he needed money. When he read about you in the *LA Times* they also mentioned the Booze Bible and how you'd been creating drinks your whole life and recording the recipes in it. He thought he could get us to pay for its return."

"So is he behind bars?" He glanced over to the sofa where she'd set her purse. "Do you have the Booze Bible?"

For once Kiki and the others had kept quiet. He knew nothing of

Phillip's murder yet.

"By the way, you don't look so good," he said. "Wait. I've got something for you."

He held up his index finger and turned to some bags on the counter. He pulled out a bottle of Patron. "I got this to thank you for what you tried to do last night. That was dangerous, Em. I wish you hadn't done it on your own, but thanks for trying."

He poured two shots. They clinked glasses in a toast. Louie sipped his. Em knocked it back and grimaced.

"Does Roland have the Booze Bible?" he asked.

"No. The police have been looking for it, but even if they find it, they'll have to hold it as evidence in a murder investigation."

"Murder? Who was murdered?" He looked confused, raised the Patron, and offered a refill.

She shook her head no. "Phillip. He's dead. Someone killed him."

"When?" Louie came around the kitchen bar and sat on a barstool beside her.

"Sometime last night. They called me to the scene this morning to identify the body. I'm so thankful Roland is here. We spent the rest of the day tracking down the extortionist's identity and trying to figure out who killed Phillip and why."

"Aw, Em. I'm so sorry."

"Thank you. Even though there was no love lost between Phillip and me, I'd have never wished him dead. Not in a million years." She blinked back tears.

"Of course not. If you want to go back to Kauai, we can leave tomorrow."

"You'd drop out of the contest for me?"

"I'd do anything for you, honey. You came to my rescue and pulled the Goddess out of debt when I needed you. You say the word, and we're outta here."

Em hugged him for a moment. "I wish I could, but I can't leave right now. The police need me to stay, and I may have to make arrangements for Phillip. His fiancée is out of the picture, and he had me listed as next of kin on an old emergency card."

"His fiancée is out of the picture? Why?"

"She has an alibi. There are only two other suspects the police are looking at right now. One is a guy who lived next door to a seedy apartment Phillip had just rented. The other is me."

Louie slammed his palm on the bar. "That's nuts. I'm going down to the HPD and have a little talk with whoever is in charge of the investigation."

Em could just imagine Louie sitting down with Bardon. "No, you are going to focus on winning that contest tomorrow. I'm going to try my darnedest to be there to cheer you on. What time do you think you'll be mixing?"

"They'll post the schedule in the morning. I'll let you know." He studied her carefully. "You must be in shock, honey. I mean, you just had lunch with Phillip yesterday, and now he's dead."

She nodded. "It's pretty surreal. When we were divorced I never wanted to see him again. When he called to say he was coincidentally going to be here during the contest week and asked me to lunch, I thought it would be good to have some closure. He seemed happy and acted like he had his act together, but that was all just another lie."

Afraid she would break down and upset Louie, Em paced over to the windows. She drew back the drapes far enough to see the water and steady herself before she let the drapes fall back into place and walked back to the bar.

"How did you find out he stole the Booze Bible?" Louie wanted to know.

"Roland and I viewed the front desk security video and saw him drop off two large envelopes like the ones that held the extortion letters. That was around the time your letter was supposedly delivered."

"Is Roland coming back here? His overnight bag is still on the floor."

"I hope you don't mind if he sleeps on the sofa tonight. He can't get a room."

"No problem. I'll be turning in early. Tomorrow's a big day."

"I think I'll head into my room now, if you don't mind."

"You must be exhausted. You go right ahead and climb in bed and relax. I'm just gonna put a few ingredients together and see what happens. I shouldn't be up long."

She gave him a hug and a kiss on the cheek.

"Thank you. I can't make any promises, but we're doing everything we can to get your Booze Bible back."

"There are far worse tragedies in life. I didn't think I'd ever say this, but I'm over it. I'm excited about creating a brand new cocktail without any references. The challenge has revved me up. Why, if Letterman's not careful, I may not need him to taste test anymore."

She found herself smiling back at him. Louie would never give up his precious parrot.

"Don't stay up late," she advised before she headed for her room.

He picked up a wand lighter. "I won't. And with any luck at all, I won't blow my face off."

34

AT EIGHT THE next morning, Kiki and Pat were in the hallway outside the door to Em and Louie's suite.

"Don't knock yet," Kiki told Pat.

"How'm I supposed to knock? I got the boom box in my good hand, and other one is history." She held up her bandage.

"Lower your voice. Do you know what to do?" Kiki whispered.

"You told me seventeen times. I made sure the tape is loaded and ready to roll. Once we get in there and you start asking Em stuff about the missing neighbor slash suspect, I push play, and we record the whole conversation."

"Right." Kiki shifted her large black leather purse higher on her shoulder. Her hands were full of grocery bags. "Ready?"

"As I'll ever be," Pat said.

Kiki knocked on the door. No one answered. She knocked again, and Em opened the door.

"Whoa, Em. You look like bad road kill," Pat said.

Em shoved her hair back off her face. Her eyes were red and bleary. There were pillow creases on her cheeks.

"Sleep in, did we?" Kiki strode in past her and looked around the sitting room. "No Roland?"

She took a few more steps and glanced into Em's bedroom. It would have made a real nice piece of gossip for the girls if she'd caught Roland in Em's bed.

Em looked around the sitting room. Worry etched itself onto her expression. She said, "He was going to bunk on the sofa, but his backpack's gone. I guess he got a room." She walked over to the bar.

Kiki followed her. Em picked up a piece of Hilton notepaper lying on the bar, read it, and smiled.

"He did manage to get his own room. He'll call me later."

"Bummer," Pat said.

Kiki gave her a hard look. Pat set the boom box on the bar.

Em yawned. "What are you two doing up and around so early?

How was your performance at Tiki's?"

"The performance was fabulous as usual. We did about ten numbers, and the crowd kept yelling *hana ho*. One man tipped us fifty bucks and said he'd never seen such precision. We're here to make breakfast for you," Kiki said. "The prices are ridiculous in this place, so we went out and bought some eggs, milk, and fruit at the ABC Store. Didn't think you'd mind us using your kitchen. We only have a standard room."

"Help yourself." Em walked over to the coffee pot and stared at it.

"You go sit down. I'll do that." Kiki bustled around, found the coffee, filled the pot, and turned it on. Then she started unpacking sacks. "Where's Louie?"

"He said he was going over to the convention center early. He's presenting his entry in the contest today."

"He finished the recipe?" Pat slipped onto a barstool next to the boom box.

Em said, "I guess so. He's not here, and the kitchen is all cleaned up. It's a flaming something."

"That's just downright scary," Pat said.

"This place is pretty well equipped for an efficiency kitchen." Kiki held up a frying pan and set it on the cooktop.

"So, tell us about the murder." She turned around, caught Em staring out the front sliding windows at the beach, and signaled Pat to turn on the boom box.

Pat made a loud coughing noise to disguise the click of the play button. It wouldn't have mattered. Em wasn't paying attention.

"Em?"

"I'm sorry. What did you say?"

"Tell us about the murder. Any new developments?" Kiki opened a carton of eggs. "By the way, did you tell Louie yet?"

"Last night."

"Good. He would have found out sooner than later and wondered why you didn't say anything. How'd he take it?"

"He was shocked at first, but he seemed more shocked about Phillip stealing the Booze Bible than the murder. We still haven't found it, by the way."

"Who are the suspects again?" Kiki found a bowl and started cracking eggs into it. "I'm making scrambled," she told Em.

"Scrambled sounds great." Em thought a moment. "As far as I know, the only suspects are me and the neighbor Phillip argued with."

"What about the *fie-on-say*?" Pat asked.

"She's got an alibi that's pretty airtight," Em told them.

"What's the neighbor's name again?" Kiki tried to sound as if she didn't care what the guy's name was, as if her whole plan didn't hinge on it.

"Damian Bautista." Em reached over the counter toward a wheel of Laughing Cow cheese and opened it. "What are you doing?" she asked Kiki.

"I'm using coconut oil to scramble the eggs."

"That's the stuff you rub on to get a tan. Or I should say a burn." Em stared at the bottle in Kiki's hand.

"It's pure coconut oil. I use it for everything—cooking, facial moisturizer, and hair conditioner."

"That the same stuff they sell by the other suntan oils and stuff?" Pat wanted to know.

Kiki shot her a glare. "This is the cooking stuff. Same thing."

"So, what about this Bautista?" Pat got the hint and steered the conversation back on track.

"Sounds Portugee." Kiki turned the stove on and started whisking the eggs with a fork and then added some milk out of a pint container.

"I haven't been an islander long enough to know what kind of a name that is. It's definitely not Hawaiian." Em pulled the red tab and unwrapped a wedge of cheese.

"Flora might know some Bautistas." Kiki carefully poured the eggs into the hot oil in the skillet.

"You promised you wouldn't do anything, Kiki," Em reminded her. "The HPD doesn't need your help."

Kiki pressed her lips together and focused on the eggs. Then she said, "Open the rest of those cheese wedges for me please, Em."

Em started opening. The coffee was almost finished brewing.

"Do they think maybe it was a random killing?" Pat asked. "This Bautista guy, why would he kill your ex?"

"They got into it over a parking space on the street. From what we learned yesterday, Phillip's fiancée broke up with him and kicked him out of their suite at the Moana. He must have been carrying enough money to rent one of those day-week-month studios in a seedy neighborhood. It's in a building called the Lokelani. Phillip was probably enraged at that point. Maybe the neighbor didn't like his attitude. Maybe he followed Phillip. Phillip had a gun—I have no idea why—but maybe the guy went to Phillip's apartment, and they got into it again. Phillip ended up dead. I really don't know."

"That's a lot of maybes," Pat said.

Em had finished opening the cheese wedges. "I've never put this in eggs."

Kiki shrugged. "Me either, but it was the only cheese they had at the ABC Store." She started chopping up the wedges and tossing cheese into the eggs.

"So the guy hasn't been home? The missing neighbor?" Pat prodded.

The coffee was brewed. Em got up and poured some for all three of them. She said, "The police searched his place and discovered he uses it for storage. He doesn't live there."

"What were they looking for?"

"Something that would connect him to the murder. They found the murder weapon at the scene. It turned out to be a gun that Phillip owned, and it had been wiped clean of prints. They didn't find the Booze Bible at Phillip's or Bautista's."

"Is the place easy to get into?" Kiki peppered the eggs. "Maybe someone else took it."

Em said, "The building has a very over-zealous apartment manager."

"Why would Phillip steal the Booze Bible?" Pat asked.

"He needed money. I guess he thought Louie would pay anything for it. Roland and I found out he delivered the extortion letters to Louie and one other man before he was murdered. So Phillip had to have stolen it, or at the very least he was in on it. He must have had it in his possession at one point. Very few people would know what it's worth."

"Unless they were a bartender or they read the same article Phillip did," Kiki said.

"That was in the *LA Times*," Em said.

"What if he had a partner in on the thievery with him? Maybe the partner killed him and took the Booze Bible so he could get all the money himself." Pat ran her palm over her buzz cut.

Kiki started pulling plates off of a shelf. She dished up the cheesy scrambled eggs and opened a couple of banana nut muffins, divided them with a knife, and set some slices on the plate next to the eggs.

"Boy, those look good," Em said. "This was a great idea, Kiki."

"Eat up," Kiki said. "Lots to do today. We'll need some protein."

"Like what are you doing?" Em forked up more eggs.

Kiki paused, careful not to raise Em's suspicion.

"What time is Louie's demonstration? We should be there to cheer him on."

"I'm not sure yet. He said he'd let me know." Em sounded less than enthusiastic.

"Is there a problem? Louie's still in the contest, isn't he?" Kiki knew when Em was being evasive. The woman couldn't lie to save her soul.

Em said, "Oh, he's still competing. It's just that . . ."

"Go on, spill it," Pat said.

"I'm afraid all of you might be too big of a distraction," Em said. "Everyone recognizes you now, and, truthfully, you aren't exactly a low key group. This is Louie's big day, not a Hula Maidens event. I think the spotlight should be on my uncle."

Kiki's initial reaction was anger, but it quickly cooled and pooled into hurt, mostly because she knew Em was right. She ate a couple of bites of egg in silence and thought about what Em said.

"You're probably right," Kiki finally admitted. "It is Louie's big day. I would imagine all those bartenders and cocktail experts would get pretty excited if we all walked in. They'd probably want us to endorse their bars or their new drinks or whatever." She wagged her fork in Em's direction. "We'll steer clear of the competition, but as soon as he's finished, call my cell and let me know how it went."

She and Pat tried to hurry breakfast and the clean up afterward and not act like they wanted to get away quickly. The other gals were waiting for them in Suzi and Trish's room.

Once they were in the hall, Kiki shushed Pat until they were inside the elevator alone and the doors slid shut.

"What now?" Pat said.

"Now we join the girls, make sure we have the information we need, and coach Flora. I hate to think getting into Bautista's apartment hinges on her, but she's the only one local enough to get us inside. Once she's well-rehearsed, we'll load everyone into the van and head over to the murder scene."

"We takin' Little Estelle?"

"She's one of our biggest diversions, but if she rolls off and disappears, we'll waste valuable time looking for her. It would be better to leave her here."

"Then what?"

"Then Flora and I will go inside the apartment while the rest of you create a diversion outside. If you didn't have that cursed monkey bite, you'd be going in with us. As it is, you'll have to keep an eye on the rest of the Maidens and man the boom box."

"While you and Flora do what, exactly?"

"Look for clues in the apartment."

"Like what kind of clues?" Pat pressed.

Kiki shrugged. "I'll know them when I see them."

35

"EVER'BODY IN?" PAT called off the names of the Hula Maidens in the rental van. "Kiki? Big Estelle? Trish? Flora? Precious? Lillian?"

When they heard their names, each of them hollered back, *"A'i!"*

Pat pushed the button on the automatic sliding door and drove out of the Hilton parking structure. Riding shotgun, Kiki punched the coordinates for Damian Bautista's apartment into the GPS tracker they had rented with the van.

Pat drove with one hand, navigating the crowded streets as Waikiki melded into Honolulu. Kiki leaned between the seats to give last minute instructions to the women in back. The Maidens were all outfitted in the same style muumuu in various bright floral fabrics.

"Flora, put the water bottle away. You need a clear head for this caper. Do you know what you're going to do?"

"This is not just water. It's 'special' water for my nerves. I know what to do, don't worry." Flora shoved the plastic Gatorade bottle into her straw bag. "I gotta tell the manager I'm the guy's cousin and get us into the apartment."

"What's the *guy's* name?"

"Damian Bautista," Flora said.

Kiki turned her gaze on Lillian. "What's step one, Lil?"

"Step one. Get out of the van. Make sure we get noticed."

"Perfect." Kiki nodded. "Big Estelle, what's step two?"

"Step two. Engage anyone and everyone we can in conversation while you track down the manager," Big Estelle said.

"Step three? Precious?"

"Step three. When you give me the high sign, I yell 'How about a dance?'"

"Step four, Trish." Kiki nodded at Trish.

"Step four. Pat gets the boom box ready, and we line up while you and Flora head into the building."

"Step five? Everyone say it all together." Kiki wagged her finger at them.

They shouted in unison, "Dance as long as we have to and don't leave the vicinity of the van no matter what."

"And what's the one thing you are *not* to forget?"

They answered in unison, "At all times be ready to *run!*"

Kiki smiled. "Perfect. Remember, we are venturing into unchartered territory. This is *not* Kauai. This is a sketchy area. These people only know what they've seen of us on television. They are not our friends. Anything could happen. If anything bad starts to go down, I want you all in this van and ready to roll." She turned to Pat. "If perchance something were to happen, say the police show up, load up the van and get the girls out of there ASAP. Don't wait for Flora and me. Got it?"

"I got it, but I don't like it. I don't like leaving one of our own behind," Pat grumbled.

"Flora and I didn't just fall off the taro truck. If we get in a fix, we'll get ourselves out of it. Right, Flora?"

Flora burped.

Big Estelle waved her hand around in the air until Kiki noticed.

"What, Big Estelle?"

"Speaking of getting out of trouble, do you have any idea how long this is going to take? I'm hoping we can get back to the hotel before Mother gets herself into any jams."

"Why isn't she with us? I forget," Lillian said.

"The Shriners are breaking up in to group sessions today. Last night one of her friends invited her to be a guest panelist," Big Estelle said.

Kiki said, "I'm sure that seemed like a great idea when they were all closing down the bar at one a.m."

"What in the heck is *she* gonna talk about?" Flora asked.

"Her duties as First Lady of the TajMaHaLay Lodge."

Pat made a left turn. A cab behind them started honking like crazy as it drove by. She glanced in the rearview mirror. "What's his problem?"

The computerized voice on the GPS tracker lost its cool and started yelling, "Danger. Pull over now. You are going the wrong way on a one way street. Danger. Danger. Pull over now!"

A lowered white Honda Civic came barreling toward them. Everyone in the back started screaming. Pat pulled over in time. She turned to Kiki and grinned. "So far so good."

Pat backed down the block to the corner and headed off the right way. Within five more minutes they were on a street that was a far cry from Waikiki. Overflowing trash cans lined the curb. Faded stucco apartment buildings built from lot line to lot line stood next to weather-beaten wood frame houses constructed in the twenties. There were no landscaped yards or fountains here, no shiny cars, limos, or open air busses full of tourists snapping photos. Nor was there the laid-back country feel of Kauai.

"We're in the gritty city now," Pat observed.

In the far back seat, Trish snapped photos. Lillian's face was no longer thick with makeup now that the Mindy's ladies were gone. She fluffed her pink bouffant with a hair pick. Precious silently moved her arms, practicing her hula to a tune in her head. Flora snuck a sip out of her water bottle while Kiki pointed out an empty parking space. Pat whipped the van into it. They both looked at the address on the GPS tracker and checked it against the slip of paper Kiki was holding.

"You have arrived at your destination," the computerized GPS voice informed them.

"We're here," Kiki said, staring across the street at a mint green building with the word Lokelani painted above the arched entry.

Pat surveyed the street. An old Chinese man was sweeping the sidewalk in front of a wooden house next door to the Lokelani. There was no one else around. "What are we gonna do now?" she asked Kiki.

Undaunted, Kiki had her hand on the door handle. "We're going to stick to the plan. Let's get out. We'll start by questioning that old man sweeping. Mark my words, once anyone sees us, he won't be the only one out here for long." She tried the handle, but the door was locked. "Let me out, Pat."

Pat clicked off the safety lock. Kiki climbed out. Pat opened the sliding door for the others, and soon the Maidens were all standing on the sidewalk near Phillip Johnson's last known address.

Kiki walked up to the old man. He stopped sweeping but didn't smile or say a word.

"A-loha," she said in a tone sweeter than coconut syrup. "Do you live here?"

The man said nothing. He merely stared at her and the others.

"We're looking for Damian Bautista. Do you know him?" Kiki watched the old man's eyes. There was a flicker of recognition there, but his expression remained passive.

"Grandpa!" A woman's voice called out from behind the screen door of the faded wood frame house. "What you doing out there, Grandpa?"

The screen door banged open, and a young woman with a toddler on her hip stepped out onto the porch.

"That's my grandpa," she called out to Kiki. "Is he bothering you?"

"On the contrary," Kiki said, relieved to see another sign of life on the otherwise deserted street. "I was asking if he knows where Damian Bautista lives. We have one of his cousins here, and she'd love to talk to him."

The young woman walked across the porch, down the two steps to the ground, and then came over to the low picket fence that surrounded a postage stamp yard.

"Everyone's been looking for that Bautista guy lately." She looked Kiki over. "You don't look much like a cousin."

"Not me." Kiki pointed to Flora. "Her. She's the cousin."

"You know the police are looking for him." The young woman hefted the chubby toddler higher on her hip. "They been all over this place. We're ready for them to leave."

"We heard about that. Flora wants to tell him that she's here for him, if he needs any support."

"That's nice." The girl looked at Trish and Lillian, then Precious and Big Estelle. "Hey, I know where I seen you all. You're those ladies who dance at that bar on Kauai."

"That's us." Kiki almost grabbed the girl and hugged her, but she was afraid she'd end up with toddler slobber on her muumuu. Further down the sidewalk behind the young woman, a couple had stepped out of the door of an apartment. They stared a minute and then started walking toward the knot of Maidens.

"Hey, Terri," the toddler's mom shouted to the other woman. "You recognize these ladies? They're on the television. That Kauai show at that bar."

"Yeah, I remembah." The couple had reached them by now. The woman looked to be in her late forties. The man about the same age. "I remembah the pink hair lady. And the midget."

"Little person," Precious said. "I'm an *LP*, not a midget."

"That one is that guy, Bautista, she's his cousin." The younger woman pointed at Flora. "They need to find him," she said.

"Nobody even knew him until that big argument with the *haole* guy who got shot," the other woman said. Her husband nodded.

Kiki was elated when she saw a few more people leave their homes and apartments and walk toward them. She stepped closer to Flora and patted her shoulder.

"Poor Flora just wants to leave a message for Damian. Is there a manager at the Lokelani?" Kiki looked at the faces on the people surrounding them.

"Sure. That would be Melvin," one of the men said. "I'll go get him."

"Oh, mahalo. Mahalo." Kiki nodded. "You're so kind, bra."

Then she caught Big Estelle's eye and mouthed the word *engage.*

"Would you like an autograph?" Big Estelle asked the mother with the toddler.

The girl shrugged. "Sure. Why not?"

Big Estelle whipped a stack of publicity photos and some Sharpies out of her purse and handed them out to the other Maidens. "Here you go, girls. Engage."

Kiki smiled when she saw three more people walking up the street to join them. The Maidens started milling around, laughing and chatting up the crowd and signing photographs. Pat gave Kiki the thumbs up. The door of the van was open, the CD cued up already.

Within three minutes a short, pudgy *haole* man came hustling out of the Lokelani apartments. His navy blue trucker's ball cap with the word MANAGER emblazoned across the front matched his navy blue polo shirt. His first name, Melvin, was embroidered in yellow on the left side of the shirt above his heart. An emblem on one sleeve said SECURITY. A heavy, official-looking ring full of keys dangled from a chain hooked through his belt loop.

He drew in his belly and puffed up his chest as he approached Kiki. Then he stuck out his hand. Instead of shaking it, Kiki pressed it between both of hers.

"You're the manager of the Lokelani?"

Melvin lifted his hat, ran his hand over his bald head and centered the hat again. "That I am. I'm Melvin Kline."

"I would imagine that's a heavy responsibility," she said. "Especially lately."

He hooked his thumbs into his waistband and rocked forward onto his toes and back onto his heels. "That's for sure. How can I help you lovely ladies?"

She introduced Flora as Bautista's cousin. "She flew over here to help him, when we got the word and all. She says *no way* is he guilty."

"I been lookin' all over for him," Flora said. "Thought maybe I could leave him a note so he knows I'm on island."

"He hasn't been around," Melvin said. "The police told me to keep an eye out, but I haven't seen him."

Kiki reached around Flora and gave Precious a thumbs up.

Precious clapped her hands and called out to the crowd, "How about a dance?"

The Maidens were encouraged with nods and scattered clapping.

Pat hit the play button, and a favorite song sung in Hawaiian began to play. "Kokee" wasn't something they danced for the tourists.

Kiki nudged Flora. Flora leaned over and yelled to Melvin over the music. "I'd sure like to see my cuz's place." Then she sniffed and wiped an invisible tear from her eye.

"He doesn't really live here," Melvin said.

"I know. That's okay. I just like to feel close to him."

"Seeing how it's you famous ladies, sure. Why not?" He tapped the keychain.

While the growing crowd watched the remaining Maidens hula, Kiki and Flora followed Melvin into the Lokelani. Crime scene tape was still draped across one of the doors on the balcony level.

They walked up the stairs with the sounds of everyday life surrounding them. Pots and pans rattled on a stove; a baby cried. Music poured out of one apartment, and the sound of a television show boomed out of a place right below them. They were standing right in front of the taped-off door when what sounded like gunshots went off.

Flora grabbed Melvin and held him in front of her like a shield. Kiki hit the ground.

Nothing happened.

"Don't worry, ladies," Melvin extricated himself from Flora's grasp. "That's just Mrs. Alexander's television. She lives right below this apartment and she's deaf as a post. The TV is always blaring."

"Help me up." Kiki extended her hand. Melvin grunted as he pulled her up off the walkway.

She stared at the taped-off door in front of them and turned up the drama. She pressed a hand to her heart.

"Oh my gosh! Is *this* the apartment where that poor man was murdered?" She clasped her hands between her breasts and hoped she looked suitably horrified.

"Sure is," Melvin said. "It's an official murder scene."

"Oh, Flora. It's right next door to your cousin's apartment." Kiki stared at the front door to Em's ex's apartment.

"You wanna see inside?" Melvin was already flipping through keys on the huge ring.

"Oh, could we?" Kiki tried to sound breathless.

"I don't wanna look." Flora was digging for her Gatorade bottle.

Kiki poked her in the hip.

"Oh, sure," Flora said. "I'll take a peek."

Melvin opened the door. Kiki ducked beneath the crime scene tape and stuck her head and shoulders inside. There was nothing in the room but a few pieces of beat up furniture, a stripped bed, and a bloodstain on the floor.

"Yuk," Kiki said.

"No worries," Melvin assured her. "I've got some stuff that takes blood out of a carpet in a snap."

Flora reneged on peeking. Kiki pulled her head out, and Melvin closed and locked the door.

"Okay, now for Bautista's place." He took a few steps to the next door over. "The police have already been through the whole place. Well, as far as they could get, that is. Murder weapon was on the floor in the victim's apartment. There were no prints on the gun. I don't know what they were looking for in Bautista's apartment. I think they're just trying to pin the murder on somebody, and since Damian really got into it with the guy earlier, they're trying to connect him."

Kiki motioned for Flora to put her "special water" bottle away.

Melvin turned the key and opened the door as far as he could, which was only half way.

"Holy Moly!" Kiki said when she saw inside.

Flora leaned closer to look over her shoulder. "Holy Moly, for shua. I cannot fit in there."

"You want to go in and look around?" Melvin asked.

Kiki had already kicked off her slaps and was wedging herself through the door. Once inside, she shoved a couple of boxes back and opened the door all the way. Boxes were piled up to the ceiling in some spots. The windows were shut tight, the air stifling.

"You can get in now," she told Flora after she pushed a couple more boxes out of the way. "Come on."

Flora stepped inside and hovered there. She and Kiki stared around without moving. Except for a narrow path between piles, the room was literally packed floor to ceiling with precariously leaning stacks of old newspapers, brochures, signs, maps, and magazines. Kiki picked up a few pieces and noticed none had been printed after the 1970s.

Kiki walked down the narrow aisle between stacks. Flora didn't move past the entrance.

"You're gonna die if that stuff falls over on you," she warned.

"I'm fine." Kiki opened a box full of rubber hula dolls and parts of hula dolls. Next to it was a plastic bin containing old chalkware bobblehead dashboard dolls from the thirties and forties. She opened yet another box that contained carved coconuts and old Hawaiian postcards with edges trimmed like rickrack.

She took another step, tripped over a bamboo wine rack, and landed on a stack of Dole pineapple labels. There were chipped State of Hawaii collector's plates, monkey pod bowls of all shapes and sizes, and ceramic ash trays. Tiki masks made of wood and plastic were piled among the boxes. Tiki mugs were crammed into every nook and cranny in the efficiency kitchen. Boxes were piled high in the sink.

"I get claustrophobia." Flora fanned herself with a 1954 map of Honolulu. "This place is way more crowded than the storage shed where I keep my shop inventory."

Kiki stared at the hoard and knew the police couldn't possibly have gone through everything in the place, let alone find a clue that would tie Bautista to the murder. The air was hot and close and tainted with the smell of mildew. She hated to admit defeat, but she had to get out.

She thought she was being careful as she turned around to head for the door until her bare foot connected with something small and very hard. She shifted away from it, let out a squeal, lost her balance, and fell sideways into a box that crashed to the floor and flew open.

Kiki rubbed her foot and bent over to pick up a three-inch plastic tiki with green rhinestone eyes dangling from a rawhide string. She tossed the tiki over her shoulder. The box had spilled its contents, and a host of paperback books was scatted in her path.

The one on top had a colorful cover displaying people dressed in retro outfits from the sixties enjoying food and drinks. She picked it up. *How to Have a Luau Indoors.*

She read the title to herself and flipped through the contents of standard luau recipes revamped for tourists to make when they went back to the mainland. She leaned over and tried to shove the other books into the box. They were all vintage cookbooks.

She pawed through them, reading the titles and tossing them aside. Grabbing another handful, she noticed the copy on top was *Favorite Tropical Drinks.*

Kiki dropped the books. "We gotta get out of here."

Flora yelled, "Did you see a rat?"

"No, but we've *got* to go."

"You want to leave your cousin a note?" Melvin asked Flora.

"Nah, he'll never find it in this mess."

"Leave it with me," he volunteered. "I'll see he gets it if he ever comes back."

"Leave a note," Kiki said as she scrambled off the pile of cookbooks. "Leave a note and let's go."

Flora dug around in her purse until she found a wrinkled cocktail napkin. She smoothed it out and scribbled *I was here cuz* on it and handed it to Melvin.

"I'll give this to him the minute I see him," he promised.

"Thanks, bra," she said.

"No problem. I'll escort you ladies back to your group." He made quite a show of rattling his keys as he locked the door.

Kiki slipped into her sandals and took a deep breath of fresh air. She wiped sweat off of her face with the hem of her muumuu.

"Where does Damian work, Flora?"

Flora wrinkled her forehead and said nothing.

Kiki prodded, "Did you *forget*?"

"Oh, yeah." Flora turned to Melvin. "I forget. Where does my cuz work?"

"La Mariana Sailing Club," Melvin said. "I make it a habit to know where all my long term renters work in case I have to track them down for payments."

Kiki could still hear hula music blaring out of the rental van. She'd seen all she needed to see here.

"We'd better get going." Kiki started for the stairway.

"You ladies have a lot of personal appearances to do while you're here?" Melvin asked.

"We sure do." Kiki was almost at the bottom of the stairs. "In fact, we've got a gig we should be getting to right now."

"No, we don't. Do we?" Flora huffed down the stairs behind them.

Kiki glared over her shoulder. "You are getting *so* forgetful, Flora. Hurry out to the car and get the girls loaded up." Kiki stepped aside and motioned Melvin over. Flora had picked up speed lumbering down the stairs and charged toward the van.

"I can't thank you enough, Melvin. That meant so much to Flora. May I get a photo of you?" She pulled her phone out of her purse. *Might as well leave the guy happy.*

Melvin shoved the bill of his hat back so it wouldn't shade his face. "Sure!"

His smile was wide as a rainbow when Kiki snapped the picture.

"You think I could end up on TV? I mean, if your show ever comes back on?"

"Oh, I'm pretty sure we won't be back on the air, but you never know," Kiki said.

"Keep my photo on file just in case," he said. "If you ever need extra security, then I'm your man."

36

IN NO TIME AT all they'd bid aloha to their fans and were loaded up in the van.

"Where to, boss?" Pat asked Kiki.

"Trish, can you find La Mariana Sailing Club on your notebook? I'll punch in the address."

"Looking," Trish called from the back seat. "It says something about Sand Island."

Precious wanted to know, "Are we going sailing? Or to the beach?"

"You know I can't sit on the beach," Lillian whined. "I can't take the sun."

"We are not going to the beach," Kiki said. "We're going to La Mariana Sailing Club. It's a restaurant at a marina. I guess it's near Sand Island."

"Great. I'm starvin'," Flora spoke up between sips of "special" water.

Trish called out from the way-back, "This says Sand Island used to be called Quarantine Island. They used it to quarantine ships carrying contagious passengers."

"Good idea," Pat said. "Somebody should make all the mainland planes stop there."

"During World War II they used it for internment camps for Japanese Americans, Italian and German expatriates living in Hawaii."

Lillian clapped her hands over her ears and started singing la la las.

"What's she doing?" Flora asked Precious.

"She does that when something makes her sad and she doesn't want to hear it," Precious said.

"So where are we going exactly, Trish?" Kiki shouted. "We need to get moving."

"Take Nimitz Highway to Sand Island Parkway," Trish said.

"We're not far," Kiki told them.

"Why are we even going there?" Lillian asked. "I don't want to see old internment camps where they locked up Americans."

"We're going there to search for Bautista. I'm pretty sure he killed

Em's ex to steal Louie's Booze Bible from him."

"How do you know that?" Flora crossed her arms and rested them on her stomach. "I saw everythng you did in that garbage dump. I didn't see one single clue."

"That's because it was *all* one big clue." Kiki lowered the visor and checked her makeup in the mirror. "Is there an address for the La Mariana, Trish?"

Trish was silent for a few seconds then said, "It's not on Sand Island. It's on Pier Street right before you cross over to the island." She gave Kiki the address, and Kiki punched it into the GPS.

"Whew." Lillian was smiling again. "No camps."

"So what did you see that convinced you this guy has Uncle Louie's Booze Bible?" Trish asked.

"He's a hoarder, but he's selective. He doesn't hoard just anything. The place is full of Hawaiian memorabilia from the forties, fifties, and sixties. When I literally fell into a box full of old retro recipe books, I realized that if Bautista even laid eyes on the Booze Bible, it was the kind of thing he'd covet. Louie started writing back in the sixties when he opened the Goddess. All those old legends he made up, all the drink recipes, the doodles in the margins, why that notebook would be like a platter of poopoo to a fly for a guy like Bautista."

"Do you think he wanted it enough to kill Em's ex to get it?" Precious clutched the armrest as Pat made a sharp left in front of a city bus. Lillian squealed and covered her eyes.

Kiki went on unfazed. "I think he may have gone to Phillip's because he was still mad about losing a parking space. Maybe Phillip asked him to step inside, or maybe Bautista strong-armed his way in, saw the notebook, and things got out of hand."

Pat added, "Em said Phillip had a gun. Maybe Bautista somehow wrestled it away, shot Phillip, and wiped off the prints."

"Then he saw the notebook and couldn't resist taking it. Unfortunately, that was a big mistake. A big one. If he has the Booze Bible, that will connect him to the apartment and the murder," Kiki said.

"That and the fact that he disappeared the day of the murder," Trish reminded her.

The lady inside the GPS said, "You have reached your destination."

Kiki turned to look out the window as Pat pulled up in front of La Mariana Sailing Club.

"Oh my gosh," Precious said.

"Wow." Trish started snapping photos.

"Look at all that *bamboo*," Lillian marveled. "And those tiki torches."

"I haven't seen a place this classically tiki since Eisenhower was alive. Talk about truly tacky tiki." Kiki smiled at the sight even as she blinked back tears. "Ladies, stick to the classics. Don't think of ordering anything but a Mai Tai, a Tropical Itch, or a Blue Hawaii once we're inside, or it just won't be right. We're gonna party like it's 1955, and we're gonna catch a murderer while we're at it."

Pat let them all out and drove off to park. Kiki and the others passed beneath the Kon Tiki Room sign as she entered the open restaurant space full of tables covered with tapa-print tablecloths and surrounded by high-backed peacock wicker chairs.

The walls were lined with woven *lauhala* and bamboo. Lights made of glass fishing floats hung from a ceiling dotted with strands of mini twinkle lights. There were shell chandeliers and booths book-ended by carved tikis.

"Wow. It's like the Goddess," Lillian said.

"On steroids." Kiki checked out the room. A hostess greeted them and said she'd put some tables together for them.

In no time at all they were comfortably seated and sipping on the restaurant's world famous Mai Tais out of official La Mariana tiki mugs.

"What now?" Pat asked Kiki.

"Now we eat lunch and ask about Bautista."

They ordered either the ahi *poke* or burgers. While they waited for their lunches and congratulated each other on their flawless street performance in front of the Lokelani, Kiki picked up her drink and slipped away to chat up the bartender.

"Aloha!" she greeted him with a smile as she slid onto a bar stool.

The tall, dark-haired local gentleman wearing a red and white aloha shirt flashed a smile. She guessed he was in his early sixties, not much younger than she. His nametag said Joe.

"What can I do for you?" he said.

"I'm from Kauai. I just wanted to tell you this Mai Tai is wonderful."

"Lucky you live Kauai, eh? Just visiting?"

"My friends and I are here for almost a week. I just love this place. There were so many tiki bars around years ago. It's a shame to see them all disappear. I hope this one lasts."

"We're holding on. The old crowd is dying off, though."

"I hear you." Kiki allowed a sympathetic note to creep into her tone. She waited a minute before she asked, "Is Damian Bautista working today? He's an old friend."

"Really?" He looked doubtful.

"Yes. Does that surprise you?"

"Damian hardly says two words to anyone." He reached beneath the back of the bar and pulled out a damp towel and proceeded to wipe down the bar top. "Comes in, does his job, and goes home."

Kiki shifted around on the stool and leaned closer. "Where's home?"

He shrugged. "Your guess is as good as mine. Like I said, he doesn't say much."

Kiki handed him her empty tiki mug. "I'd love a refill, Joe."

"Sure." He started mixing ingredients. "I hate to tell you this, but the police are looking for Damian, too."

Kiki made her eyes wide. "They *are*? Why?"

"He's wanted in connection with a murder."

"No way."

The bartender nodded. "Yeah."

"Gosh, then I *really* feel sorry for him. Like you said, he's always seemed like a nice, quiet sort." Kiki was flying by the seat of her granny panties and she knew it, but she pressed on. "You don't have employee home information that you could give me, do you? I'd really like to try and touch base. At least leave a note at his place."

When she was young she never would have believed being a senior would have advantages, but no one suspected a harmless little old lady could be up to anything shifty.

He hesitated a minute, then topped off her Mai Tai with dark rum, shoved in a straw, and pushed the tiki mug back across the bar.

"Hang on a minute. I'll see what I can find." He glanced around the room. It was still early yet, and the lunch crowd was light. He left the bar and was back in two minutes with a sticky note in his hand.

Before he handed it to Kiki, he made sure no one was watching.

"Here you go. I took this off Damian's emergency card."

Kiki looked at the address in Honolulu.

"That's somewhere in Chinatown," the bartender said. "Don't go wandering around down there at night, okay?"

"Of course not. Thank you *so* much. I do appreciate it."

"I'd rather you find him before the police do. If he's innocent, he must be scared to death. See if you can talk him into turning himself in."

"If he's innocent?" Kiki lowered her voice. "Do you think he did it?"

Joe shrugged. "Nothing surprises me anymore."

"He certainly doesn't need to be scared of a little old lady like me," Kiki said. "I sure hope he didn't do it."

37

LOUIE CALLED TO let Em know his demonstration was set for eleven a.m. in the Coral Ballroom, so she showered, slipped into the sundress she'd worn to lunch with Phillip, and left for the conference center.

The minute she walked in, she was approached by Lamar dePesto. Outwardly Em smiled. Inwardly she groaned. He was just as smarmy as she remembered. His participant's badge dangled from a lanyard around his neck with eight miniature gold swizzle sticks clipped to his nametag. Everyone who didn't know already would have no doubt he'd won the Western Regionals every year.

"Ms. Johnson." DePesto was decked out in an aloha shirt and a straw Fedora with a seashell hatband. "I just heard you're a 'person of interest' in your ex-husband's murder investigation. I can't say I'm surprised after catching you red-handed in my suite."

She tried to hide her shock. She hadn't seen a paper or the morning news. The HPD must really consider her a prime suspect if they were officially announcing she was a "person of interest."

What next? An arrest?

She half expected a SWAT team to descend on her any minute now.

"I was all set to apologize to you, Lamar, but since you didn't catch me doing anything but looking around your room, I've changed my mind. The only thing I regret at this point is that my impulsiveness might have jeopardized my uncle's chances of winning your contest."

"Are you accusing me of rigging the contest? That's as insulting as your accusation of my involvement in theft and extortion. Besides all this slander, we've never had so many problems at this contest. *Never.* The hotel is all over me because your uncle lost a stupid monkey. The Shriners are up in arms because one of their members desperately wants that monkey back. They're demanding *I* do something about it. Those old hula dancers of your uncle's are not only a constant nuisance, but there's now an Internet petition circulating around demanding they be allowed to perform whenever and wherever they want, a petition that also asserts this hotel is down on locals. You can imagine how *that's* going over with management."

Apparently, dePesto wasn't finished. "Thanks to your uncle and his entourage, once word gets out, the contest committee will be lucky if we can even contract with any hotel in Waikiki next year."

The lights flickered. It was time to find a seat for the next demonstration.

"You'll have to excuse me, Lamar," Em said. "I'm here to support my uncle."

She turned on her heel and walked away. There was one empty seat at the end of the first row of chairs. Em slipped into it, pulled out her cell, and set it on vibrate. She shoved the phone into her pocket and set her purse on the floor beneath her chair.

The stage lights were off, and the room lights dimmed. Four hotel workers carried in two potted palms and set them beside either end of the bar, adding a touch of tropical ambiance. She knew that had to be Louie's doing and part of his presentation. They had no sooner exited when a couple of seconds later, the exotic strains of Martin Denny's "Swamp Fire," complete with monkey howls, ululations, and bongo beats accompanying a vibraphone, drifted through the ballroom.

The crowd hushed at the first note. A tall, buxom woman with flowing black hair dressed in a leopard-print sarong stepped out of the wings carrying a flaming torch. She walked to the bar and touched the flame to the wick of a short tiki torch standing in a bucket of sand. As soon as the tiki torch caught fire and blazed steadily, the woman sexily strolled to the other end of the bar and lit a second torch before slinking off stage. No sooner was she out of sight than a muscular bongo drummer with a low-slung *malo* tied around his hips strode in. He sat cross-legged on the floor beside one of the potted palms.

The crowd applauded in appreciation. If their reaction was any indication, Uncle Louie would definitely garner extra points for his "delivery" portion of the competition. An entertaining and confident delivery coupled with confidence, knowledge, and hygienic preparation were vital elements toward a final score.

Louie waited in the wings long enough for the applause to die down, and then he appeared on stage wearing his signature baggy white linen pants, an original silky—a vibrant red and yellow vintage aloha shirt from the 1940s—a black *kukui* nut lei, and his white Panama hat.

He paused dramatically near one of the burning torches. His voice boomed out of the clip microphone attached to his shirt collar.

"A-looo-ha!" he called out.

"A-looo-ha!" the audience echoed.

Em smiled and relaxed back into her chair. Her uncle had the audience, and hopefully the judges, in the palm of his hand—and he hadn't even started mixing a drink yet.

He turned around. From the end of the bar, he picked up a pith helmet Em hadn't noticed before. Louie removed his Panama hat, set it on the bar, and donned the pith helmet.

"I'm Louie Marshall," he said. His voice easily carried to the back row. "I'm the owner of the Tiki Goddess Bar and Restaurant on the North Shore of Kauai, a northern island in our beautiful island chain. I've been creating cocktails for our patrons' pleasure for sixty years. It's my great honor to be here mixing it up for you today."

As Louie walked behind the bar, the crowd applauded again. Once he was in position, he began lining up martini glasses. The bongo drummer started a slow, rhythmic beat.

"There is a legend behind each and every cocktail I create," Louie began. "These legends are essential additions to our menu at the Tiki Goddess. Not only do our guests love reading them, but the stories make it easier for them to remember the names of their favorite drinks."

Louie pulled out a bottle of Kahlua and held it up. He said, "Kahlua—rum based, coffee flavored with a hint of vanilla—inspired by the jungles of Mexico. Whenever I see one of these tall brown bottles, I'm reminded of a harrowing trip to Brazil, to the Amazon rainforest to be exact. There, I was part of an expedition in search of a centuries-old relic, an amethyst skull known as the Manic Monkey."

He set the bottle down, reached below the bar again, pulled out a pear-shaped bottle of amber liquid.

"This is Trader Vic's Macadamia Nut Liqueur. You probably all know mac nuts grow in Hawaii, but they also grow in Brazil and other tropical climes."

He set the bottle on the bar and then pulled out another. "This is Bacardi 151 proof rum. No mixologist should be without it. It's not just Bacardi rum. 151 proof is an essential ingredient if you're going to flame a cocktail, which is what I'll be demonstrating today, although the Manic Monkey can either be flamed or shaken. That's between you and your customer." He winked at the audience.

He held up his index finger and said, "Ah! I almost forgot one more ingredient."

There was a wooden calabash on the bar. He picked up the bowl and tipped it so that the audience could see the silver foil wrapped objects inside.

"These are chocolate kisses. Everybody needs a kiss now and then. One kiss is essential for each drink."

Louie had already unwrapped a dozen kisses and had them ready and waiting on a small monkeypod tray beneath the bar. He pulled it out and set it alongside the liquor bottles.

"Now we're really ready to begin." He flexed his fingers and picked up a teaspoon and a shot glass. "You'll also need these. The flame will be the only garnish you'll need for the flaming version. I have a few ideas for rimming the glass for the shaken version, which I'll clue you into later."

"I'll start by placing one chocolate kiss in the bottom of each martini glass."

Louie launched into a tale of his trip up the Amazon with explorers from the Museum of Natural History in search of the Manic Monkey, a monkey skull carved of pure amethyst not seen since it was reported stolen from a jungle temple in Paraguay in the 1800s.

As he continued to spin the tale, he measured, poured, and drizzled the liqueurs into the martini glass over the chocolate kiss. Then he carefully topped them off with an ounce float of 151 rum and picked up the wand lighter.

"So, I was asleep on deck of the riverboat one night when the earsplitting screams of Capuchin monkeys shattered the silence. Not to mention our nerves. I bolted out of my hammock and staggered to the rail. Through the dense jungle growth, I saw the flickering light of torches bobbing along, parallel to the shore. We could barely make out the silhouettes of the fierce Yanomami, the indigenous people of the rainforest. They were not only carrying the torches, but a raised platform.

"Upon that raised platform was a shrine that held the skull of the Manic Monkey. Its mouth was open wide, as if forever locked in a scream. The skull's eyes were lit by an eerie interior glow. We watched in silence as the Yanomami and the skull slowly disappeared into the depths of the forest. Then to a man, with no discussion, we voted to turn back."

Louie whispered into his mic, "Here's where you have to be both careful *and* dramatic."

He flicked on the lighter and held it above the rum float. The lights dimmed on cue. The liquor caught fire, and the flame danced above the martini glass, glowing blue and beautiful in the low light of the ballroom.

The audience clapped wildly. Photographers snapped photos. The judges hunched over their score sheets. Louie slowly scanned the audience and asked for silence. Everyone immediately complied.

The cocktail was still flaming as he lowered his voice and said, "No living soul has ever reported seeing the Manic Monkey skull again."

The drummer started beating with a frenetic pace. The crowd was on its feet. Louie was taking a bow when the door to the left of the stage flew open, hit the wall, and slammed shut again. Loud screeches brought a halt to the drumming. The bongo player jumped up and hid behind the bar as the fugitive monkey Alphonse came loping into the ballroom with a fez on its head. The animal kept screaming as it leaped onto the bar and ran toward the flaming martini glass.

Everyone in the room watched in shock and awe. Em couldn't believe what she was seeing. Nor did she have the vaguest notion how her uncle managed to get the monkey to enter on cue. Then the door banged open again, and Little Estelle swooshed in on the Gadabout.

"Come back here, you disgusting rodent! Give me back that hat!" Little Estelle screamed. Em immediately realized the monkey's entrance wasn't scripted. They'd gone live and uncensored.

A second later the flame died, but not before the tassel on the fez caught fire. The monkey threw the hat at Little Estelle, grabbed the martini, and knocked back the drink. Then it smacked its lips and jumped onto Louie's shoulder, kissed him on the cheek, and jumped on the floor. It raced out the opposite door.

Little Estelle batted out the flaming tassel and shoved the fez on her head. A fishing net with a bamboo handle was shoved into her handlebar assembly. She grabbed the net and waved it over her head.

"Don't worry, Louie, I'll get that furry sucker if it's the last thing I do!" She revved up the scooter engine and drove out the open door, hot on the monkey's trail.

The crowd went absolutely wild. The press surged forward and crowded around the bar. DePesto was seated down the row from Em. She saw him slump forward and bury his face in his hands.

Behind the bar, Louie calmly filled the line of martini glasses for the judges' taste test. Taste was the final score element.

The audience remained on its feet as Louie touched the wand to one "Manic Monkey" after another until the entire row of drinks flamed like a host of tiki torches at sunset.

Em was thrilled for Louie and so proud she was about to burst when her cellphone vibrated in her pocket.

She pulled it out and glanced at the caller ID.

38

"HERE YOU GO, ladeeeze. We're now in Chinatown." Pat negotiated the van around a turn and passed a public parking lot on Beretania across from the Chinatown Cultural Plaza. "All fifteen blocks of it."

Kiki stared out at streets crowded with shops displaying signs written in Chinese characters. Boxes of goods and produce were stacked on the sidewalks. Shoppers crowded around the boxes inspecting the fruits and vegetables. Apparently they were on the fringe of a street peoples' settlement. Two beat patrol cops rolled by on battery-powered Segways.

Lillian had her nose pressed to the window of the rental van. "I'm certainly not in Iowa anymore." She sounded amazed. "I won't have to go to China now that I've seen this. I can't wait to get back to Kauai and tell MyBob."

Precious piped up, "Are we going to eat some dim sum?"

Flora said, "For sure, and den some!"

Kiki rubbed her temples. The drive from La Mariana Sailing Club hadn't taken all that long, but it was far longer than she liked being cooped up with the Maidens.

"So where does Damian live?" Pat asked.

"*Damian?* What is he? Your best friend now? You mean Bautista the murder suspect?" Kiki looked at the GPS screen. "According to this thing, we're almost there."

Pat followed the GPS instructions, made another right on to Smith Street, and stopped across from a small grocery store. The windows were cloudy but not enough to hide the piles of goods inside. Pat pulled into a ten minute parking space and killed the engine.

"I'm goin' with you," she told Kiki. Then she ordered, "Everybody stay put."

Precious and Flora started chanting, "Dim sum! Dim sum!"

"What's dim sum?" Lillian wanted to know.

"Steamed or fried Cantonese food served in bite-sized pieces," Trish said.

"Good lordy, how can you possibly be hungry? We just had lunch," Kiki reminded them.

"Always room for dim sum," Flora said.

"And den some!" Precious shouted. "Dim sum! Dim sum!"

Everyone joined in except Kiki and Pat.

"We aren't getting any if ya'll keep that up," Pat warned.

The chanting abruptly stopped. Kiki looked at the scrap of paper, stared at the store, and reread the address.

"Maybe there's an apartment upstairs," she said.

"Maybe. Then again, you said this Damian was a hoarder. The inside of that store looks about right. Maybe he sleeps somewhere in those piles."

They walked in past fresh produce that was mainly tropical fruit, rambutan, papaya, coconut, pineapple, and bananas. Kiki saw a box full of huge mangoes and paused as she debated buying one.

"Would'ja look at this?" Pat was staring though the glass of a small meat case.

Kiki forgot about the mango and joined her.

"What the heck?" Pat pointed. "Gross."

"Pig feet," Kiki said. She pointed to the tray on the left. "Pig head."

"Now that's just some kind of sin," Pat said. "That would put me off eating if I saw it on a plate."

A man in a butcher's apron stepped up behind the meat case. "Hep you?"

"I'm looking for a man who lives upstairs." She pointed at the ceiling. "Damian Bautista."

"Nobody rive up there," he said.

Kiki waved the piece of paper. "This is the right address." She read it aloud.

"No. Nobody." He shook his head. "Ask owner."

"I will. Where is he?"

The butcher pointed across the store at a short Asian man wielding a pole with a hook on the end. He was balancing a prom dress on a hanger, lifting it toward the ceiling. By the time Kiki reached him, he had hung the blue chiffon gown from the ceiling above a triangular stack of canned bamboo shoots.

"Need a fluffy prom dress?" Pat whispered to Kiki. "Maybe we'd get a discount if ya'll ordered ten of 'em."

Kiki ignored her. She gave a slight bow and said, "Hello. I'm looking for Damian. Damian Bautista. He lives upstairs?" She held out the paper.

The old man started shaking his head. "No. Nobody dat name rive here."

"I was told this is his address."

"Police a'ready here rooking for him yestaday. No apartment here. Onry storage upstairs."

"Damian stores stuff here?" Kiki figured finding Damian was now a matter of linguistics.

The man raised his voice, as if Kiki hadn't heard him the first time.

"Onry me. Onry my stuff. My things up there. Things for shop. Now you buy or go."

Kiki sighed. Maybe the guy was covering for Bautista.

"I'm his friend. I need to see him. Are you *sure* he is not here?" she said.

"No. Why somebody say he rive here? He don't. He don't rive here."

"Do you know if he lives anywhere else? Maybe next door?"

By now a small cluster of old Asian women had gathered and were listening intently.

"How I know? I don't know heem. You go now." The man shook the long pole at them.

Pat looked at Kiki. "Give up. He don't *rive* here."

Kiki gave up. She bowed again and said, "Mahalo. So sorry. Mahalo."

They virtually backed out on to the street, bowing as they went. While Pat stopped a passerby to ask if they knew where to find the best dim sum, Kiki pulled out her cell and dialed La Mariana.

"A-*lo*-ha," she said and asked to speak to Joe. When he came on the line she said, "Hi, Joe. This is Kiki Godwin again. Apparently Damian doesn't live at the address you gave me."

Joe said, "I got it off of his emergency card. Maybe he faked it." There was a pause and then, "After you left, I got to thinking. Today's Saturday, so he wouldn't be at home anyway. On Saturday and Sunday he works a booth at the Aloha Stadium Swap meet before his shift here. I know 'cause I've seen him there."

That would explain the piles of Hawaiiana, Kiki thought.

"Aloha Stadium Swap Meet? How long does it last?"

"I don't know. Maybe ten to three or so."

"Mahalo, Joe." Kiki hung up and told Pat what he'd said.

"If the police are looking for him, would he be there?"

"He needs money. He's not working at the restaurant right now. Besides, that swap meet is huge. He could be wearing a disguise, hiding in plain sight."

"I hope he hasn't sold Uncle Louie's Booze Bible." Pat glanced across the street. The Maidens were hanging out of the van windows waving and yelling for them to hurry.

"We'd better go. There's gonna be an insurrection if we don't get some dim sum."

"And den some."

39

PAT DUMPED THEM out in front of Mei Sum Dim Sum a block from the grocery. Kiki instructed them to order take-out because they had to get to the swap meet before it closed, and they still had to tackle Sunday afternoon traffic. The restaurant was clean but crowded, and surly was the only word that aptly described the squadron of waitresses.

Precious turned out to be a dim sum expert. Kiki was relived. Pat didn't know a dim from a sum, and after four days, Kiki was exhausted from wrangling the Maidens 24/7. She was in no mood to educate them on the finer points of ordering the bite-sized dumplings.

Since they'd all had lunch, they settled on tasting the house specialty—deep fried garlic eggplant—and two desserts, the custard tarts and sweet coconut balls.

"Sweet coconut balls" quickly replaced "dim sum and den some" as the phrase of the day.

Armed with Styrofoam take-out boxes of stinky garlic eggplant and sweets, the Maidens piled back into the van and headed for the swap meet in the parking lot of Aloha Stadium, a short walk from the USS *Arizona* Memorial at Pearl Harbor.

"Do we have time to go to the Memorial?" Lillian asked around a mouthful of custard tart. "I've never seen it."

"This from the woman who didn't want to see the site of an internment camp," Trish said.

"No time," Kiki said. "Have MyBob take you sometime."

When they reached the stadium, Lillian said, "It's too hot to wander around this parking lot." She had her nose pressed to the side window. "It looks like the asphalt is melting. I can't take all this sun. It will ruin the color of my hair." She patted her pink bouffant.

"So buy a hat," Kiki told her. She turned around to address them all. "Make sure your cell phones are on. I want you to spread out in twos. Flora and Precious. Lillian and Trish. Big Estelle and Pat. We don't have much time before this thing closes down. Go different directions and check out all the booths. I think Bautista, if he's here, will be in a booth that sells secondhand Hawaiiana. Collectibles, old newspapers, things like that. Any antique thing that says Hawaii. Old plates. Whatever. If you find a booth like that, do not approach. I repeat, do not approach. Call me, and I'll hightail it to wherever you are. I'll alert Pat, and she'll call all of you. Got it?"

"Got it!" They shouted.

"We gotta get outta this van," Pat said. "It smells like the inside of a rancid garlic clove. I can't breathe."

"It costs a dollar to get in the gate," Kiki said. "Get out your money and let's go. We've only got forty-five minutes."

"This'll be a good way to get your exercise." Pat made sure they were all out and then pressed the auto lock.

"Who exercises?" Flora checked to see how much "special" water she had left.

They each paid their dollar and went through the entry gate.

"Sweet coconut balls!" Pat hollered. "It's hotter'n Hades out here. I think Lil's right. The asphalt is meltin' my shoes."

"I'm heading for a hat stand." Lillian charged off with Trish at her side. They looked right and left, checking out the various booths as they flew past. The swap meet consisted of a sea of silver awnings stretched over aluminum frames. Folding tables lined up beneath were loaded with every kind of tourist trinket imaginable, not to mention some local favorites.

Kiki hustled along as fast as she could without getting distracted by straw bags lined with Hawaiian print fabrics and knock off Prada backpacks. She finally had to stop for five minutes at a stand that sold hula implements. She chatted up the seller, asked about used stuff and Hawaiiana, found out that kind of thing was mostly sold early Sunday mornings. He said if she went around the circle to the far side she might get lucky.

It wasn't long before she noticed the exact same items were for sale every half a dozen booths or so. It was like being trapped in a recurring nightmare. Huge beach towels with colorful flowers, dolphins, and scenic wonders of Hawaii flapped in the trade wind breeze that gave little relief from the heat waves emanating from the asphalt lot.

She paused to catch her breath in the shade of one booth and watched a tourist with huge feet let a vendor try to shove a toe ring onto her little toe. The vendor was nothing if not determined. Kiki left when the tourist started screaming.

Passing a bread booth, she was tempted to stop again when her cell rang. It was Pat.

"I found a booth that sells old stuff. Used stuff. Looks like garage sale stuff, not the souvenir crap."

"Where are you?" Kiki tried to see around the sea of awnings but found herself trapped in the maze of aisles.

"Head away from the sun, that's all I can tell ya. Wait a minute . . ." Pat mumbled to someone. "Booth 1211. Ask somebody which way."

"Don't tip off Bautista if you see him."

"No worries. I'm not right in front of it."

"Call the others." Kiki was already on the move.

"Roger that. Then I'm gonna get me some wrinkle cream while I'm waitin' for ya'll."

"Wrinkle cream?"

Pat didn't respond. She'd already ended the call. Kiki checked the time on her phone. They had a little under twenty minutes until closing.

She rounded a corner and found an intersection, then crossed over to another aisle where the numbers were getting closer to 1211. She saw Flora, Pat, and Big Estelle in front of a dried fruit booth. Big Estelle had a bag of shrimp chips in her hands. Precious was in the aisle leaning against a carved wooden tiki as tall as she was. Flora dipped a plastic spoon into a jar of *liliko'i* butter spread and ate it.

"How are you going to get that thing to the van?" Kiki asked Precious.

"Roll it. I've rolled it down every aisle so far."

Kiki said, "Estelle, pay for those chips pronto. Where is Lillian?"

"There they are." Pat pointed down the row of stalls. Her face was coated in some kind of oil.

Kiki asked, "What have you done?"

Pat showed her a small plastic bag with a logo of some kind on it. "I bought me some *kukui* nut oil. It takes out all your wrinkles overnight."

"You look like a greased pig at a county fair," Kiki said.

"You'll be wantin' to borrow it tomorrow when my face is smoother than a baby's butt."

Trish and Lillian came panting up to join them. Trish hadn't purchased anything. One look at Lillian's hat, and the rest of them were goggle-eyed. Flora stuffed another spoonful of *liliko'i* butter in her mouth.

"What's with the hat, Lil?" Pat asked.

"What's with that oil on your face? If it's sunblock I need some."

Trish shifted her camera strap.

Lillian raised a hand to her wide straw hat brim. "What's wrong with it? I thought the colors were very tropical, and I love these big leaves."

Kiki closed her eyes and counted to ten. The hatband was knitted green, yellow, and red yarn with a spray of green plastic leaves attached to one side.

"For one thing, those are Rasta colors, Lil," Big Estelle said gently.

"Rasta?"

"Rastafarian. As in Bob Marley. As in Jamaica and reggae music."

"As in marijuana," Precious said.

"As in, those are plastic pot leaves stuck up there on your hat, Lillian," Pat said.

Lillian slapped her hands on her cheeks. Her mouth formed a huge O.

"Am I going to be arrested?" She was poised to run.

Kiki grabbed her by the shoulders. "*Plastic* pot leaves, Lil. *Plastic.* Get a grip on yourself."

"MyBob will have a fit if I take this home," Lil cried.

"MyBob don't have to know," Big Estelle said. "It's keeping the sun off your face. When we get back to the hotel you can give it to Mother. She'll love it. Maybe it'll inspire her give up rap and get into reggae."

"Ten minutes to closing," Pat announced. "If we're gonna catch that Bautista guy we'd better get goin'. Kiki, what do you wanna do?"

While Lillian continued to sniffle, glancing around to see if anyone was staring—no one was—Kiki gave orders.

"Let's saunter back down to that booth with the Hawaiiana Collectibles sign. I didn't see Bautista when I walked by, but that doesn't mean he's not there. Pat, find something to ask the vendor about, and I'll scope out the back of the booth. Precious, roll your tiki down there and wait for us in the middle of the aisle. Lillian, stop crying and have your cell phone out. If we see him, you'll call 911, but you have to be sneaky about it. Trish, have your camera ready. I want this whole take down photographed. Big Estelle and Flora, if he makes a run for it, you two grab him." Kiki was pretty certain their combined weight was well over five hundred pounds. If they didn't want Bautista to go anywhere, then he wasn't going.

"Let's go. Look casual, don't be nervous," Kiki advised.

They had walked about two yards when a couple of teenage gals walked up to Kiki. One of them said, "Is it really you? Are you those old hula ladies from Kauai?"

Kiki kept walking, but Lillian stopped. "*We're* the Hula Maidens."

"You know, you folks can't really dance," the other girl said with the kind of snotty smirk only a teenager can pull off. "In fact, you're the worst hula dancers I ever saw."

Lillian gasped. Kiki stopped in her tracks, turned around, and marched up to the girls.

"Maybe we're a little *challenged* when it comes to hula, but at least *we* know enough to respect *kupuna*."

"'Cause you are *kupuna*," the first girl said. "Not many people older than you alive."

"Six minutes," Pat said.

Kiki envied the girls' long, silky dark hair, their smooth, coffee-colored skin, and lovely features. She tried to remember she was a smart-mouthed kid herself once. Who was she kidding? She prided herself on being a smart-mouthed old lady.

Kiki leaned closer to the teenagers and lowered your voice. Her smile never dimmed.

"Remember this moment someday when *you're* old, 'cause if you're lucky, you'll get old one day, too." She shoved past the two girls, and the Maidens trailed after her toward the antique booth with Precious rolling the tiki down the aisle behind them.

Pat perused the piles of old show posters and Hawaiian album covers. She picked up an old 33LP of Elvis' *Aloha from Hawaii via Satellite* and waved it at the vendor, a wiry Filipino man in his forties.

"How much for this, bra?" she asked. "It's says fifty bucks, but you can do better, yeah?"

The man took the LP from her, turned it over, turned it back, and stared at it.

"Fifty bucks. No can do better."

"You kiddin' me?"

While Pat bartered and got louder with every question, Kiki wandered around inside the booth. She stopped at an assorted pile of old hotel china with a banana leaf pattern. She picked up a plate and pretended to inspect it while she took in the van parked behind the booth. The sliding door was open. Someone was seated inside, but all she could see was a pair of Nike tennis shoes and two skinny legs.

Pat kept up the banter with the vendor. Big Estelle and Flora milled around, filling up the inside of the booth. Trish was casually moving around the exterior edges snapping photos while Lillian nervously paced the aisle, and Precious signed autographs and posed for pictures next to her tiki.

Kiki leaned over the table and called out to whoever was in the van.

"You hoo! Hooeee! I need to know about this plate," she yelled.

The feet inside the shoes moved. The vendor working with Pat glanced over his shoulder.

"One minute," he said. "Wait one minute."

"It's almost time to close," Kiki said. "This matches a bunch of plates I inherited, and I'd give anything to have it. *Anything.*" She stepped around the table and got close enough to stick her head around the edge of the van door. "Can you *please* help me?"

There was a man sitting inside the van. The shadowy interior hid his face from view until he hunched over and walked toward the opening.

"I can help you." He scanned the scene before he stepped out.

He was about Kiki's height and weight with curly dark hair sticking out from under a baseball cap, huge sunglasses, and a couple days growth of moustache. The moustache didn't disguise him much. It was Damian Bautista.

Bingo!

She shoved the dinner plate at him. "This is just what I was looking for, but I can't make out the price on the sticker."

He glanced around furtively, uncomfortable out in the open. When he lifted the plate to study the sticker, Kiki waved to Lillian, put her hand up to her cheek and mimed talking on the phone. The faux pot leaves on Lillian's hat bobbed as she nodded in understanding and punched in 911 on her cell.

Shoppers were filing down the aisle toward the exit, sauntering mostly, stopping to purchase last minute impulse buys. Lillian bounced around, nervously talking on the phone and glancing back at Kiki.

Right on cue, Pat started yelling at the vendor.

"That's insane. I ain't paying fifty bucks for that album. I seen them on eBay for thirty."

"Then go buy it on eBay!" the vendor shouted back. "I gotta pack up. You go now."

When he turned around and saw Bautista standing in the middle of the booth, his eyes bugged out.

"What are you doing, man? Are you nuts?" the vendor said.

Kiki played innocent. "He's being so kind. He's helping me read the price on this label."

"I'll handle this. You get back in the van." The vendor grabbed the plate and motioned to Bautista. Bautista started to turn away.

"I'm also looking for old cocktail recipe books," Kiki said. "Drink recipes, you know? I'm a collector. I'm always looking for something really unique. Money is *no* object if it's something I've never seen before."

Just as Kiki expected, greed won out. Bautista paused.

The vendor gave a slight shake of his head as if to warn the other man away. Bautista paid no attention.

The vendor whispered to Bautista, "Get in the van, I'm tellin' you, man."

Bautista whispered back, but it was loud enough for Kiki to hear. "She's just an old lady with money. No worries."

He ducked into the van, and as the vendor was quoting a price of fifty dollars for a plate clearly marked at twenty-four, Bautista was back with an insulated grocery bag. Kiki ignored the vendor and watched Bautista slip Louie's Booze Bible out of the grocery bag. Trish was standing beside the front table. She held up a vintage pillowcase and pretended to take a photo of it, but aimed the lens right at Bautista and the notebook.

By this time Big Estelle, Flora, and Pat were no longer pretending to shop. They watched as Kiki reached for the Booze Bible. It was almost in her hands when Lillian came running up to the booth waving her cell and yelling, "They're on the way. The police are through the front gate."

Bautista pushed Kiki out of his way, tossing her against a table. He darted toward the front of the booth. Faster than a mongoose, he sidestepped Big Estelle and Flora. Pat tried to grab him by the sleeve and missed. With all three of them on his heels, he barreled around the front table and out of the booth.

He shoved Lillian aside and headed down the aisle. Lillian started screaming. Precious knocked the tiki on the ground and gave it a shove with her foot. It rolled right into Bauista's path. He pitched forward, flew through the air, and dove across the hot asphalt face first.

Big Estelle and Flora came barreling out of the booth and sat on Bautista before he could get up. Kiki was right behind them carrying the insulated shopping bag containing Louie's Booze Bible.

"Do not let him up!" she hollered. "Keep him there."

"Good job, ladeeze! Way to go," Pat hollered.

The crowd closed around them. Kiki bounced up and down to look over them and saw the police round the corner of the aisle. The officers saw the commotion and started running.

Kiki looked at Bautista, what she could see of him anyway. Except for his head and his Nikes sticking out from beneath the ruffled flounces on Big Estelle and Flora's muumuus, he was completely hidden.

Lillian was still crying. She'd managed to end up with three of her fans surrounding her. They patted her on the back to comfort her.

Kiki walked over to her and said, "Get a grip, Lillian. You might want to get that hat off of your head. The police are here."

"But they're *fake* leaves," Lil whined. "How was I supposed to know what pot leaves look like?"

"And call Em," Kiki added. "Now."

Lillian yanked off her hat and shoved it into her straw bag. "What should I tell her?"

"Tell her to bring Roland and get over to the Aloha Stadium ASAP. Tell her we've got her husband's killer all wrapped up for her, and we recovered Louie's Booze Bible, too. Then get the mayor of Honolulu on the phone. I'm gonna ask him about giving us a proclamation."

40

WHEN EM SAW THE caller was Lillian she decided let the call go to voicemail and watched her uncle bask in the glow of success. The standing ovation went on and on until finally the MC waved everyone back to sitting except the press.

They shouted questions and compliments to Louie as he took it all in stride. Everyone was convinced the monkey in the fez and Little Estelle were part of his shtick.

"Mr. Marshall," one of the reporters shouted.

Louie acknowledged him. "It's Louie. Just Louie. Or Uncle Louie," he said.

"Louie, you did so much more than shaker juggling and drink mixing here. You really set the mood before you started and ended with a real bang. How did you decide on the theme?"

Louie nodded. "Tiki's not a theme to me. It's the symbol of a lifestyle. Tiki culture is all part of a myth that came out of the mindset of the 1950s . . ."

As the interview went on, Em decided to slip out. She went out the same door the monkey used for its exit, hoping it might be somewhere nearby. With the deposit Louie had riding on its return, she wondered if there might be someone from the Honolulu Zoo she could hire to catch it.

Her phone vibrated. When she saw it was Lillian again she answered.

"I'm sorry, Lillian. I was in Louie's presentation and . . ."

Lillian was sobbing too hard to speak.

Em said, "Calm down, Lillian. What's going on?"

More sobbing.

"Is everyone alive?" Em pictured an overturned van with Maidens trapped inside.

"Yes. Kiki told me to call you. You have to get over here now!"

"Where is here? Where are you?"

"The swap meet. The big swap meet. We tracked him down. We got him. First we went to his apartment, then we went to the tiki restaurant by that marina.”

“What’s that screaming?”

“That’s him. Your husband’s killer. We got him.”

“Do you have someone tied up in the van, Lillian? Who is screaming?”

“We found him. Kiki found him.”

“Is someone torturing him? That kind of confession won’t stand up in court.” She could just picture Pat wielding wires attached to a battery and clipping them to Bautista’s privates.

“No, no torture. Big Estelle and Flora are sitting on him right now. The police are here somewhere. Kiki wants you to get here fast. Oh!”

“Oh, what?”

“They’re here. They’re sealing off the area with crime scene tape.”

Em heard scratchy sounds, as if Lillian had muffled the phone. Then Lillian said, “Okay, okay.”

“What’s going on?” Em realized she was shouting. People outside the convention ballroom were staring.

“They said we can’t leave the scene. Kiki just waved at me. What? She says you need to get over here ASAP.”

“Over where?”

“The big swap meet. I gotta go. The police are rounding us up.”

“Lil, wait! Lillian . . .”

Em tried calling back but Lil didn’t answer.

Why me? Em wondered. Kiki and the girls had rounded up Phillip’s killer? Did they mean Bautista?

She hit Roland’s number. He’d told her that he’d be in the gym.

When he answered she heard weights clanking in the background.

“What’s up?” It sounded as if he was breathing hard.

She’d seen him oiled up for his knife dancing routine, clothed in nothing but a skimpy piece of tapa cloth print fabric tied around his hips. It wasn’t hard to imagine what he’d look like in a gym pumping iron.

For a second she almost forgot why she’d called.

“Lillian just phoned and said the Hula Maidens had captured Phillip’s killer. She said we had to get to the swap meet right now.”

She could tell Roland was already on the move. “What do you mean? Did they find Bautista? He could be armed and dangerous. Are they crazy?”

“Of course, they’re crazy. That never stopped them before. I heard a man screaming. Flora and Big Estelle had him pinned down.”

“Ouch. Where?”

"Lil said something about a big swap meet. I couldn't get anything else out of her."

"Aloha Stadium Swap Meet?"

"I have no idea. The *big* swap meet was all she could tell me."

"That's it then. I'll meet you in the reception area in five minutes."

"Roland, we've got to hurry. The police are already on the scene."

As Em rushed toward the reception area she saw Little Estelle headed along the walk in front of the shops near the pitiful Penguin Pool. She had five minutes to spare, so Em ran down the stone walkway to catch up with her. Luckily Little Estelle hadn't floored the Gadabout.

"Little Estelle," Em called. The Gadabout stopped. "Where's the monkey?"

"Alphonse? He had an appointment."

Em couldn't do anything but stare. The woman was seriously losing it.

"Are you shocked we're on a first name basis?" Little Estelle asked.

"That's his only name," Em reminded her.

"As far as we know."

"About the monkey. Where is he?"

"I think he's at another wedding reception. He's hooked on receptions. Besides, he's in demand just like me. When he does his cha cha wearing a fez, he's a real showstopper. He loves the limelight as much as Kiki. If you hang around the bar long enough, I'm sure he'll swing back through."

"I can't wait around. Roland and I have to rush off to an emergency."

"Who's dead now?" Little Estelle squinted behind her glasses.

"No one, I hope," Em said.

Little Estelle was staring at a point over Em's shoulder. She said, "Me, too. Roland's headed this way, and he's still handsome as heck, but he sure doesn't look happy."

41

BY THE TIME EM and Roland arrived at the swap meet, the HPD had the entrance cordoned off. Cars were allowed to exit but not enter. Roland pulled up to the officer in charge of traffic control and flashed his KPD badge.

"Is Detective Lieutenant Bardon here? I'm working on an investigation with him."

"He just arrived." The officer waved them through.

The parking area was huge and nearly empty except for the line of cars waiting to exit. Roland headed around the stadium, and they saw a group of white HPD cruisers circled up near the tent city of booths. There was a line of officers blocking the scene though no one was trying to get past.

"How did they find Bautista?" Roland wondered aloud.

"How do they find anyone? Kiki is a force to be reckoned with when she wants something." Em leaned forward. "I can't see what's going on beyond all those navy blue uniforms."

Roland pulled up and parked. They both exited the rental car and headed for the gathering on the edge of a row of booths. One officer noticed them. Before he could stop them, Roland flashed his badge and said he was working with Bardon. Two officers parted to let Em and Roland slip into the inner circle. They headed up the aisle. Em saw the rainbow splash of muumuus against the silver gray of awnings and lines of tables. Vendors who had left until tomorrow had draped tarps over their goods and closed up.

"There they are," Em said.

They hurried toward the action.

"There's Bautista." Roland nodded toward a man sitting on the ground in the middle of the aisle with his hands cuffed behind him. His forehead, nose, lips, and chin were skinned and bleeding. He leaned over as if his side was causing him pain. He looked confused and miserable.

"Kiki's talking to Bardon," Em said. She saw Pat, her face covered in shiny oil, standing behind Kiki. Lillian was in the shade of a booth that was blocked with crime tape. Her face was as pink as her hair. She was fanning herself with what appeared to be a bouquet of marijuana leaves wrapped in straw.

Precious sat on a toppled tiki in front of the booth. Trish was not far, showing one of the officers the photos on her camera.

"Em!"

Em turned around and saw Big Estelle and Flora sitting on two folding chairs across from the collectibles booth. Each was snacking out of a bag of dried fruit.

"Wanna banana chip?" Flora held up her bag. Em noticed her water bottle was on the ground beside her chair.

"Not now."

"We got 'em." Big Estelle smiled. "He tried to run, but we put the skids on that idea."

Flora nodded. "Sure did. Sucker didn't know what hit 'em."

Roland nudged Em's elbow, and they moved closer to where Bardon was interviewing Kiki. Kiki was saying, "So we went to Chinatown, where we found out he'd given a false address on his employee card at La Mariana Sailing Club. I called the bartender, and he said Bautista might be here at the swap meet, which made perfect sense."

"How did that make sense?" Bardon's expression looked like he hadn't yet made much sense out of any of her story.

Kiki shrugged. "Because after we saw all that stuff in his apartment—"

"You broke into his apartment?" Bardon stopped taking notes and stared at her.

"Sure. That part was child's play."

"I'd call it breaking and entering," the detective said.

"We didn't *break* in. We were escorted by the manager, Melvin. Nice guy. A little taken with himself though."

"So Kline let you in." Bardon was writing again.

"Don't blame him, though. Flora is Bautista's cousin. That's why he let us in. Aren't you, Flora?" Kiki yelled to Flora across the aisle.

"Aren't I what?"

"Damian's cousin."

"Sure."

"I doubt that," Bardon said. "I seriously doubt it."

Flora stood up and ambled over to where Damian was seated. She nudged him with the toe of her rubber slipper then leaned over him. "Say you my cousin," she said.

Bautista looked over at the detective.

"We're cousins," he mumbled through swollen lips. "For shua."

Bardon stared at the slight Portuguese man and then rotund Flora.

"Exactly how are you related?" he asked Flora.

"Way back," Flora said.

"Must be way, way back." Bardon frowned down at his notes. "So go on," he prompted Kiki. "You saw the stuff in his apartment and then what?"

"I could see that he was a collector. All the stuff in there was old Hawaiiana. There's a big market for that kind of thing online. There has been for years." She waved her hand at the collectibles booth. "That booth is full of it. Same stuff I saw in his apartment. When I saw what was inside the apartment I thought, ah, ha!"

"Ah, ha." Bardon nodded. "Ah, ha what?"

"Ah, ha, Bautista probably has the Booze Bible. The one piece of the puzzle that ties him to the murder. He saw it when Em's ex-husband had it, he wanted it, and he wanted it bad enough to kill for it. He was pissed at her ex anyway."

"I didn't kill anyone," Bautista yelled and winced.

"He was angry enough to kill Phillip Johnson without the notebook," Bardon said.

"If he wasn't guilty, why would he run?" Kiki asked. "But you still need something to link him to the apartment. Right?"

Pat stepped closer and held up an insulated bag. "Here you go. He had this in his possession. The minute we saw it, we took him down," she said. "It's Uncle Louie's Booze Bible. Bautista had to have taken it from Em's ex's apartment after he killed him. Whether the murder was because he wanted the notebook or 'cause he was mad don't really matter, does it? He still killed Johnson, and Em sure as heck didn't."

Em grabbed Roland's hand and squeezed it. Louie's notebook was safe.

"They found it," she whispered. "They did it."

Bardon took the bag from Pat and looked inside before he handed it off.

"I didn't kill anybody!" Bautista shouted, struggling against the handcuffs.

"Fat chance," Kiki yelled back.

"Okay, I've heard enough for now," Bardon announced. To one of the uniformed officers he said, "Read him his rights. We'll take his statement at headquarters." Then to Kiki, "What you ladies did today is wrong on so many levels."

"We were just looking out for one of our own, that's all. No way did Em kill her ex. That's ridiculous. You boys were taking too long. We have to *hele* on back to Kauai on Monday and we needed to find Bautista before then. You really should just say *mahalo* and stop glaring like that. You're gonna get creases on your forehead."

Pat held out the jar of *kukui* nut oil. "This might help with those crow's feet around your eyes."

Bardon ignored her. Two officers helped Bautista up. The man groaned and whimpered. The Maidens collected their bags and purses.

Kiki spotted Em and Roland for the first time.

"We got Louie's Booze Bible," she called out.

Em hurried over and hugged her. "I saw, and I can't thank you enough." Aware of Roland standing right behind her, Em said, "I can't thank you enough, but you shouldn't have done this, Kiki."

Bardon was still within hearing distance. He turned to Em. "I should have known you were behind this somehow."

"I had no idea they were going to do anything," she said.

Kiki backed her up. "She didn't. She'd never have condoned this. She's not into covert action. Is she, ladies?"

"Never. No way." The Maidens all piped up from wherever they were in the area.

All around the immediate vicinity officers were questioning other vendors. The skinny man who had been in the collectibles booth with Bautista was in the process of being handcuffed. Other vendors were helping to pack up his things.

"What did he do?" Em asked Bardon.

"Aiding and abetting. He had Bautista hidden in the white van in back."

"Can we go now?" Kiki asked the detective.

Bardon didn't hide his frustration. "That's it for now. Don't leave Honolulu until I give you the okay."

Kiki was smiling as she turned away.

To Em he said, "Unfortunately, you can't have your uncle's notebook, but I'll personally make sure nothing happens to it. Ms. Godwin was right. It does tie Bautista to your husband's apartment, since Johnson was trying to extort money for its return." He watched the officers lead Bautista's cohort out of the booth. "I'm sure Bautista will cave and confess once we get him to the station."

"I'd like to observe the interrogation," Roland said. "As a visiting police officer."

"Sure, whatever," Bardon said. Then he looked at Em. "But not you."

"Of course not." Em would like nothing better than to sit in on the interrogation. She hoped Bautista would be chained to table in a room with a two-way mirror.

Roland said, "She'd coming with me, though. She'll wait outside the room."

"Fine."

They started to follow Bardon as he walked along the aisle toward the squad cars. The Maidens were making their way along as well. Precious trailed behind them, hunched over the wooden tiki as she rolled it down the aisle. The sun was relentless. Sweat was streaming down her face.

"I'll take that," Roland said.

Relief wreathed her face in a wide smile. She stepped back, and Roland upended the tiki and picked it up with no effort.

"Where's your van?" he asked.

"Pat ran ahead to get it. We're going to wait by the police cars, and she'll pick us up. The girls can help me get the tiki inside."

Roland carried it to the end of the aisle where the others were waiting.

"You two go on. Make sure Bautista doesn't give them the slip at headquarters," Kiki urged.

"No way he's going anywhere," Roland assured her. "You ladies sure did a number on him."

"Mahalo." Kiki smiled.

"That wasn't a compliment," he said.

"Oh."

"I'm afraid for you to return to Kauai." Roland wasn't laughing.

Em was amazed at how Kiki remained undaunted by his dark expression.

"You could always deputize us," she said. "I think we're better at fighting crime than we are dancing hula."

42

ONCE THEY REACHED Honolulu Police Headquarters on Beretania Street in downtown Honolulu, Em told Roland she'd wait for him on the front steps. The sun was setting, and she needed some fresh air.

"I think you should wait inside," he said.

She shook her head no. "There's probably not a safer place to wait than on the steps of police headquarters. Besides, need to give Louie a call and check in."

Roland went inside, and Em sat down on the top of the wide concrete steps and pulled out her cell.

"Where did you say you are?" Louie yelled into the phone. "I can't hear you."

It definitely sounded like he was in the middle of a wild celebration. She told him she was at HPD headquarters waiting for Roland.

Then she added, "The police have your Booze Bible. It's safe, but they're holding it as evidence."

"Are you kidding? They found it?"

"The Hula Maidens are responsible. They tracked down Bautista, that's Phillip's neighbor suspected of the murder. Since he had the notebook, he had to have been in Phillip's place. Are the girls back yet?"

"No."

"They should be there any minute. I'm sorry I'm not there to celebrate with you." She didn't know if he heard her. There was a loud roar on the other end of the line. "What's everybody yelling?"

"Cha cha cha, cha cha cha!"

"Is that a conga line?"

"No, Little Estelle is dancing with Alphonse. She's the only woman he can tolerate. Maybe because she's not much taller and they're both wrinkled."

"Maybe she can she coax him into his cage."

"What?"

Em was the only one on the steps at the moment so she yelled,

"Can she coax him into his cage so you can get your deposit back?"

"Oh, I doubt it. He's smarter than that. Are you going to be able to make it back in time for the awards ceremony?"

Em rubbed her forehead with the heel of her palm. She'd nearly forgotten all about it.

"I hope so. What time is it again?"

"Not until eight."

"Great. I'll meet you there."

She hoped they could make it back in time. At the very least she might be able to slip in before it was over. The lights of Honolulu were starting to going on. As in any large city, people were on the move. The traffic was bumper to bumper. Some of the cabs sneaked in and out of lanes while others just sat and waited.

A handful of minutes away down in Waikiki people were enjoying the end of a beautiful day with cocktails on the beach or sailing on sunset cruises. Oahu had the same cooling trade winds as Kauai, the same sunsets and velvet air, but the pace of life and heartbeats of the two islands were polar opposites.

She thought about Sophie, Tiko, and Buzzy working the Goddess dinner hour and hoped all was going well. She doubted Sophie would call to bother them and was thankful that for such a young gal, Sophie had a great head on her shoulders. If a crisis arose, she'd try to handle it.

Em seriously doubted there would be much going on, nothing that might spell disaster. After all, the Hula Maidens were on Oahu, doubly ensuring all was well on Kauai.

Almost an hour went by before Roland appeared. Em even didn't realize he was there until he sat down beside her. He didn't volunteer any information, just sat there with his shoulder pressed against hers.

"How did it go?" she finally asked.

"Bautista swears he didn't kill Johnson. I don't think he's going to break. He's sticking to his story."

"Which is?"

"He confirmed he and Phillip got into a shouting match over a parking space outside the Lokelani. Bautista was about to back into a spot when Phillip honked once and snaked his smaller car into the space. Bautista waved and yelled, but Phillip flipped him off."

"That sounds like Phillip." Back when she was starry-eyed she saw Phillip's confidence and assertiveness as assets. She'd come to realize he was really an arrogant ass.

Roland went on. "So Bautista left his car in the middle of the street, got out, marched up to Phillip, and got right in his face. Called him an effing *haole* among other stuff. The neighbors heard the hassle going down and came out. Phillip was a lot bigger than Bautista, so he didn't back down, either. More neighbors ran out to watch. Finally the building manager came out and told them both to cool it or he was going to call 9-1-1."

"Which is exactly what Melvin said happened."

He nodded. "Right. So then Bautista drives off furious and heads for work. The next day, around five thirty a.m., he went back to his apartment, which he uses as a storage shed, and notices the door next to his is slightly open. That place had been empty for a week prior. He listened and heard nothing. Then he pushed the door open with one finger and looked in. He didn't see anyone at first, but he saw your uncle's recipe notebook on a side table directly across from the door.

"He figured the asshole he got in the argument with had rented the apartment and maybe left it open."

"So Bautista couldn't resist," Em said.

"Exactly. He wanted to get back at Phillip at that point. So he slips into the apartment, focused on stealing the notebook off the table. He got halfway across the room and sees Phillip's body, face down in a pool of blood. He was in shock for a minute or two—but not so much that he didn't go ahead and grab the notebook before running out the door."

"Why didn't he call 9-1-1?"

"He panicked. He knew everyone had seen him screaming at Phillip the day before, and he was sure they'd think he went back and killed him. He admitted running was a terrible idea."

"The worst. That, and he kept the notebook."

"Next thing he knew his face was all over the news, and he was afraid to go anywhere."

"He still could have turned himself in and explained."

"Could have but didn't. He says he was just too scared. He left his car where the police found it up by Punchbowl and took a bus over to his vendor friend's place. He begged the guy to let him sleep in his van."

"If not in the Lokelani apartment, where does he actually live?"

"On different boats in the La Mariana Marina, though that's illegal. The moorings are not for live-aboard owners. He doesn't own a boat, he just slips aboard them to sleep. He eats his main meal at the restaurant before or after work and showers at the beach. He said if he had another apartment of his own he'd just end up filling it floor to ceiling with stuff and have to move out, and he can't afford it."

"So he was hiding out at the swap meet?"

"He wasn't supposed to get out of his friend's van. It was closing time when Kiki asked for help, and then she mentioned she loved recipe books and would pay top dollar for something unusual. He thought of the notebook and figured that was a way to get rid of it. He never suspected someone like Kiki was setting him up. He was a sitting duck."

"Kiki isn't exactly the stereotypical *Hawaii Five-0* babe, but she always seems to get her man. Or woman."

A breeze ruffled the loose strands of hair that had escaped Em's ponytail.

"You know, I think he's telling the truth," Roland said.

"You do?"

"I do. Bardon isn't sure. He'd like to pin this on Bautista and have it wrapped up, but I can tell he's hesitant."

"Why don't they give him a lie detector test?"

"They can, but there's no consensus that polygraph evidence is reliable. They'll probably find DNA in the apartment. He admitted he was there, but not when anyone was around to see him. There's every chance there might be a hair sample or fingerprint somewhere, but he still swears he's innocent."

"If Bautista didn't kill Phillip, then who did?" She turned to face Roland.

"Besides you?"

"Not funny, Roland."

"It could have been a random killing. Someone saw Phillip, a *haole*, obviously with some money, moving in and surprised him. Somehow Phillip came up with the gun. There was a struggle, Phillip was shot."

"The robber wiped down the gun and accidentally left the door open? No one heard or saw anything?"

"In that neighborhood they probably wouldn't say anything even if they had. The old lady next door keeps her TV booming. No one would know if the shots were coming from the TV or the apartment."

Em fell silent, picturing Phillip lying in a pool of blood in the seedy apartment.

"Are you okay?"

"What a horrible way to die."

"Hopefully the case will be solved, and he can rest in peace."

"Hopefully."

"Will you have to make arrangements for him?"

Em shook her head. "I gave the coroner his brother's name, and they'll contact him. They probably already have."

When she heard Roland's stomach growl, she realized it was completely dark already.

She got to her feet and brushed off the back of her pedal pushers. "Do you feel like eating?"

"I promised Louie I'd be there for the Shake Off award ceremony."

"You should have a bite. It's been a long day," he said.

She pictured the noise and crowds at the Hilton. The last thing she needed right now were the Hula Maidens and a dancing monkey.

"I've got an idea," he said. "How would you like something low-key and local?"

"Low-key and local? Are you talking about you or dinner?"

He drove back toward Waikiki and a little beyond, turned down what looked like an alley, and pulled into a lot behind a chain link fence across from a wall of graffiti art.

"Okay, I give up. Where are we?"

"Home Bar and Grill. Trust me."

"I trust you." She learned early on that the most humble places in Hawaii usually had the most delicious food.

The place was packed, but they were seated within minutes. They ordered beer and wine, and before Em knew what was happening, the table was covered with food. Roland's smile had been on full power megawatt since they walked in.

Naturally someone on staff knew his cousin and his aunties and that he was from Kauai. Word of his presence quickly circulated, and young lovelies kept appearing at the table bearing free appetizers.

"Just a little *pupu*," was the excuse waitresses made each time they set down another delicious dish for them to sample.

Having dinner in the local hangout was low-key, comfortable, and sane after the nightmare and drama she'd been living all weekend. She looked across the table at the handsome detective and didn't know how to thank him for being there for her. He'd been an island of calm and strength in an ocean of upheaval.

Never in a lifetime would she have guessed Phillip would be the one to bring them closer. Or that Nat would ever call Roland to come to her rescue. But that just proved what a great guy Nat was too. Despite everything that had happened, she considered herself one lucky girl.

She smiled when she noticed his pork chop dinner was nearly demolished. They'd had so many great *pupus* she'd barely made a dent in her Korean fried chicken.

"Another glass of wine?" he asked.

"No, thanks." She still had a long night ahead of her. "I'm going to the awards ceremony," she reminded him. "Even if I just slip in at the end."

He signaled a waitress for the check.

"We've got time. Finish your dinner," she told him.

He had another couple of bites. "I'm *pau*."

While he finished up and polished off his beer, Em said, "I can't thank you enough, you know."

"Hey, we took an oath to protect and serve with aloha." He shrugged off her thanks and then smiled. "This is the serving with aloha part. What can I do for you now?"

"How about passing me that last hunk of Tater Tot nacho?"

"You got it." He slid the plate across the table. "If you think of anything else, maybe later in the evening, just let me know, and I'll be there."

43

EM MADE IT BACK to the Hilton with enough time to freshen up and grab a *pareu* to use as a shawl in case the air conditioning was cranked up in the ballroom. She arrived at the Shake Off awards by eight thirty, entered through a side door, and scanned the room. Pat saw her and waved her over to a row of chairs filled with Hula Maidens. They'd saved a seat on the end for her.

"Sweet coconut balls! We thought you'd never make it." Pat was doing her form of whispering, but her voice was still audible to most of the folks sitting around them.

"Sorry. We stopped for dinner," Em whispered back.

Kiki leaned over Pat. "Tell me Bautista is locked up nice and tight."

"He is, but he still hasn't confessed to murder. Did I miss the awards?"

"Nope," Pat said. "So far all they done is blah-blah about next year's event. It's gonna be held on the Big Island."

Kiki started to say something else, but Em put her finger to her lips and indicated the stage where dePesto was handing the microphone over to the awards chairman.

The demonstration bar was still set up, but the palms and tiki torches that had been part of Louie's presentation were gone. Five trophies were lined up on the bar now: three bronze, a silver, and one gold. She located her uncle seated among the other contestants in the first three rows. He was tall and stately, and his distinguished white hair made him easy to spot.

DePesto took a seat as the awards chairman began the ceremony. Em guessed he was in his late thirties. He was dressed in what would be standard issue bartender wear on the mainland: a gold brocade vest over a white shirt with a black bow tie and black trousers.

"And now, finally, the moment you've all been awaiting is finally here," he said. "It's been quite a Western Regional Shake Off this year. I'd say one of the best ever. What a great way to celebrate the tenth anniversary of the national contest founded by Lamar dePesto. Let's give Lamar another round of applause."

Em guessed it wasn't the first, nor would it be the last round of applause for dePesto.

"Without further ado." The host turned to face the right side of the stage. A tall, slender blonde in red stilettos, red cat's eye sunglasses, and a 1940s two-piece swimsuit sauntered out carrying the judging results envelope. She handed it over to the awards chairman and then perched on a barstool near the trophies, crossed her long bare legs, and folded her hands on her knees.

Em was certain there wasn't a man in the room watching as the awards chairman opened the envelope. But open it he did. He read the results to himself, and at first his expression was blank, then Em thought she saw a hint of a smile. He called the names of the five finalists. Four men and a woman walked onto the stage and lined up in front of the bar. Louie and dePesto were among them.

"I'll start with fifth place," the chairman said, and he read off the name. The trophy girl handed the fifth place winner one of the bronze trophies while the crowd applauded.

Tension mounted between applause for the fourth and third runners up. Before the second place winner was announced, a heavy hush fell over the ballroom. Only Louie and dePesto remained on stage.

Em found herself holding her breath. Pat took hold of her hand. Em looked down the row and realized all the Hula Maidens were perched on the edges of their chairs holding hands. The awards chairman gazed dramatically at the audience. Then he looked at the two contestants left on stage. Louie was calm and smiling, holding his favorite tiki mug. DePesto just looked nervous.

"In second place"—the young man paused dramatically and then looked down at the card—"Lamar dePesto!"

There was a heartbeat of stunned silence, and then the room went berserk when everyone realized Louie had won and dePesto had been dethroned. The Hula Maidens started screaming, and all jumped to their feet. Pat put her thumb and forefinger in her mouth and let out shrill, earsplitting whistles until Em and Kiki elbowed her into silence.

Louie actually looked stunned until the leggy blonde walked over and handed him a two foot tall golden trophy with a three-foot-long swizzle stick on it.

"What the heck is that?" Pat squinted toward the stage. "A penis trophy?"

Em laughed for the first time in almost a week. "It's a swizzle stick."

"What's a swizzle stick?" Pat asked.

"A long plastic thing you stir drinks with," Kiki said.

"That don't look like a spoon."

"Because it's not. It's a swizzle stick."

"Like those plastic things with palm trees on top that they stick in drinks at the Goddess?"

"Yes, those," Kiki said.

DePesto was still on the stage holding a silver trophy. It was like Louie's first place prize only smaller. Em almost felt sorry for him. Standing beside Louie, he appeared to be shrinking.

"How about a few words from our champion, Louie Marshall!" The awards chair tried to hand Louie the microphone. With his drink in one hand, Louie had to hand his award back to the trophy girl, then took the mic. As he waited for the pandemonium to die down, he took a sip out of the tiki mug.

When the room was finally quiet he lowered his voice and captivated the audience again. "A-looo-ha," he said.

"A-looo-ha!" the audience shouted back.

"This is quite an honor, believe me. Coming from the North Shore of Kauai after not being out in the world can be a little intimidating. Oahu is one thing, but I haven't been to the mainland for forty years. Or maybe more."

For some reason everyone in the room started cheering, though the majority hailed from the western mainland states.

Louie continued. "After this week, I'm in awe of most of you young bartenders. You mixed up some quality drinks, and I'm proud to have met you. Heck, I'm thankful you even let an old geezer like me enter this event."

He turned to dePesto. "I want to thank not only the judges, but Lamar dePesto. Ten years ago he founded a top notch contest, and despite a couple of personal hitches while I've been here, I've had a great time. That being said, winning the Western Regional Shake Off is a great honor and more than enough for me. So with your permission, I'd like to ask you, Lamar, to take my place in the National Competition in St. Louis. I just can't see myself packing up and heading to the mainland to compete for the national title."

For a moment or two no one moved. The crowd couldn't believe what they'd heard. The winner of the Western Regional Shake Off had abdicated and was sending his runner up off to the nationals.

When Em realized what Louie had just done, she started

applauding. The Hula Maidens joined in and whooped it up, chanting Louie's name. Soon the entire room joined in.

DePesto was staring at Louie with a stunned expression. Louie waved the trophy girl over, handed her the mic, took back his golden swizzle stick, and started taking bows.

"That was way cool," Pat said. "Kinda like they both win."

"I was just thinking the same thing." Em watched as the audience left their seats to congratulate the winners.

"Time to hit the bar," Kiki said. "After the day we've had, I think a celebration is in order. Not only did we capture Damian Bautista, but we recovered the Booze Bible, and Louie won the contest."

"A triple crown," Pat said.

Kiki was all smiles. "It doesn't get any better than that." She looked over at Em. "Where's that hot hunk of detective you've been with all day?"

"He turned in early. Said he wanted to check in with one of the guys he works with on Kauai and find out what's been happening over there."

Em turned to concentrate on the stage when she felt her face burning. She wasn't about to tell them that when Roland left her in the atrium, he'd not only kissed her in public for the first time, but he pressed his key card into her palm and whispered, "No pressure, but if you want to join me later, *komo mai*, come on in."

44

THE NEXT DAY, Em rolled over, pulled the sheet over her naked breasts, realized where she was, and propped herself up on her elbows. Roland was up, dressed, and moving around in the dressing area of his room pouring a cup of coffee.

"They only have packets of powdered creamer," he said. "How do you take your coffee?"

She'd spent the night with him, had the most incredible sex she'd ever had, and the first thing he asks is how she takes her coffee as if nothing spectacular had happened.

Her insecurities kicked in. Maybe for him, it hadn't.

"Black with sugar." She saw her sundress draped over the back of the desk chair, her sandals on the floor. "What time is it?"

"Almost seven thirty."

"I slept in. I can't believe it."

He approached the bed with a steaming cup and set it on the bedside table. Then he reached over her and gathered up all the extra pillows. Em leaned forward, and he propped them behind her.

"Mahalo," she said as she leaned back. He handed her the coffee.

"A'ole pilikia." No trouble.

He sat on the edge of the bed next to her hip and then reached over and smoothed her hair back away from her face and tucked it over her shoulder. She wished she could think of a spectacular word for the way he made her feel. Maybe something in Hawaiian.

Leaning back like a princess against the pile of pillows sipping coffee served by a handsome man was something she could get used to. So she warned herself not to make any more of last night than it was.

The trouble was she had no idea *what* it was, other than a word she couldn't come up with.

She decided that for now she would simply enjoy the moment. Something she rarely had time to do.

Last night she'd told Louie not to worry, that she might not be spending the night in their suite.

"You mean with any luck you won't be spending the night in the suite," he'd said. "I won't worry, as long as you're with Roland."

"Okay, then you don't have to worry."

He winked and said, "You're a big girl now. Have fun."

She was glad he'd given her his okay. She was thirty-five, divorced, and hadn't slept with anyone since she'd moved to Kauai.

She wasn't a one night stand kind of gal.

But what about Roland? With his good looks and the way women of all ages threw themselves at him, Em figured he had to have collected a string of hearts by now. She saw him glance at his watch and warned herself not to be insulted. He was a busy man.

"Are you going somewhere?" she asked.

"Connecting with Bardon. I want to talk him into letting you leave with the others. As it is, Kiki and whoever went into Bautista's apartment with her will have to stay until he gives them the okay to leave too."

"I have a feeling if some of them stay, all of them will stay."

She sipped some more coffee, self-conscious wearing nothing beneath the sheets while he sat there in a black golf shirt and slacks. The draperies were open all the way, the slider open to let in the balmy trades and the sound of the surf. Voices of beachgoers were carried on the wind.

"If you'd like breakfast, I'll be happy to order room service for you before I leave."

"No, thanks. Louie is going to treat everyone to the Sunday buffet at the Rainbow Lanai to celebrate his big win. He said you're welcome to join us."

"I would, but I'm bribing Bardon with food."

"Are you taking him to Home Grill?"

"Nope. The place for breakfast is Sweet E's. French toast stuffed with cream cheese and blueberries."

"By rights you should weigh four hundred pounds. It's not fair."

"Good genes."

She didn't tell him he looked *really* good in jeans. Not when he was smiling *that* smile. The man already knew he looked good.

"Go ahead and go," she said. "I'll finish my coffee and take off."

"You sure?"

She smiled. "I'm sure. I have the feeling you're not the type to ever want to lounge around in bed, not even the morning after. Am I right?"

"Believe me, I'm tempted this morning." He rested his palm on her hip. "But I know where lounging would lead, and then we'd both be late." He leaned over to kiss her and took his sweet time.

When they came up for air, Em was the one who was smiling.

He lifted her chin with his fist. "You enjoy that?"

"You bet."

"Me too. I enjoyed every minute of last night, too. Mahalo."

Whew, she thought. No worries.

He kissed her again, but this time it was quick.

"Be sure your cell is on. I'll call as soon as I can."

She followed him out of the room with her gaze, heard the door shut behind him.

Em finished her coffee, took a quick shower and dressed, then headed back to the suite to change before she met the others downstairs.

The Rainbow Lanai was next to the beach. The Kauai contingent had taken up a very long table on the water. Louie had kept a seat open beside him for her. The Golden Swizzle Stick trophy was on display in front of Louie in the center of the table. As Em slid into her chair, the Maidens greeted her with their usual smiles and alohas.

She leaned close to her uncle. "You didn't tell them, did you?"

The last thing she needed was for them to know she'd slept with Roland. She'd have to suffer relentless teasing and speculation if they did.

Louie's expression was perfectly blank. "Tell them what?"

"Mahalo," she whispered, relieved.

"For what?"

Relief went to worry. Had he actually forgotten already?

"Head over to the buffet," he told her. "I want everyone back here for a toast."

She noticed everyone was there except Little Estelle. Even Suzi was there with crutches propped up behind her chair. They were all sipping Mimosas and Bloody Marys and had apparently just filled their plates. Em hurried through the extensive buffet line, opting for a veggie omelet with bacon and skipping a wide array of temptations: Portuguese sausage, smoked salmon, French toast, *pipikila*, and baked goods galore.

"You missed it, Em." Trish stirred her Bloody Mary with a celery stick as Em took her seat again. "We closed down the bar last night."

"Why am I not surprised?" Em spread her napkin on her lap and waited for Louie to make his toast.

"The Kamakanis showed up to play for us, and the late night crowd went crazy. It was the Shriners' last night, and they were on a roll. Then things got mellow later when the guys started playing old doo-wop songs from the fifties and sixties. No one wanted to leave. The manager had to turn off the lights and threaten the bartenders if they poured one more round. Too bad you turned in early," Kiki said.

"Oh!" Louie perked up. "Now I remember. She spent the night—"

Em kicked him in the shin, and he let out a yelp. She gave him a *say nothing* glare.

"She was exhausted," he said before he shifted the topic by raising his champagne glass. "Here's to all of you. You have made winning the Golden Swizzle Stick a blast. Here's to my motto: Never be boring!"

Everyone took a drink then Kiki clinked her spoon on her glass to get their attention.

"Here's to Louie, the Western Regional Shake Off champ! And remember girls, whatever you do . . ."

They all chimed in, "Don't fall down!"

Kiki turned to Suzi. "You broke our number one rule."

Pat hollered, "Should we vote her out?"

Everyone pretended to vote Suzi out of the Hula Maidens until Suzi shouted, "You think I wanted to break my freaking foot? How about a little compassion?"

A waiter hurried over to the table and told them to keep it down. They were frightening the tourists.

"Where's Little Estelle?" Em noticed the nonagenarian was missing again.

Big Estelle said, "She had to meet with someone this morning and decided to have breakfast in the room first."

"How's the rap career coming along?" Precious asked.

"She decided to give it up when she put her song up on a rap website and got some nasty comments. It burst her bubble to find out there were a lot of haters and competitors out. She said she can't stand the heat, so she's getting out of the kitchen."

"That's too bad," Em said.

Big Estelle leaned in so she didn't have to shout. "Oh, not to worry. One of the Shriners is a self-published novelist, and he convinced her to write her life story. She was up there making an outline when I left."

Em stopped listening. The aqua waters of Waikiki were so tempting Em decided she had time to take a swim. Louie and the others flying back to Kauai had an extended check out and didn't leave until later this afternoon. After that she'd be getting her own room rather than keep the suite. She asked Kiki if she'd heard anything from Bardon yet.

"Not yet," Kiki said. "I told Kimo I might not be home tonight, and he said to stay and shop. Maybe I'll find a hula class somewhere I can drop in tomorrow and observe."

Em knew it was a sure bet Kiki would observe for about five minutes before she jumped in and tried to dance.

Brunch ended with a round of hugs and kisses. Anticipating a great float in the ocean, Em was upstairs changing into her swimsuit when her cell rang. It was Roland.

"Can you meet me at the curb at reception in five minutes?"

"Of course. What's up?"

"Hasigawa's son called. They want to talk."

"I'll be right there." She grabbed her purse and headed out again.

45

ROLAND PULLED UP in his rental car at the same time Em reached the curb. She hopped in and said, "Where are we going?"

"We're meeting them at Duke's. It's next door to the Moana in the Outrigger Waikiki."

"Good. That's public enough that I won't have to worry about having my head cut off with a Samari sword."

"I don't think we'll need to worry about that yet."

"Why did Hasigawa call you?"

He shrugged. "I gave Felicity my card. Maybe he's calling for her."

"Maybe he understood more English than she thought."

He wove in and out of traffic the few blocks to the restaurant tucked beneath the high-rise hotel. Like every popular spot, Duke's was perched right on the beach. Em liked the tiki ambiance, the bamboo and rattan, the photos and memorabilia dedicated to Duke Kahanamoku, the father of international surfing who won Olympic gold and silver medals for freestyle swimming in 1912.

She was reading a plaque on the wall when Roland nudged her toward the hostess. They were quickly escorted to a table in a corner where Hasigawa and his son, a younger carbon copy, waited. They rose and bowed. Em and Roland bowed, and Roland pulled out a chair for her.

"Thank you for joining us," the younger Hasigawa said in carefully worded English.

"How may I help?" Roland was attentive, formal, but not solicitous.

Em glanced at Hasigawa, who was watching the exchange intently. She decided that he didn't speak English, or at least not enough to understand completely.

"My father is afraid he may have become inadvertently enmeshed in a delicate situation. He said you questioned his dinner companion. He is uncertain what the interview was about, but he now feels it may be of a more serious concern than he first deduced."

"Which is?"

"He thought perhaps Ms. Duncan was being questioned about illegal prostitution. But no money changed hands, my father assured me."

"Ms. Duncan was not questioned about illegal prostitution."

"That is good to know."

"We were determining her alibi for a time period during which her fiancé, Phillip Johnson, was murdered." Roland spoke clear, precise English without a trace of pidgin so that Hasigawa could understand.

The son turned and translated for his father in rapid-fire Japanese. Hisigawa's expression never wavered, but it darkened. His eyes grew icy cold. Em hoped she never got on the bad side of anyone like him.

"How did your father know to contact me? I wasn't aware that he understood any English."

"His bodyguard speaks but few words, but he made a point to remember your name and that you were from Kauai. His is paid well for such things. It was easy to find your name and phone number on the Internet."

"Why not call the Honolulu Police?"

Hasigawa's son's gaze dropped to Roland's aloha shirt. "Let's just say he felt he would be more comfortable talking with you."

"About what?"

"He has a reason to believe he may have been drugged the night of my wedding reception, the first night he spent with Ms. Duncan. So you see, he cannot be entirely sure that she was in the suite all evening."

Without moving a muscle, his father radiated controlled anger.

"Why does he think he may have been drugged?" Roland hadn't pulled out his notebook, which surprised Em. No doubt he wanted to keep the information flowing.

"He and Ms. Duncan went back to the suite after the wedding reception and opened some bourbon. She poured two drinks." His gaze flicked over to his father and back to Roland. "My father is used to being served. He left the room, changed into a robe. He came back. He recalls getting into bed."

"With Ms. Duncan?"

"Yes, of course. But the rest is a blur. He slept very deeply and didn't awaken all night. He woke up early the next morning with a headache and blamed it on having too much to drink at the reception and afterward. Ms. Duncan was in bed beside him. Both of them were nude. They had sex again. All day he felt odd and again, blamed alcohol and perhaps jetlag. Following Ms. Duncan's interview he has been troubled.

He wants to leave this country as he entered, with no encumbrances, so to speak. He wants you to know that he cannot honestly say that Ms. Duncan was in his suite all night long the night in question."

"She could have gone anywhere," Em said aloud.

The older gentleman looked at her and then away.

"The other day your father had a man I presumed to be his bodyguard with him."

The younger man said, "Yes."

"Was he or someone else on watch that evening?"

During a pause, the son glanced at the father. "Yes. The same man was on watch. Unfortunately, after my father questioned him somewhat intensely today, he admitted that he may have fallen asleep at his post."

"Which was?"

"In the foyer outside the suite."

One look at elder Hasigawa's face, and Em hoped the bodyguard had survived the intense questioning.

Hasigawa's son studied Roland for a moment, as if sizing him up. She realized he was weighing whether or not he could trust Roland when he said, "We are scheduled to fly back to Japan in three days. My father has much business to attend to, and a delay would be a hardship. I'm sure that you might imagine he would not be comfortable testifying in your court."

"Yes. I thought as much," Roland said.

"If there is any way to prove Ms. Duncan left the room that evening—"

"If we're in luck there is." Roland looked at Em.

"The hallway video feed," she said.

He nodded. "Exits and elevators too."

"One of them is bound to be working."

"Don't count your chickens," he said.

"On Kauai we have too many to count. Let's hope that holds true here."

"Have you seen Ms. Duncan today?" Roland asked them.

"My father saw Ms. Duncan for the last time last night."

Roland thanked the Hasigawas and told the son that either he or detective Bardon of the HPD would contact them. The police might still need a statement if they found a time-stamped video tape of Felicity leaving the hotel during the time of Phillip's murder. The former fiancée would become one more person of interest. A lot of interest.

They hurried out of Duke's and entered the Surfrider wing of the Moana.

"What if Felicity's checked out?" Em scanned the reception area.

"I told my cousin to call me if she did. He's working until Wednesday night, so he's got it covered."

"She was supposed to check out on Wednesday. If she's still here, what if we run into her?"

"I'll detain her, tell her Bardon wants to talk to her again, and then we'll call him."

Roland's badge and smile worked on the same manager who connected them to the security office before. The Moana surveillance cameras had been working on Thursday night, and with the help of security officers, the replay was cued up in no time.

Em leaned over Roland's shoulder as he scrolled through on fast forward. She held her breath as they watched and had to remind herself to breathe. Felicity and Hasigawa entered the penthouse suite around nine thirty. The bodyguard took up his post outside the door. There was a chair in place, but he ignored it and stood still as a stone staring at the opposite wall. As time passed he paced the foyer, then finally sat down. Around eleven thirty his head nodded and fell forward. He apparently fell asleep.

A few minutes later Felicity slipped out the room with her shoes and bag in her hand.

"She left the room. She wasn't there all night long," Em said.

"Got her," Roland said. "She lied. She's using the emergency exit stairwell. No elevator door bell."

"How did she get past the guard later? The exit door would be locked from the other side. I can see walking *down* all those flights of stairs but not up all those stories?" Em's legs burned just thinking about it. "Surely the guard would wake up if she used the elevator."

They pressed fast forward. At one thirty-seven the elevator door opened, and Felicity stepped out. The guard sat up and looked around, confused. Felicity stared the man down until he finally stepped aside without a word. She used the key card to let herself in.

"That's weird. Why didn't he stop her?"

"She'd entered with Hasigawa. If he stopped her and disturbed his boss, he'd have to admit he'd fallen asleep and didn't see her leave. She caught him sleeping. It was safer for him to let it go, and she knew it. If he let her go in without a hassle, Hasigawa wouldn't be any wiser. If the guard admitted she'd gone out but he hadn't seen her leave, he'd be toast."

"I have a feeling he's toast anyway," Em said.

"Wherever he is, I don't think he's having fun."

"What now?" She stepped back.

"We're calling Bardon. We'll need a photo of the frame when she left and when she returned with a time and date stamp."

She smiled at the use of *we.* "Am I an official partner now?"

"Not on your life, Nancy Drew. At least not as a detective."

While Roland called Bardon, the manager went to check the reservation. She waved Roland over to the desk when he finished his call.

"Sorry to tell you, but it looks like Ms. Duncan checked out forty-five minutes ago. She was booked until Wednesday but left early."

"In a rush no doubt," Em said. To Roland, "I thought your cousin was supposed to call if he saw her leaving."

"I'm about to find out why he didn't."

Roland thanked the manager, and together he and Em hurried toward the main entrance beneath the porte-cochere.

"Are they going to arrest her?" Em asked.

"They're definitely going to keep her from leaving and haul her in for questioning."

They reached the valet stand. His cousin was on duty. A smile broke out on his face when he saw Roland. "Hey, cuz."

"Felicity Duncan checked out already. How come you no call?" Roland demanded.

"I jus' got here, bra. There was an accident on the H1. If I'd seen her I'd have called you."

He described Ms. Duncan to the other valets.

"Oh, yeah. I remember her," one of them said.

Another said, "Me, too. Hard to forget."

"She took a limo to the airport," the first added. "I held the door for her and heard her tell the driver United Terminal."

46

ROLAND CALLED Bardon before they jumped into the rental car and raced to Honolulu International Airport. Traffic was heavy headed that way as visitors were headed home. Em could tell Roland was used to a squad car with a siren and was frustrated with the slow crawl. She had to close her eyes more than once as he changed lanes and passed cars.

Once they reached the airport he pulled over outside the United Terminal where three HPD cruisers were already parked at the curb. It was a restricted area, and they were immediately approached by an airport traffic officer.

Roland flashed his shield and explained he was working with Detective Bardon. They were able to leave the rental car there and head into the terminal. Roland saw one of the HPD uniformed officers and identified himself. The police officer was hefty, with salt and pepper hair. He told Roland that Detective Bardon was speaking with a ticket agent and pointed down the lobby.

They walked further inside. Roland was on a mission when Em grabbed his arm and they stopped.

"Roland, I've *got* to use the lua." She found herself thinking, *oh great. Fine time to have to go.* But nature wasn't just calling, she was screaming out loud.

"Go." Roland pointed toward the restrooms.

"What if I lose you?" She started to panic. She *so* wanted to be there when they nabbed Felicity.

"You have your phone. Stay by an officer. You know what Duncan looks like. If you see her, point her out to him. She may have already checked in and is up in the boarding area."

Em ran toward the restroom, unwilling to miss the action. She was already washing her hands with her back to the room when Felicity stepped out of a stall. Em almost didn't recognize her in what Em thought of as standard "movie star" disguise. She'd seen it enough in the Goddess to know: sunglasses, hair pulled back in a ponytail, a white Roxy baseball cap. Instead of her usual body-hugging clothing, Felicity wore a paisley India gauze top, white slacks, and she had a scarf artfully draped around her neck. She must have already checked her luggage. All she carried was a Hermes bag.

Em ducked her head as if concentrating on washing her hands but decided she could sneak a glance or two. Felicity wasn't paying attention to anyone around her, and besides, it was the last place she'd expect to see Em. She walked to the basin farthest from where Em was scrubbing as carefully as a surgeon before an operation. She was tempted to look again, but afraid Felicity might see her in the mirror.

Phillip's former fiancée finished up quickly and dried her hands on a paper towel before she walked out. Em wiped her hands on her capris to save time. She counted to three before she headed out the door.

She nearly ran smack into Felicity's back. The woman had halted just beyond the restroom exit and was watching the cop. He walked around a corner, and Felicity surveyed the ticket lobby, then put her head down and walked swiftly toward the TSA screening line. She entered the first class aisle and must have had priority security screening because she was already entering the x-ray machine.

Em ran after the cop who had gone around the corner and didn't see him anywhere. She scrabbled for her phone, finally dug it out of her purse, fumbled, and nearly dropped it.

She took a deep breath and tried to calm down. She kept eyes on Felicity while she hit Roland's call number. She didn't see him anywhere and figured he'd found out Felicity had checked in and gone upstairs.

The call went straight to voicemail.

"Roland, I saw her. Call me," Em said.

Two seconds later he called her back.

"She's just cleared TSA and is going upstairs right now," Em said.

"Okay. We have her gate number. We're here."

"Don't let her see you. She skirted the cop—he disappeared somewhere. She's got on a white baseball cap, aqua print blouse, white slacks, big black purse. Her hair is in a ponytail."

"Got it."

He was gone without a goodbye.

Without a ticket or a badge there was no way anyone would let her upstairs. Helpless, she turned around, looking for the officer again, and spotted him at the other end of the lobby. She wove through passengers with their luggage waiting in long lines and ran up to him.

"Hi. Remember me? I was with the officer from Kauai who just spoke to you about meeting Detective Bardon? I had to use the *lua* and we got separated. He's upstairs now. Could you escort me up?"

"No, ma'am. Not without authorization."

"Would you call Detective Bardon? Please?"

She could tell by his expression he was wavering, so she turned up the heat.

"It's really, *really* important that I get up there."

He pulled his two-way radio off his belt and clicked it on. His rapid fire pidgin was almost unintelligible, but she heard enough to know he'd asked if he could escort the blonde *haole* lady with the Kauai guy upstairs.

She heard Bardon loud and clear when he answered no.

The officer clipped his radio on again and shrugged. "Sorry."

"We tried. Mahalo."

Em wandered over to a low wooden bench and sat down. She thought about crowding to the front of the line and charging a ticket to anywhere just to get upstairs but then thought better of it. Last minute ticket, one way, no bags, traveling alone. Bad idea. With her luck she'd get flagged as a terrorist.

A party of eight tourists with enough bags to field a safari for a month rumbled by. She was always amazed by how much stuff people thought they had to take on vacation. Then again, the Hula Maidens not only packed flowers, frozen fish, and poi but costume changes for impromptu appearances.

Em was wondering how long she'd have to sit and cool her heels when her cell suddenly vibrated. It caught her unaware, and she nearly fell off the bench. It was Roland.

"We have her," he said. "We're on the way down."

Em worked her way over to the interior exit from the upper level and waited. Within three minutes she saw Felicity walking between Roland and Bardon as they escorted her through the glass doors and into the main lobby.

As much as she would have loved to have seen Felicity in handcuffs, she wasn't cuffed. She was only going in for questioning, but as far as Em was concerned, the woman was as guilty as hell. Why else would she have lied about leaving the Moana the night Phillip was murdered? Em very much doubted Felicity had run out to an ABC Store for some last minute necessity. Besides, when she'd returned to the suite she hadn't been carrying anything but her purse and a key card.

She was staring straight ahead. Even with sunglasses on, even flanked by two detectives, Felicity gave off an aura of hautiness. Without thinking, Em stepped right in front of the trio and they were forced to stop. When Felicity recognized Em she couldn't hide her anger. She looked down her nose at Em, and her posture stiffened.

"Em." Roland's tone held a warning.

Em was too upset to listen. "You lied when you said you hadn't left the hotel the night of Phillip's murder."

"I didn't lie."

"You left Hasigawa's suite that night," Em said.

"I went to my room."

"That's easy enough to prove on the video surveillance, but we both know that's a lie."

"Em . . ." Roland said again.

Bardon took a hold of Felicity's elbow as if to steer her past Em, but Felicity shook him loose. That obviously didn't sit well with the detective.

"You wanted revenge because Phillip conned you into believing he was wealthy, because you were humiliated and embarrassed. Phillip was a player and a liar, but he didn't deserve to die."

"What makes you think I hated him enough to shoot him through the heart?" She faced Bardon, made certain her fake breasts were front and center and pointed at Em. "She had more reason to want him dead than I did."

Bardon reached for the cuffs in his back pocket and in a split second snapped them around Felicity's wrists.

"Felicity Duncan, you have the right to remain silent. Anything you say can and will be used against you in a court of law. You have the right to an attorney. If you cannot afford an attorney, one will be appointed for you."

"What are you doing?" Felicity tried to tug her hands free, but it was too late. Roland held her firmly by one elbow as Bardon took hold of the other. "What's going on? Why are you doing this? I thought you were only taking me in for questioning."

"We've never publicized that Phillip Johnson was shot in the heart, just that he died of a gunshot wound."

"Let me go!" Felicity cried. "I'm calling a lawyer. We'll see about this. I'm calling my lawyer. I'll sue this city for every penny I can get. I'm innocent."

"That's what they all say," Bardon said. He nodded to Em, and she took it as a compliment. At least he wasn't frowning for a change.

"Mahalo, Ms. Johnson," he said.

"My pleasure, Detective. I had to get myself off your persons of interest list so that I can go home."

He actually smiled. "Just to be on the safe side, I'd say you will probably be able to leave by tomorrow afternoon at least. Will you spend one more night here in Honolulu?"

She glanced at Roland. He looked perfectly happy about her staying another night. Suddenly the inconvenience seemed worth it.

"Sure. You have my cell number," she said.

Bardon pulled Felicity toward the exit. Roland hung back with Em.

"You have to go to the station with him," she said. "I'd give anything to hear what Felicity says. You can tell me later."

"How will you get back to the hotel?"

"Believe it or not, I'm a college graduate. I know how to catch a cab. There are plenty lined up outside."

"If you're sure."

"I'm positive."

She thought for a minute he was going to kiss her goodbye. There were still officers milling about in the lobby and beyond the front door, so she urged him to go.

Just as the doors closed behind him, her cell vibrated again. This time it was Louie.

"Em!" He sounded as if he were in a crowd. "Where are you?"

"Right now I'm at the airport, in the United Terminal."

"We checked out of the hotel, everyone but Kiki and Pat, that is. A detective called and told them to stay over tonight just in case he needed another statement."

"Same with me. Hopefully we'll all be home tomorrow sometime."

"What are you doing at United?"

"It's a long story. Where are you?" she asked.

"We're at the Hawaiian terminal waiting in the TSA line. It snakes all the way out the front door."

"I'll walk over and say goodbye." She hung up and hurried outside.

47

BUSSES, CARS, TAXIS, and vans circled the airport beneath the concrete overpass in a never-ending dance as they dropped off departing passengers and picked up new arrivals.

Em spotted Louie and the Maidens once she crossed over from the mainland and international flight terminals to Inter-island. The gals were all wearing their "YES! We are the Hula Maidens" T-shirts while standing in a long TSA line inching its way toward the terminal doors.

Precious was perched on her new tiki. Big Estelle was fanning herself with a woven *lau hala* fan. Little Estelle was on her Gadabout busy scribbling in a composition notebook while Trish moved up and down the line documenting their departure with her camera. Suzi sat in a wheelchair with her crutches resting across the arms of the chair. Lillian was digging in her purse, completely oblivious to what was going on.

As Em drew closer she noticed that Louie was holding his Golden Swizzle Stick trophy. A small group of fans had gathered to stare at the Maidens. People passing by snapped phone photos. Occasionally someone asked for autographs.

Em walked up and gave Louie a hug and wished she could fly home with them. "Where's the cooler?" She looked at the heap of baggage around them.

"Pat and Kiki will bring it back." Louie's brow wrinkled. "What if they don't clear your name by tomorrow? What if they lock you up?"

"They're not going to lock me up," she assured him. "There's been a late-breaking development."

"Bautista confessed?"

The others heard him and turned around.

"No. Another suspect has been apprehended. The authorities are confident it's the murderer this time." If they weren't, she was.

"We sat on Bautista for nothing?" Big Estelle snorted.

"Most likely," Em said.

"The paper said he had three broken ribs. How does that make you feel, Big Estelle?" Trish wanted to know.

"Darned proud. He might not be a murderer, but he stole Louie's Booze Bible. He should have to pay."

"Actually, he stole it from the thief," Em said.

"Speaking of my notebook, I'd sure appreciate it if you could get it back before you come home, Em," Louie said.

"That's probably impossible, but I'll do what I can."

"Is Roland staying over too?" Precious asked.

"Yes. He's at the interrogation right now." Em felt herself blushing. Thankfully no one but Louie seemed to notice. He winked at her.

"I sure hope you find a room," he said.

"I have one. I made a reservation this morning before I joined you for brunch." She didn't add that if she got a better invitation she still had time to cancel it.

The line moved a foot, and so they scooted their bags along the walkway. Late Sunday afternoons when locals were heading home from visits to the outer islands were the worst time for interisland flights.

"You don't have to wait with us," Louie said. "Go on back to the Hilton, and maybe you can get a swim in."

Nothing would be better. A dunk in salt water was the perfect way for her to rejuvenate. She pictured herself floating in the Pacific thinking about Felicity Duncan behind bars. Em was about to tell him that was a great idea when the image of the Hilton pools and gardens flashed through her mind, and she thought of Alphonse swinging through the palms.

"Louie! What about the monkey? Did anyone ever round him up so you could return it?"

"I did." Little Estelle looked up from her notebook.

"You did?" Em stared down at her. "Was it easy?"

"Sure, it was easy. He never missed a wedding reception, so all I did was figure out what all those receptions had in common."

"Besides Japanese brides and grooms," Precious laughed.

"Champagne and sushi," Little Estelle said. "And cake."

Big Estelle explained. "We all went down to the Hilton Hau Tree Bar. It's on the beach right out in the open."

"I remember," Em said. "Where you were arrested that first night."

"Either management is a lot more mellow on Sunday afternoons, or the online petition worked. Anyway, we took the cage along. The Kamakanis started playing the "Hawaiian Wedding Song" over and over, and sure enough, pretty soon we spotted Alphonse in the trees overhead, listening. We ordered a plate of sushi and slid it into the cage and left the door open."

"Alphonse was hanging out right over our heads," Little Estelle added. "We bought some champagne, some dessert cake, and made a big deal of the wedding song. We popped the champagne, filled a plastic cup, and slid it in the cage with the sushi and cake."

Precious added, "I was hiding under the table next to the cage."

"We waited and waited and pretended to be partying," Lillian said.

"Pretended?" Big Estelle laughed.

"Pretty soon Alphonse sneaked down and darted into the cage, and Precious slammed the door shut." Little Estelle brushed her hands together as if brushing off sand. "Voila! One manic monkey to go."

48

EM HUGGED THEM all goodbye, said she'd see them on Kauai, and caught a cab back to the Hilton. Phillip was dead—may he rest in peace—his murderer was hopefully confessing at that very moment, and all Em wanted was to live the dream pictured on Waikiki postcards. She wanted to experience the balmy trade winds, salt water drying on her skin, a beach towel on the sand, and a frothy cocktail in her hand.

She collected her carry-on from the porter and headed for her new room to change into her swimsuit. There wasn't a Shriner or a fez in sight. They'd departed as fast as they'd descended. Hilton handymen were hanging a new banner near the bar: WELCOME PACIFIC INK ARTISTS. She pictured a gala art show in the lobby until a man literally covered in tattoos strolled by, and she realized what "ink" artists were.

She decided the hotel business wasn't that different from running the Goddess. The one constant was the tourists who kept coming and going. Every day there were new faces, new experiences, and behind the scenes the staff and the loyal locals made the place what it was.

She was on the beach in record time. She swam out through the smaller surf, bobbed around in the salty water, and floated around on her back staring up at the clouds until all the tension soaked out of her and she decided on a thick, yummy Danno Bannao cocktail.

The sun was warm, the trades gentle, and the tropical concoction worked its magic. Em stretched out on her beach towel and fell asleep to the sound of the waves underscoring the sound of kids squealing the first time they ever dipped their toes into the ocean.

When she opened her eyes, Roland was sitting beside her in the sand. Her sunglasses hid the fact that she was awake, so she enjoyed watching him without his knowing until she couldn't wait to hear what happened at police headquarters any longer. She stretched, sat up, and shook out her hair. It was almost dry.

The sun was low in the sky. Sunset wasn't far away. He'd been gone three hours.

"Please tell me Felicity confessed," she said.

"Finally. She shot him, but claims it was in self-defense."

"What do you think?"

He shrugged. "Her story made sense, but she's had time to figure it all out. It'll be up to a jury to decide if they believe it or not. Bottom line is she won't be running around free any time soon."

"I hope she looks good in orange. Details, please."

"After he left the Moana Phillip kept texting her incessantly. He said he had to see her. He wanted her to hear him out. He threatened to go back to the Moana and make a stink until she listened to him. She didn't want to blow her chances with Hasigawa, figured he was good for some gifts and jewelry in exchange for her time, so she slipped a sedative in his drink. She exited out the side entrance at midnight and walked next door to catch a cab."

"Smart."

"Right, none of the valets saw her leave the hotel."

"She got to Phillip's place, saw where he was living, and realized he was more desperate than she'd suspected. He tried to convince her that he was coming into a hundred thousand right away, and he'd be back on his feet in no time."

"The extortion money."

"Right. In the meantime, while he's talking, she notices a gun on the table and a letter beside it. She thought he might be contemplating suicide and started to feel sorry for him and asked about the gun. He told her it was for protection and that he'd been in a beef with one of the neighbors already. Then she took a look at the letter and saw that he'd written it to you, declaring he still loved you. She blew."

"She was mad enough to shoot him?"

"No, but she was furious. Called him a bastard. He said he was desperate, and you were his last option if she didn't help him out. He had nothing left after spending everything to impress her. He was up to his eyeballs in debt."

"I knew that letter was a lie. He wasn't in love with me, and he hadn't been looking at me as if he was in the restaurant that day, either. Why would she say that?"

"To put the blame on you and take the heat off of her. She knew the letter would be found in the apartment with the body."

"So she did go there to kill him."

He shook his head. "No. Everything went down when she tried to leave. Phillip got between her and the door and demanded she give him back the engagement ring so he could pay off some of his debt. He said that was the least she could do and reminded her that she broke up with him.

"She told him to get out of the way, that she was leaving. He said he'd take the ring if she didn't hand it over. She grabbed the gun off the table and told him to move. He wouldn't. His anger escalated. She was frightened. He took a threatening step, and she shot him."

"Through the heart? What are the chances?"

"At a close enough range, better than you'd think."

"If it *was* self-defense, her mistakes were not calling the police, wiping off the gun, and fleeing the scene. She ran a couple of blocks over to a busy corner, caught a cab, and walked back into the Moana. More video tapes will provide the time line. If she'd have reported the shooting and claimed self-defense at the scene then her fate wouldn't be in the hands of a jury."

Em sighed. "Only she knows if she acted in self-defense or if she walked in, saw his gun, and decided to pay him back for what he did to her."

"She could get off, you know. A beautiful young woman, a few alligator tears, and she walks."

"I know." Em took a deep breath, stared at the ocean, and let it out. "But at least she's admitted she shot him. What happened to Bautista?"

"He'll probably get off with probation since he has no record. Not even driving citations. According to Bardon, Bautista figured he wasn't actually stealing the notebook. Phillip didn't need it anymore."

"So I'm free to go home?" She'd never felt so relieved.

He looked at his watch. "If you want to catch the last flight to Kauai we could probably make it happen. By the way, Bardon had me call Kiki and tell her she and Pat could take off if they wanted. She said they were going to scramble to get on stand-by and said to tell you goodbye."

"I thought they'd have tracked me down by now for a sunset cocktail. No wonder I haven't seen them."

She thought about leaving for a nanosecond and wondered what he was going to do but didn't want to make any assumptions.

"I've already checked into my room," she said.

"Seems like a shame to have it go to waste." He smiled.

"That's what I was thinking."

"Probably a good idea to make the most of it, I guess."

Em stood, picked up her towel, and shook out the sand.

"You could spend the evening in. Order room service. Rent a movie."

"I could."

"Might be kind of lonely all by yourself."

She met his gaze. "Are you free tonight?"

He slipped his arm around her shoulders and steered her in the direction of the walkway to the towers.

"I thought you'd never ask."

49

BY THE TIME KIKI and Pat landed at Lihue airport it was darker than dark. Pat ran to the parking lot to get her Jeep while Kiki waited for the bags and ice chest and dragged them out to the curb. They'd parked close to the baggage claim, so by the time she had everything collected at the curb, Pat was pulling up.

"I brought a tarp over to cover all the bags in case it's raining." Pat hefted her suitcase into the Jeep bed. She was reaching for Kiki's bag when they heard a loud thump.

"What the heck was that?" Pat looked around.

"I just heard it again," Kiki said. "Did that come from the cooler?"

"Maybe the Spam cans are rattling around."

"Did you hear that? It was a definite thud." Kiki tapped on the lid of the ice chest.

"I don't hear anything," Pat said.

"Open it."

"Aw, heck. Let's do it tomorrow morning."

Kiki shook her head no. "I'm not taking that thing all the way to the North Shore if somebody put something in it. It was out of our possession, you know. We handed it over to the baggage people. No telling what they did with it. Cut that duct tape and let's look inside."

Pat huffed and puffed as she stomped to the Jeep and took a Swiss knife out of the glove compartment.

"It just thumped again," Kiki said. "You think it could be a bomb?"

"What? A thumping bomb maybe?"

"Maybe we should get security over here before we open it." Kiki saw an airport police officer walking along the curb a few yards down and waved.

"Excuse me," Kiki called out. "Can you come down here a minute?"

The female officer sauntered along and told a couple by the curb in a rental car to get moving. Finally she walked up to Kiki and Pat.

"You gotta get this vehicle moving," she said. "You been at the curb too long, you know."

"Look lady, we're still loading up. We got a problem. Maybe." Kiki pointed to the cooler. "Something's thumping around in there."

"Something that's not ours," Pat said. "All we put in there was Spam."

The police officer looked at them for a minute. "You those crazy *wahine* that's on TV?"

"Crazy?" Pat planted her fists on her hips.

"Yes," Kiki said. This was no time to get huffy. She wanted to get home, make a martini, and put her feet up. "This is our cooler. Pat's going to open it, and I thought we might need back-up."

"Go ahead. Open it." The officer stared at the cooler.

Pat opened her knife blade and sawed through the duct tape.

There was no thumping, but Kiki took a step back. "Well, open it."

Pat lifted the lid very slowly. There was no warning at all until they heard a loud scream, and Alphonse flew out of the ice chest. Kiki took one look and started running down the sidewalk. When she glanced back and saw the monkey running after her, she started screaming for help and ran faster.

Pat hollered, "Run, Kiki, run!"

Huffing and puffing, Kiki knew she was no match for the monkey. She glanced over her shoulder and saw it take two great leaps before it finally caught up. Kiki screamed again as Alphonse vaulted onto her shoulders. He clamped his arms around her head.

Blinded, she veered left into the lobby and headed for the Hawaiian Air ticket counter still screaming for help.

The last thing Kiki saw before she fainted was a swarm of airport security agents rushing across the lobby. The last thing she heard was Pat hollering, "Sweet coconut balls! Don't shoot! *Do not shoot!*"

The End

Drink Recipes

Even More Tropical Libations from
Uncle Louie's Booze Bible

Flaming Manic Monkey

Author Jill Marie Landis creating and testing the Flaming Manic Monkey.

Here is the recipe for Uncle Louie's winning entry in the Western Regional Shake Off Competition in Waikiki. This stunning flaming cocktail commemorates Louie's trek to the Amazon in search of the legendary Amethyst Monkey Skull.

Per cocktail you will need:
1 oz. Kahlua
1 oz. Macadamia Nut Liquor
1/2 oz. Bacardi151 Proof Rum
1 Chocolate Candy Kiss

Glass: Martini (The thicker the glass, the better.)
Long Reach Lighter
Bar Spoon

WARNING: LIGHT ALCOHOL AT YOUR OWN RISK!

PROPERLY EDUCATE YOURSELF ON FLAMING DRINK SAFETY BEFORE ATTEMPTING!

Drop a Chocolate Kiss into the martini glass. Pour 1 oz. Kahlua down the back of a small spoon into the glass. Next, slowly pour in the Macadamia Nut Liquor over the spoon onto the Kahula trying not to mix, but to layer them. Do the same with 1/2 oz. of 151 Proof Rum. (151 Proof is preferred for flaming.) There should be 2 distinct layers with the dark layer on the bottom. Stand back and use a long reach lighter to ignite the flame. The flame will be blue so it's easier to see if the lights are low. Blow out the flame after a few seconds of enjoyment. Don't sip until it cools.

Sweet Coconut Balls!

Uncle Louie returned triumphant from winning the Western Regional Shake Off Competition and promised to dedicate this drink to Pat Boggs if she promised to stop yelling "Sweet Coconut Balls!" in crisis situations.

Per cocktail you will need:
1-1/2 oz. light rum
1-1/2 oz. coconut cream
1-1/2 oz. half and half
Splash of orgeat syrup
Tablespoon of shredded coconut
Maraschino Cherry
Ice

Optional: 1/2 banana
Plastic cocktail monkey to hang from rim of glass.

Glass: Highball

Measure all ingredients into a blender and add 1-1/2 cups of ice. Blend on high until frothy. Pour into a highball or tall glass, add a maraschino cherry, hang a plastic cocktail monkey on the rim and enjoy.

Frozen Banana Stash Tip

Never toss out those soft bananas again!
Uncle Louie has Chef Kimo keep a zip lock bag full of frozen bananas on hand to make his blender drinks extra icy. When you have too many bananas and they're getting over-ripe, peel them first and place them in a zip lock bag in the freezer. Use as needed for cocktails and fruit smoothies. You can chunk them up with a knife before you toss them in the blender. They'll make the drink colder, too.

About the Author

JILL MARIE LANDIS has written nearly thirty novels which have earned distinguished awards and slots on such national bestseller lists as the USA TODAY Top 50 and the New York Times Best Sellers Plus. She is a seven-time finalist for Romance Writers of America's RITA Award in both Single Title and Contemporary Romance as well as a Golden Heart and RITA Award winner. She's written historical and contemporary romance, inspirational historical romance and she is now penning The Tiki Goddess Series which includes MAI TAI ONE ON, TWO TO MANGO, and THREE TO GET LEI'D.

Visit her at thetikigoddess.com

CPSIA information can be obtained at www.ICGtesting.com
Printed in the USA
LVOW12s0808150714

394395LV00002B/3/P